J.Q. DAVIS

Published: J.Q. Davis 2021
jq.davis@yahoo.com
Editing: Precy Larkins
Cover Design: Murphy Rae, www.murphyrae.net
Formatting: Elaine York, www.allusionpublishing.com

The B
&
B

To all my fellow worriers. I see you.

1st Floor

Music Room
Bathroom
Cellar
Study
Kitchen
Foyer
Parlor
Dining Room
Veranda

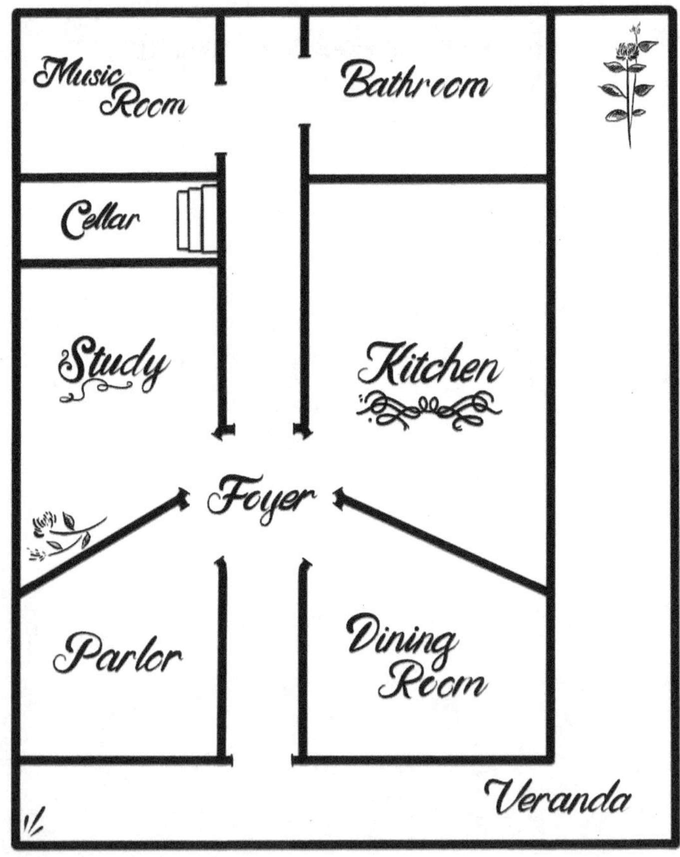

2nd Floor

Library
Bathroom
Bedchamber
Bedchamber
Bedchamber
Bedchamber

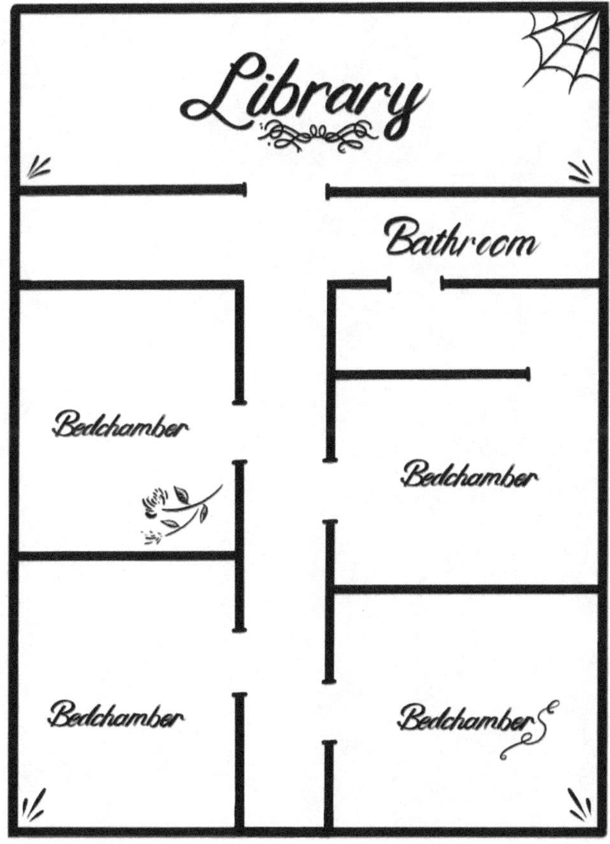

Chapter One

There was a long, windy road ahead of us. Our bodies bounced slightly on the cushioned leather seats against the suspension of the bus, and we moved and swayed with the twists and turns of each bend around the mountain. Although the street itself looked to be freshly paved, the scenery around us showed no evidence of human life. Nothing to signify anyone had ever even ventured down this way. Tall, mature trees surrounded us in all directions, their long, lean trunks and lush green leaves standing strong under a clear, cloudless sky. The forest was dense, offering no chance of exploring what might be hidden within as we zoomed past.

The old school bus was certainly out of commission, the wear and tear of the interior a clear indication that it hadn't been used to pick up children for years, if not decades. I suspected that the rattling of the engine and its components was proof that the guts of the bus were also worn away, probably containing eroded parts that hadn't been updated anytime recently. I questioned whether it could even make it all the way up this mountain without breaking down. Just as importantly, I wished the jostling would stop long enough for me to keep a steady hand to jot down some notes. The landscape was inspiring me, and I had to take advantage of that, which was why I always had my trusty notebook of story ideas on hand.

It wasn't really a surprise that the hotel would send such a rickety mode of transportation to carry its guests from the airport. I wouldn't have expected anything better after booking the cheapest place I could find on the entire Internet. In the entire country. And the entire state of Maine. To be fair, my vacation (which should properly be named my writing retreat since I plan to write the whole time) choices were pretty limited considering the tight budget I had set for myself. It didn't help that most places still weren't even open yet after the global pandemic had finally gotten under control. People were still worried about the deadly virus, even though a vaccination had successfully been developed, approved, and available to the public.

Well, there was really no choice in the budget, either. Being labeled a starving artist wasn't a figure of speech; there was literal truth behind it. The royalties from my three self-published books could barely pay for my monthly cellphone bill, and the paycheck from my part-time job as a receptionist at the animal clinic was just enough to afford me my claustrophobia-inducing studio apartment.

If it wasn't for my parents agreeing to foot the grocery and utilities bills for another year, I'd be forced to buy greasy ninety-nine-cent cheeseburgers and live on the watered-down coffee we offered clients at the vet's office while trying to read and write in the dimness of my candlelit six-hundred-square-foot hole because I couldn't afford the light bill.

"McCall, you're...what now? Twenty-five?" Mom had asked one Saturday evening I'd decided to unsuccessfully sneak into their sprawling estate to raid the Sub-Zero refrigerator in search of some expensive organic fruits the maid bought from Whole Foods. Running into my parents meant that I would have to pretend like I was listening while she gently counseled me on the importance of having a social life, especially on the weekends.

Just as I'd popped a robust, red strawberry into my mouth, Mom startled me mid-chew, and I stepped from behind the large fridge door to find her setting down her purse and a bouquet of flowers on the Quartz countertop.

"Yes?" I replied through a mouth full of mushy sweetness.

"Don't you think it's time to do something with your business degree? I know someone who can—"

I swallowed quickly to stop her before the rant began. "We made a deal, Mom, remember? You and Dad said you'd help me out just one more year. I know it's taking a while, but it will happen. I will write THE book. The one that's gonna get my name out there." The one that I promised them would definitely put my name on a bestseller's list and skyrocket my writing career.

Dad's voice carried into the kitchen before he made his appearance. "Well, didn't that *Harry Potter* lady make tons of money? And she wrote it while living inside a cardboard box on the street!"

I rolled my eyes. "No, Dad, that's not...listen, just please give me some time. Please."

Otherwise, they were going to have to cut off their twenty-five-year-old college grad daughter because it was time for her to grow up and get a "real job" using that business degree, which they pushed and paid for. After all, I was the only one of four children who didn't have a traditional career.

Drifting back into reality, I rested my head against the cool window of the bus, the vibrations of the tires rotating on pavement massaging my scalp, and stared at the blue sky. Movement to my left caught my eye, and I glanced over at the empty space beside me, then at the bucket seat across the aisle. A man, possibly in his late twenties or early thirties, sat against his window, head bobbing forward then back against the cushion, his eyes fluttering partially open then closed as he struggled to keep his head from falling forward again. He was failing miserably at trying to stay awake, and I wondered why he wouldn't just allow himself a short nap. He was alone after all; only his camouflage-printed backpack rested on the spot next to him.

This bus was pretty much empty. Besides the sounds of the wind finding its way through the poorly sealed frame of the windows and the rusted coils inside the seats springing under my butt, it was quiet, and that surprised me. I would have figured since the quarantine lifted and a vaccine had finally become available, people would be flocking to vacation destinations all over the place, cheap or not. It had been a whole year of illness and death and wearing masks everywhere. But now we didn't have to worry about whether we were standing too close to people in the grocery line. We didn't have to cover our faces or dry out the delicate skin of our hands from constantly using hand sanitizer. We were finally...free again.

But I suppose this particular place wasn't very popular. And though I'd spent most of my time as a loner even before we were forced to self-isolate, solitude mixed with the quiet didn't bode so well for me. Too much quiet had the potential of producing unwanted thoughts of the past. Or create new thoughts. Ones that would try to convince me into thinking only the worst could happen. The faint sounds of a TV or radio normally kept me company in my lonely apartment. The tip-tap of my fingertips typing the letters on my keyboard created a sense of security. But that was usually in the comfort of my own home. Right now, I was pretty far from home. About a five-hour plane ride away and an hour up a very steep mountainside.

I closed my eyes and breathed deeply, trying not to focus on the distance away from what I considered my safe zone, which was my apartment back in Florida. I pictured myself lying on the beach, the sound of the Atlantic waves gently brushing up against the shore. Florida beaches didn't have waves that crested some odd-feet high before crashing down, generating a roar that could almost feel intrusive. No. These waves were smaller, more tranquil. A subtle white noise that created the perfect soundtrack for relaxation.

The beach was beautiful, but I had never been in the mountains before. Fall was in the air, and I could spot the color of the foliage in the trees beginning to change into the brilliant oranges and yellows I thought I would only ever see on postcards. Where I was from, autumn looked the same as spring and summer.

A ray of golden yellow sunlight sliced through the trees that lined the ridge in the distance, and I leaned my cheek against the beam to feel its warmth. We were venturing high up in elevation, miles away from any city. I could just feel myself detaching from the hustle and bustle of metropolitan life. Miami was not an overpopulated urban city like New York, but it was fast. Even living right near the beach was fast. People were always going, going, going. Working. Partying. Vacationing. Which was probably why I stayed to myself in the confines of my apartment.

This place, here in the mountains, was slow. Slow and peaceful. The last time I saw someone other than the people on this bus was back at the airport. The journey up this path through the miles of trees was deserted in a serene but eerie way. It felt almost as if we were encroaching on nature, and we should not have been here because absolutely no one else was around.

Even during the pandemic and mandatory stay-at-home orders from the government, people still went out to ride their bikes or exercise or shop for food. Only, most of them wore surgical masks and gloves. But here, there wasn't a soul in sight. The anxious bubbles were beginning to form in the pit of my stomach. The gnawing anxiety was beginning to nibble a little too hard. What the hell was I thinking when I decided to take this trip?

My left knee began to bounce—the apprehension rising from my toes and moving through my body was trying to convince me to stand up and pace the aisle, but I wrung out my hands and continued to breathe instead. When I shifted that bounce to my right knee, my foot kicked the duffel bag under my seat, and I was reminded of the fact that I had another option.

I have other options. It was what my therapist and I decided would be my mantra whenever I felt a panic attack coming on. Having a fight-or-flight response to situations wasn't exactly the best coping mechanism. Many people felt it best to fight, and most of the time I did. Or at least tried. That was if I had my feel-good meds at the ready. If not, I was getting my ass out of there.

There were some other little exercises I did to reduce the symptoms associated with my post-traumatic stress disorder, such as grounding techniques, but popping a fasting-acting benzo usually did the trick. The overwhelming need to run away was coming on strong, but I couldn't exactly jump off the bus at the moment. Clammy palms and bile rising to my throat were clear indications that I needed to get that pill into my mouth ASAP. I tried to hold off as much as I could, but I needed to get it under control before it got control over me.

I reached down into my bag to retrieve the prescription bottle, shaking its contents to hear the pills ping together before I opened it. It was a soothing sound. After swallowing one, I eyed the little white, round tablets crowding the bottom of the bottle, mentally counting how many I had left. Visual satisfaction. There were more than enough tabs to get me through this weekend-long trip.

A bump in the road bounced me in my seat, forcing me back into the now and away from possibly worsening the panic. The tricky thing about anxiety was that as many times you tell yourself it was going to be okay, the possibility that it wasn't became much greater. Eventually, my brain would convince me that anything could happen at any time, and there was nothing I could do about it. The exact thing was happening now. Anything could go wrong because I was so far away from home—the exact negative thought that I mustn't dwell on.

I wiped my hands on my jeans to clear the sweat away and tried my best to relax. I took three long, deep breaths through my nose and exhaled out of my mouth.

Through my nose, out my mouth.

Through my nose, out my mouth.

When I was finally able to focus on the air entering each nostril, imagining my lungs expanding with every inhale, I rested back into my seat to glance out the window at the verdant trees passing us by. The aisle seat was my usual go-to on a train or plane whenever I had to travel with my parents to visit family, but I decided it would be okay this one time since the space next to me was empty.

Although the view outside offered some peace of mind, it only reminded me that we were in the middle of a never-ending expanse of trees and woodland. There was nothing and no one out here, which only added to the jitters. It was too deserted. Nowhere to go if I needed to escape. The number of options dwindled as we ventured farther up into the mountains.

The sound of a sneeze broke my concentration, and I twisted my head, peeking just above the torn vinyl seat to get a glimpse behind me. A young blonde woman sitting two rows back glanced down at her magazine. The white-haired man reading a newspaper and sitting next to her looked to be quite a bit older than the woman, and I wondered if he was her dad. But when Blondie leaned over and planted an open-mouthed kiss on the man's lips, it was obvious he wasn't—and I was thoroughly grossed out.

My eyes traveled back to the aisle across from me where the guy trying very hard not to fall asleep sat. It seemed he had finally given in. His head had fallen to the side, and I titled my gaze to get a better view of his features. To be honest, he was cute, in a geeky kind of way. His beanie had plastered his dark hair to his forehead, small chunks peeking from underneath and curling over the edge. His black thick-framed glasses had slid down the brim of his nose. For some reason, I had a hunch that he might be good with computers.

The only other people on the school bus were a couple and their two small children—a girl and a boy, one wearing her surgical-type mask over her face, the other wearing it beneath his chin—sitting a few rows directly behind me.

"You have to wear your mask the right way, sweetie," I heard the woman say. The boy made a *hmph* sound, but that was all. I was grateful that their young ones weren't kicking and screaming, forcing us all to endure an unpleasant journey.

Don't get me wrong, kids were great. I sometimes fantasized about having my own children one day if I could ever muster up the courage to date someone long enough for that to be an option. But other people's kids were not exactly my cup of tea. Most of the time they weren't disciplined to my standards. And they had germs. Too many unknown germs.

I didn't quite know what to expect from this journey but judging by the deeply discounted price of the lodging and the fact that there wasn't some deadly illness looming over everyone's heads anymore, I figured more people would have jumped on the offer. The place we were barreling down the stretch of twisty, desolate road toward seemed to look like a pretty decent hotel by the one picture of it online. Well...according to the wording on the website, it was called a bed-and-breakfast. Although, I didn't really know the difference between a hotel and a B&B.

If I had my choice, and a significantly larger budget, I would have picked an island destination. Somewhere foreign and exotic, not filled with young idiots partying on school break. I wrote an idea in my notebook, suddenly becoming inspired by the island getaway:

A woman embarks on a journey of self-discovery sailing a boat around the world all alone, only to find herself shipwrecked and stranded on a remote island in the middle of the Indian Ocean. But she isn't as alone as she thinks. There are people indigenous to the island who do not appreciate her presence, and they capture her. Torture her. Now she must figure out how to survive and get out alive.

Not too shabby.

It was too late, though. This bus was headed to the B&B I had stumbled upon while scouring the Internet in the middle of the night a few weeks ago in desperate need of finding an inexpensive and inspiring place to stay that would stimulate my creativity. There were some better-known lodging establishments to narrow the choices on my list. Places that were located in city centers and usually accommodated parents just renting a room for the weekend so their rambunctious kids could swim in the indoor swimming pool of the hotel. But those places were completely booked. Besides, there was something different about this place.

Something...intriguing. Something about the fact that I actually had to fill out an online application and wait to see if the B&B accepted my interest in coming to stay for the weekend. I swiftly skimmed through the Terms of Agreement—who'd actually read the entire fifty pages of those things?—but I gathered that an application was needed because of the historical aspect of the place. The impression I got was that the owners didn't want just anyone staying there, which was smart. And it helped my anxieties about staying somewhere unknown. Anyway, I hadn't written a book about being in the mountains yet.

The bed-and-breakfast's website brochure wasn't exactly anything special. It contained two pages: the home page and the room-booking page. No gallery of photos. No testimonials written by past guests. Just a static page with a single picture of the bed-and-breakfast itself, which was grainy and worn despite being digital, and one paragraph describing what the place had to offer in about three or four sentences. Something along the lines of: Charming Victorian-style mansion from the 1800s. Hiking trails. Free breakfast, lunch, and dinner.

There was a particular draw to that photo, though. Some kind of gut intuition that this place was unique and could really inspire my writing. The seclusion of the B&B might have also been the deciding factor in the location. On one hand, this was alarming and definitely didn't do my mental health any favors. I had nowhere to go if I needed to run away. On the other hand, people scared me. They were unpredictable, and it was why I spent most of my time alone in my apartment, writing, in a highly populous city. It was the topic of discussion at all my therapy sessions: *How do we repair McCall's aversion to humans?*

Thanks to the medication I'd just taken, my body had steadily been melting into my seat, the tension in my muscles slowly unwinding. I could almost feel the bundle of nerves in my neck and shoulders unraveling. Now that I wasn't fixated on trying to control the urge to crawl out of my skin, I decided to switch my notebook out with my laptop to see if maybe any story ideas might have been ready to find their way to my fingertips. I opened a blank document on Word and placed my palms on my computer. But after two minutes of staring at the blinking vertical line, I realized maybe it wasn't the right time.

The bus's weight shifted and plunged to the side as we curled around a tight curve in the road. The sudden movement nearly slid my laptop out of my lap and stirred the man in the row next to me awake. He perked up and his eyes popped open, immediately glancing over at me and searching my face. "You okay?"

"Uh...yeah. I'm fine," I said, biting the inside of my cheek and hastily turning my head away from his worried eyes.

That was weird. My gaze moved forward to the driver, a very dapper young fellow with wet-looking, slicked-back hair who was wearing a rather fancier coat jacket. My eyes drifted toward the windshield and what lay ahead of us. We didn't seem to be climbing the mountain anymore, but the blue skies had suddenly morphed into a grayish gloom and the asphalted road had turned into dirt. I switched my view to my window. There was no longer a luscious backdrop rich in leafy, harvest-colored trees. Instead, there were less leaves. The forest was thinning out, like it was gradually dying.

I fought the urge to glance back at the stranger who awoke from sleep wondering about my wellbeing. It was odd, but he could have just been coming out of a bad dream.

The momentum of the school bus began to slow, signaling to the passengers that we were approaching our destination, and soon the sounds of bags bustling and bodies moving filled the bus. We coasted a few more minutes down the dirt road before the high-pitched grind of the breaks reverberated around us. We pulled to a halt, our bodies jerking with the sudden stop, directly in front of a sign that read HAZELHURST MANOR.

Chapter Two

A flock of crows took flight right as I stepped off the bus, their cacophony of caws echoing into the still, frigid air. Once the birds cleared the area, it became eerily quiet. The kind of silence that you could almost feel on your skin, in your bones. It was the chilly fusion of that and the crisp air kissing my face that produced goosebumps all over my skin. I wasn't entirely used to this kind of weather, being from Miami and all.

The wheels of my suitcase refused to glide over the slightly dampened soil. It was stuck, and my duffel bag began sliding off my shoulder as I tried to maneuver the suitcase, myself, and my laptop tote through my predicament.

"Here, let me get that for you," the cute, nerdy man with glasses who sat across the aisle from me on the bus insisted, grabbing the handle of my suitcase. He lifted it up off the mud, clasping onto his own travel bag in the other hand. I probably shouldn't have had so much luggage given that I'd only be here for the weekend, but I did pack a couple of reference books as well as some copies of the books I had written. Just in case someone was interested in purchasing one. I was not above self-promotion when the time was appropriate.

"Thank you," I said. His eyes met mine for a brief moment, and I took the opportunity to examine the color of his pupils before he turned away. Not gray. Not haunting. Just normal and brown.

See, it was a thing I did. A thing to help me feel safer from my past, because it was those eyes—silvery gray and menacing—that plagued my nightmares. I couldn't forget those eyes. To this day, I still searched people's eyes. Men. Men walking past me on the street. Owners of the dogs who'd come for checkups at the clinic. Cashiers at the store. I inspected the men closely, trying to find any resemblance to those same haunting eyes that peered into mine that one fateful night. The very eyes that, for some reason, wanted me dead.

The nerd whistled. "Wow, get a load of this place," he said, his face lighting up as he stared out in front of him.

My eyes followed the dirt road that narrowed into a moss-covered path leading to the enormous, Victorian-style mansion. Had the sky and the forest remained the same as it was only about fifteen minutes back, all blue and bright green and picturesque, the derelict building would have looked out of place. But the three stories covered in weathered shiplap fit perfectly in this foggy setting. The house was snuggly nestled right in the thick of the forest. It was hard to tell if there was a backyard from where we stood, but it was unlikely. The tall trees behind the house towered directly over the gabled roof and fish-scale-shingled turret. A wide porch wrapped around the entire width of the mansion, about three or four whitewashed rocking chairs lining up against the exterior wall.

The sight of the bed-and-breakfast from where we stood was sort of giving off fairytale vibes. Despite the lack of healthy-looking trees surrounding this particular area, an abundance of lively vines climbed the side of the house, snaking up each floor and framing the dormers. The windows were encased in arched molding, with a few of the ones on the top floor stained in vibrant colors.

The book-obsessed kid in me instantly compared the house and our surroundings to a scene out of one of my favorite childhood fables. I was delighted with the idea of standing in the middle of an enchanted forest where whimsical little forest animals come to life and sing to me. My fairy godmother could be living in this house, waiting to turn my denim jeans and oversized pea coat into a sparkling blue ball gown.

However, the adult...ish...person in me—and the me riddled with worrisome thoughts—couldn't shake the feeling that something felt...off. It could have possibly also been the writer in me. My heart began to race at the thought of sitting in front of my computer surrounded by such an imaginative setting. I had to fight the urge to drop my bags and reach for my notebook of story ideas to start describing what was in front of me.

When I glanced toward the edge of the forest just a few yards away from where we stood, that elation was quickly replaced by a deep shiver of wariness inching its way up my spine. A labyrinth of dead trees lay ahead, making me question what might be lurking within.

"It's kind of beautiful, right?" Nerdy Boy asked, clearly awestruck by the same view the kid in me saw.

"It's kind of creepy," I mumbled. "What happened to all the trees?"

"Don't know." He looked up at the cloudy sky. "Maybe they don't get enough sun in this area."

"Daddy, Max won't give me the tablet!" A tiny but shrill voice interrupted my suspicious thoughts.

"It's still my turn! Tell Missy it's still my turn, Dad," Max yelled back, clutching tightly onto the tablet with one hand and repeatedly swatting away Missy's outreached hands with the other. Nerdy Boy and I both watched the little kids yelp and whine and tug on the tablet. Max and Missy's dad did not look the least bit amused by the siblings' dispute over the handheld electronic device. He huffed and fumbled with the plethora of bags and suitcases at his feet. Like this family had planned to move in or something.

"Melissa, wait your turn. Max, quit pushing your sister," he said, sighing with exasperation. "Ellen, do you have the reservation?"

Ellen, a middle-aged-looking woman wearing khaki shorts and a khaki blouse, which was the kind of uniform a zookeeper might wear, had her arms and hands buried deep inside her tote bag, frantically searching. "I'm trying to find it, Tom," she answered sharply.

Embarrassment for the couple pricked at my skin, and I silently sent a little prayer out into orbit for my future. If I ever got married one day—which would be unlikely if I didn't figure out how to let my guard down long enough to allow a man into my life, have sex with him, and pop out a baby—I hoped my husband and I would never turn into Tom and Ellen. They looked so tired. So exhausted with life. They didn't even seem bothered by the fact that their children were arguing and running around them in circles. Or maybe they did, but just gave up on trying to wrangle them.

Ellen retrieved the reservation from her bag then stopped each child to pull their masks back over their nose and mouth.

"Stop pulling these down. You've got to wear them until we get settled inside."

"Oh, man!" they both cried, voices muffled by the fabric.

I was surprised by this. Most people gave up wearing their mask in public once the vaccine became available. There were three categories of the fight against the virus a person could fit into. The vaccinated people, which my family and I were a part of. Most of the general population received their vaccinations right away when they became available. Then there were the people who had already contracted the virus, which meant that they survived it and didn't have to get vaccinated because the illness was a one-time thing. They were considered to be immune. Finally, there were the anti-government folks who refused to be told what to do or were convinced that the vaccine contained mind-controlling tracking devices that would be injected into our bloodstreams.

This family could be those people. However, Tom and Ellen could just be taking extra precautions to keep their children safe. It might have been the first time they've traveled since we were all told it was okay to. It could be that they didn't trust that this thing was under control. I certainly couldn't blame them. But I understood why the kids griped about wearing their masks. It was terribly uncomfortable.

"Ma'am, are you ready?" the nerd holding my suitcase asked.

"Oh, I'm not a 'ma'am,'" I said, my cheeks flushing red. A smile crept up his olive-complected face, stretching the dark, round mole right above his top lip near the corner of his mouth. "I mean, I am a ma'am. I'm a girl. Like, a woman, but...I'm not that old."

Now *his* cheeks blushed. "Oh, I didn't mean to call you old. It's just kind of a slang thing we use for all women where I'm from. Sorry."

"No problem," I said, adjusting the strap of my tote as I eyed him carefully. He pulled his beanie off, revealing shaggy, unkempt hair that matched the color of his brown corduroy coat, which was unbuttoned, displaying a graphic T-shirt underneath. Some kind of video game emblem or something. The nerd suspicion might have been spot on. "Where are you from?"

"The South. My family lives in Alabama."

"You don't have an accent."

"Oh, you mean like 'I reckon y'all think 'errbody sounds the same down yonder?'" he asked, country accent in full swing. I shrugged, feeling like an ass for making that comment. It might have offended him.

"I'm sorry. I just figured—"

He chuckled. "It's okay. I get that a lot. People assume that everyone from the South is a hillbilly."

"Well, no. I didn't mean to say you were a hill... I didn't mean..." *You're a dumbass, McCall.*

His smile didn't falter. "I'm just giving you a hard time. Most of the people down there do have a Southern twang. I don't really have one because I spent a lot of time with my dad, who doesn't live in the South," he explained, his eyes soft and humble. "Plus, my family is from Cuba. They kind of have their own accent." We made eye contact for another moment or two longer before I glanced away, curious about the rest of the group.

Blonde chick and her veteran boyfriend/husband were standing back, admiring the view. I took one last look at the old school bus we'd just unloaded from, taking a final glance at the driver who sat perfectly postured behind the wheel, his face stark white and expressionless, before the vehicle pulled forward in a semicircle and putted away, spraying mud in its wake.

"How often do you think that bus has to make this trip? Do you think there'll be others coming?" I questioned aloud as we trotted toward the house, more to myself than to my personal concierge carrying my bag. But my concern wasn't over who else was coming to join us. It had more to do with realizing that our only transportation out of here was slowly heading down the road and out of view, going who knew where.

"I'm not sure," nerd guy answered. "I doubt he'll be coming back, though. It's already midday."

The blonde woman suddenly spun around, stopping me and nerd guy in our tracks. "Did you know that this house is like three hundred years old?" It was obvious why an older man would be interested in her. Blondie was stunning. Captivating green eyes, high cheekbones, shining platinum hair. Her makeup had been expertly applied, and I envied the way the colors of her eyeshadow blended together, as if her eyelids were the canvas for a trained artist.

When it came to makeup, I was so out of touch. My face only ever saw the bare minimum. Not like I was going to impress the animals at work. A swoosh of mascara on my lashes and a dab of concealer to minimize the harshness of the scar on my neck, the daily remainder of what a deranged man could do to you on a night that was supposed to be cheerful and fun, was as far as I'd go. But this girl obviously knew what she was doing. If I had to critique anything about her, it'd be her overly filled lips. It was clear that she had them injected with collagen. They were too plump, too augmented to be considered natural.

Her boyfriend/husband adored her, I could tell. His eyes were blue and twinkling with the reflection of the woman holding his hand. He stood next to her and watched her intently as she spoke, like everything that came out of her mouth was the most important information he'd heard in all his life.

"My best friend's sister's boyfriend said his great aunt is from the next town over," Blondie continued. "And she said when she was a kid, she heard horror stories about this place."

Horror stories, huh? Horror like spooky ghosts, or horror as in people were murdered in this house?

"Like what?" the nerd asked, stealing my curiosity. This could be good information for a new book. Again, I fought the impulse to retrieve my notebook. I had to wait until I got settled before I could start any kind of writing.

"Like that it's haunted," the blonde woman whispered, eyes wide. I glanced back at the children, Max and Missy, grateful that they were too fascinated with whatever was on their tablet to hear what she'd said. If I was a kid, I'd be scared out of my mind to learn that I was about to sleep inside a haunted house.

"You mean like by ghosts?" I queried. A ghost story? That could work. Not that I wasn't a little alarmed. Things that went bump in the night, especially in a beautifully strange house in the middle of nowhere, did solicit a sense of unease. But it still wasn't as frightening as a real human viciously attacking you. Ghosts weren't real. And even if they were, I think I could deal with them. But people? People were real and capable of many things.

The golden-haired beauty nodded. "Apparently," she started, "there was some kind of massacre in the eighteen hundreds. A man killed his entire family. Cut their bodies into pieces and ate them." Her green eyes went wild. She was clearly shaken up by her own words.

I immediately questioned the veracity of this story. As soon as I got to my room, I would have to do a quick Internet search about massacres in the 1800s at Hazelhurst Manor. I did a brief search on the B&B when I booked the room and right before I'd gotten on the plane, but there was no literature on the place. I did learn that Maine was admitted as the twenty-third state in 1820 and nicknamed the Pine Tree State. Also, ninety percent of the country's toothpick supply was produced here. Stephen

King hailed from Maine, which posed an interesting tidbit of information in regard to these "horror" stories and where they originated. I wondered if any of the tales were influenced by his own. Maybe Mr. King started the rumors himself.

The boyfriend/husband chuckled and grabbed her hand. "Now, Gwen, let's not frighten the folks before they even get inside."

"I'm just sharing what I know," Gwen said, shrugging.

"I wouldn't worry about it," he said. "This whole area is historical. I'd imagine there have been a few old wives' tales passed down over the years."

Nerd Guy and I exchanged glances, only his expression donned a silly grin and eyebrows raised all the way up his forehead. He was intrigued by this story, I could tell. It seemed he had already mentally declared to learn as much as he possibly could about this so-called haunted mansion before he was due to leave.

"I'm Preston Prescott, by the way," Gwen's boyfriend/hubby said, producing his hand and offering to shake mine. I took it, surprised by how the wrinkles on his fingers actually felt silky smooth against my skin.

"McCall Harris," I said.

Nerd Guy set down a suitcase and accepted Preston's hand. "I'm Aidan Moreno. It's nice to meet you."

"Are you folks here for the weekend?" Preston asked.

"Yes, sir. I am," Aidan answered.

"Oh, you two aren't together?"

"No," Aidan and I said in unison.

"That's a shame!" Gwen cried out, pouting. "You look like a great couple." She reached into her expensive-looking handbag hanging off her forearm and retrieved a business card then handed it to me. I glanced down at the shimmering, metallic letters spelling out *Gwen's Galas: Add Some Glitz to Your Soiree.* "If you ever need to throw a wedding or something," she said with a wink.

"Oh, wow. I, uh...I don't even know him," I said, taking a step away from Aidan and out of the awkwardness that just blanketed us.

Gwen waved off my comment. "Anyway, I've got a portfolio if you want ideas. I have successfully planned and carried out over a hundred parties. Most of them for my very prominent clients. Although," she said, eyes drifting down to my Doc Martens and back up to the long, wavy hair spilling over my shoulders and down the front of my peacoat, "I think I can work with a tighter budget."

"Gwen, honey. We said we wouldn't be working this weekend," Preston said.

"So how about you two lovebirds? Honeymooning?" Aidan asked, and I was grateful for the change in subject.

"Just a little romantic getaway," Preston answered. "We've been married a year now."

"But every day is like a honeymoon with this guy," Gwen purred, bopping Preston's nose with her manicured finger. He flashed an amorous grin back at her before they kissed...using tongue. I quickly averted my eyes. They were cute, but in a totally weird, inappropriate way.

Preston looked like he could be Gwen's dad. Or maybe even her grandfather. It made me wonder how these two even ended up together. How did two people so far on the opposite ends of the age spectrum find each other? Preston had to at least be twice her age, probably had already been married before, maybe even fathered a couple of kids who were now well into adulthood. As for Gwen, what would a young, beautiful girl want with someone as old as him?

My initial thought was money. Wasn't that where all our minds went whenever we saw a younger woman with an older man? That the gold-digging chick must be seeking some kind of financial security, whether it'd be while her geriatric husband was alive or after he died. Besides, the bottoms of her knee-high boots did have the signature red soles of an upscale clothing brand and her luggage was covered in the distinctive plaid pattern of another equally luxurious fashion designer. It made me question why they were here in the first place. Shouldn't they be in some luxurious hotel with valet and room service?

The kissing finally stopped, but the ickiness didn't. They cooed and flirted in hushed little whispers, as if to be telling secrets. Gwen covered her husband's cheek in perfectly puckered rose-colored lipstick, and Preston reacted with a cringeworthy moan.

Gwen giggled. "We should get inside to our room before we start grossing everyone out."

Too late.

Aidan picked up my suitcase. "We should head in, too. I'm dying to see the inside of this place."

I glanced behind us, realizing that Tom, Ellen, and their kids had already made it inside. The dirt road and roundabout to the front of the manor was completely deserted, only the deep tracks where the tires of the big yellow bus sunk into the muck were left behind. The strength of a cool breeze generated crackles from the leafless branches of the trees. The distant sounds of birds and other unknown creatures in the forest sent a chill through my body and a hollow curiosity for what kind of animals might be surrounding us. The fog had thickened around my feet and the sky had darkened. I glanced down at my watch to check the time. It was only one in the afternoon and yet, somehow, it looked like nightfall had already began creeping up. It could have been because we were high in the mountains, dark shadows casted upon us by the tall, barren trees.

This place was definitely not what I expected. The website photo left much to the imagination, but I didn't realize these accommodations would be so...dismal. Naively, even though I knew it was less expensive than most of the other locations I considered, I had hoped that there might be an indoor pool or something. Maybe an outdoor one, heated to keep warm in the brisk October air. But it was highly unlikely. Unless the owners decided to have one put in, this old estate looked like it kept pretty true to its historical roots.

"You coming?" Aidan's voice knocked me out of my undiscerning thoughts. He had already walked up a few steps ahead of me.

I decided to chalk it up to the time of year. This place might have been magical during the warmer months, around springtime or early summer. I imagined glowing rays of sunshine cutting through the abundance of trees, all overflowing with vibrantly green leaves. I just chose the wrong time of year to visit.

As I carefully plodded down the slippery walkway covered in wet moss to the front porch, my eyes traveled up the three stories of aged, horizontal wood siding. And right as my gaze met one of the three windows of the turret on the third floor, or presumably the attic, my breath hitched, forcing me to pause. A figure—a very pale, ghost-like figure—stared down at me. For a moment, I thought maybe it was the outline of a white curtain and my eyes were just playing tricks on me. Some kind of optical illusion causing the curtain to resemble a person. But when the figure moved, slowly and thoughtfully passing by the second window, then stopping in front of the third to glare down at me again, I was certain it was an actual person. A pale, young woman with raven-colored hair framing her face.

I looked away for a moment and watched Aidan step through the threshold of the front door into the house. For some reason, I wanted him to see what I was seeing, for confirmation that it wasn't some kind of trickery of the eye. But when I glanced back up at the mysteriously fair-skinned patron of the bed-and-breakfast, she was no longer there.

Chapter Three

A welcoming bell chimed as the door opened and closed behind me. Immediately, I was struck with the pungent aroma of something cooking that made my stomach churn. Meat, maybe? Aidan had stopped and dropped our suitcases to gaze up at the cathedral ceiling and grand staircase rotating all the way up to the third floor.

One quick glance around and I was transported into another era. I was certainly no expert on the interior design and architecture from earlier centuries, but I did have a slight addiction to the Home and Garden network. It made no sense, really. The landlord of my apartment complex forbade anyone from even making thumbtack holes in the wall to hang up pictures, and the closest I had to a garden were the two houseplants my mother gifted me upon moving in, both now barely clinging to life. But for some strange reason, I couldn't get enough of the television shows where people transformed outdated houses into beautiful sanctuaries. I promised myself that one day, I'd flip a house all on my own, using the money from my bestselling books.

One of my favorite shows was about a woman who purchased dilapidated historic homes in Georgia and rehabbed them, making it her duty to restore its original beauty and charm. You could really learn a lot about period architecture if you watched enough of those home-improvement shows, which I certainly did.

In addition to religiously watching these shows on a weekly basis, I could recall taking trips with my parents to visit family back in Louisiana, where plantations were pretty common. In modern times, the original residents no longer occupied these estates that were used to cultivate crops. Many of the plantations were now owned by the city or the state and were turned into a museum of sorts. By paying a very small fee, usually used for the upkeep of the place, people were able to explore the plantation and learn how its residents lived centuries ago.

As a kid, my interest in how people used to live in the age before televisions and computers and toothpaste was very low. Most of the time the rooms in these plantations were roped off at the threshold of the doorway anyway, so we were only able to study the contents from afar, which was stupid. I wanted to touch things. Play with the glass trinkets sitting on the shiny piano. Jump on the canopy beds and twirl around with the sheer curtains hanging off the bedposts that made absolutely no sense to me. Brush my hair with the weird metal-looking comb on the wooden vanity.

While I couldn't remember tiny details, I did recall some of the ways our tour guides described the decor. They used words like *parlor* and *sconces* and *parquet*. And now that I was older and had developed some kind of weird home-improvement fetish, I knew what those things were and appreciated all of it way more than I did as a child. Especially in regard to my writing. My heart thumped with inspiration as descriptive words began popping into my head.

We all stood in the foyer, some of the crew from our bus audibly *oohing* and *aahing* over the interior details of this antique Victorian home. Everything either had a shiny or velvety finish, with warm, ambient light emanating from the many decorative Tiffany lamps scattered around us in various shapes and sizes. It didn't matter if it was a desk or floor lamp, a Tiffany lamp could always be identified by its distinguishing stained-glass shade. The true question was whether or not they were genuine—made by a particular designer in the late eighteen hundreds. My hunch was that since this house was historical, they were probably the real deal.

The foyer was shaped like a hexagon, each side an archway leading into another room. Straight ahead of us were the stairs, the wooden banister and steps a deep, rich brown matching the trim of the walls throughout. The Persian rug under our feet carried on into the other rooms, but parquet flooring peeked out at the edges underneath. Just like I remembered seeing on those family vacations.

The walls were completely wrapped in wallpaper—different patterns in each room—and I had to admit that I didn't hate it. Some people might have found the paisley and damask designs to be too busy, but it actually worked really well with the whole theme, in my opinion. And the creamy colors enhanced the dark tones in the furniture.

"It's so magnificent," Preston said. "Isn't it, Gwen?"

Gwen glanced around for a beat before answering. "Yeah, sweetie. It's really cool." Her tone made it sound like she was impressed, but her expression didn't. Preston was too busy admiring the ornate carvings in the crown moldings to notice the unmistakable disappointment in her frown. I didn't know what Gwen expected when they booked a weekend here, but this was not it.

"How awesome is this?" Aidan asked, and I wasn't sure if his question was directed at me or if he was speaking aloud. I chose not to answer. It might have been rude, but I wasn't here to make friends.

"Are we supposed to wait here or something?" Gwen whispered to Preston.

"I don't know."

"Missy, don't touch that," Ellen hissed at her daughter whose fingers were stretched out and just about to make contact with a very old, very valuable-looking vase placed in the center of an accent table.

"If you could please refrain from touching any of the ornamental items on display in the common areas, it would be greatly appreciated," a stern female voice insisted. The entire group turned to the source, which was the woman descending the stairs. The edges of her lacy, black dress swept the ground in a way that almost made it look like she was floating right above it. A matching shawl draped her shoulders, its tassels dangling onto her pasty arms and hands. She glided down the stairs into the foyer, passing through our little group and stopping in the archway of one of the rooms. "Please, follow me into the parlor." She turned and stepped away, and we all complied.

"Did you see her hair?" Gwen quietly asked me. "It's, like, so old school."

"I think they call it an Edwardian hairstyle, honey," Preston said.

"I wonder if all the employees' uniforms are like hers."

"It definitely makes this place seem more authentic, doesn't it?" Aidan added. I simply nodded and followed closely behind him into the parlor room.

One thing I remembered from those plantations was the abundance of chairs. I couldn't understand why people needed so many places to sit back then. The only explanation I could come up with was that they just didn't have anything else to do but sit around and read or stare at each other. They didn't have TVs to occupy their time. And by the looks of it, that might be just what guests did around here, too. I hadn't spotted any flat screens yet.

We each filed into the room and sat on the variety of button-backed sofas and chairs. Tom, Ellen, and their two kids sat across from Preston and Gwen, and Aidan and I took the loveseat. The woman enclosed our little irregular circle, positioning herself in front of the large fireplace encased in a mahogany mantel piece accented with Baroque details. The wood burning inside snapped and sparked, the orange and yellow flames dancing in a hypnotic glow.

"I would first like to welcome you to Hazelhurst Manor," she began. There was an authoritarian demeanor about her. Like she could have passed for a very mean nanny or a teacher with a sourpuss attitude who would swat you with a ruler if you misbehaved in class. But this was only an assumption based on her voice and mannerisms. Her physical features displayed otherwise. Everything about her reminded me of an old woman, except her face. While kind of pale, there wasn't a single wrinkle on her skin. Almost as if she barely went outside into the sun. She was actually quite beautiful. Her period costume did nothing for her, and if it wasn't for that, I would have pegged her at about the mid-thirties.

"I am Madame Clara, and you can address me as such. We are happy to be hosting a weekend stay for you all. As I've mentioned before, this is the parlor room. Across the hall is the dining room, which attaches to the kitchen. We have a chef and a housemaid on staff who will provide you with breakfast, lunch, and dinner, and snacks and beverages throughout the day upon request. Breakfast is served at eight o'clock in the morning, lunch is served at noon, and dinner is served at six-thirty in the evening. There should be no need to enter the kitchen quarters at any time.

"Down the hall is the study and the music room. Please do not be tempted to play the piano, as it has not been tuned in quite a long time. The second floor contains a library and your bedchambers. Please be aware that your rooms do not lock from the outside. This is not a hotel. We do not have electronic key cards."

"Excuse me," Gwen interrupted, holding her palm out as if to either raise her hand or blatantly gesture for Madame Clara to stop talking. "My husband and I have a lot of valuables."

Madame Clara cocked an eye at Gwen. "Each room is stocked with a safe and a key to that safe. It is your responsibility to ensure you do not lose that key, as we do not have extra copies. We will request them at the end of your stay." She rolled her gaze back to the rest of the group. "Now, the third floor is only an attic space and is reserved for the staff. We ask that guests do not enter. There is a door at the top of the stairs that is locked at all times, just like the cellar door down the hallway from here. That, too, is locked."

"So, are we allowed to do anything in this house?" Gwen asked with a hint of displeasure. It was obvious that she was not told what to do often and seeing as how Preston clearly doted on her, he probably never told her no. Madame Clara wasn't the least bit pleased with Gwen's spoiled-girl attitude, though. She stared a hole right through Gwen's forehead.

"You are allowed to humbly appreciate that I am offering up my historical home, one that has been carefully maintained and curated for centuries. We take pride in the items we have collected over the years, as well as the architecture of the home itself. My ancestors constructed this house with their bare hands; gallons of sweat and blood have been spilled here. If you cannot respect this, I believe there is a Best Western back near the airport that would be more than happy to accommodate your imperious needs."

For a very long minute, there wasn't a single sound in the room. Even the children became immobilized. Gwen sunk deeper into the cushion, her defiant expression falling into a glower. But Madame Clara didn't falter, and she finally broke eye contact with Gwen to address the rest of the group again.

"Does anyone have any more questions before I continue?"

Preston's hand shot up, his fingers mashed together, and he wiggled in his seat like an eager child when Madame Clara called on him. "Yes, Mr. Prescott."

For a split second, I half expected Preston to defend his wife against Madame Clara's veiled insult, which he probably should have, but his beaming smile indicated otherwise.

"Would you be so kind as to explain the history of Hazelhurst Manor?" he asked, ultra-politely. I had never heard someone speak like that in real life.

"There really isn't much of a history to speak of. Not a very notable one, at least," she said. "Over the years, the Hazelhurst family were of middle class, the men working as blacksmiths, farmers, and carpenters. Those sorts of jobs. The women worked as teachers and seamstresses. Average Americans earning an average living."

Preston nodded and half-smiled, his chest deflating. He was clearly disheartened by the manor's mediocre past. I wondered if he'd been hoping to be staying somewhere famous. I didn't figure as much. Or else we would have known well in advance.

Madame Clara inclined her head back to the rest of us. "Now, if you require that your clothes be laundered, I ask that you place them in the laundry bag we have provided you with inside your bedchambers, then place the bag directly outside your door in the hallway. Our staff will collect and return them accordingly."

"Yeah, that's not happening," Gwen scoffed under her breath. Madame Clara chose to ignore her this time, which was probably for the best.

"Are there any other questions?" Madame Clara asked again.

"Yes," Tom spoke up. "What are the activities for the little ones?"

I couldn't be too sure, but it seemed to me like Madame Clara had stiffened, her eyes narrowing on little Missy and Max. "I have taken the liberty of purchasing coloring books out in town and sorting out some child-friendly books in the library for the children."

"Dad, I don't want to color!" Max objected, his voice suppressed by the face mask. He glanced up at Tom with puppy-dog eyes, and Tom patted his head.

"It's okay, son. You have your tablet."

"Mister Humphrey, you should know that there is no Internet or phone reception this high in the mountains," Madame Clara clarified.

There was a collective groan within the group, Gwen's being the loudest. It was painfully clear that her life revolved around social media when I noticed her taking tons of pictures outside, and then whispering to Preston that she would post them later on "The Gram." I imagined this trip just went from bad to worse for her.

But unlike Gwen, my concerns didn't involve whether I'd be able to post an overly filtered photo on Instagram. Despite the medication metabolizing through my body and suppressing the anxiety, I felt like I could still be teetering on the edge from Madame Clara's admission. There was a very slight possibility that I could make it through this weekend without Internet. Having online journals and articles for research at the ready for my writing was definitely helpful. But I could look things up when I got home. And thankfully, I remembered to bring my thesaurus, which I was not the least bit ashamed to use as a writer.

However, no phone reception? I didn't remember that being in the terms. Only the section strongly advising that visitors leave their cameras at home and forgo taking pictures inside the B&B. A courtesy to the many antique items that could be damaged by a flash—as if anyone even used flash anymore. That was what filters were for.

No reception, though? No reception...

Everyone's voices warbled in and out as I stared past Madame Clara, staring into the distance and finding the memory of my last therapy session with Dr. Finn.

"McCall, this is a huge step," she'd said in her calm, therapist voice. "I'm so proud of you for coming this far in your recovery. This will be the first time you've traveled on your own. You might find that your anxiety will be magnified. But just try to remember that this is all going to come a long way toward your healing."

I couldn't look her straight in the eyes, fixating on a pill of fabric from my sweatshirt. My brain wanted to believe her, but I was having issues doing so. It wasn't like I was diagnosed as mentally incompetent. I didn't need supervision. I could still function as a normal human being. But when you were violently attacked as a teenage girl by some random hobo who broke your arm and bit you on the neck, forcing you to undergo extensive medical intervention and testing for viral diseases, only to learn from the police that the assailant somehow magically disappeared into the night never to be seen again by anyone, and you were reminded of the fact that this crazy freak was never caught every time you glanced into a mirror and saw the dark, rigid scar he'd left behind, you tended to develop major trust issues with the general public.

A multitude of talk sessions with my very patient therapist, Dr. Finn, over the past few years, confirmed the diagnosis as PTSD and depression that stemmed exclusively from the event that happened years ago on the night of my sixteenth birthday. The depression was brought on by the debilitating anxiety, and the debilitating anxiety made me depressed. It was a vicious cycle.

Duh. I didn't need a shrink to validate that.

Immediately after what happened nine years ago, the endless nights of waking up in cold sweats led to insomnia. I was afraid to shut my eyes to sleep because I would only dream about the event. Except, in my nightmares, I didn't escape like I did in real life.

Night after night, I'd sit on the accent chair in my parents' bedroom while they struggled to sleep with every single light on in the house. When my refusal to sleep began affecting my health—sleep deprivation can cause a number of severe health issues, including death—my parents decided it was time for me to get help. They contacted my pediatrician, and he prescribed a mild sleep aid, which helped. The deeper sleep seemed to keep me from having dreams, or at least remembering them. However, suppressing the memories while I slept only intensified them during my cognizant state. Somehow, everything flipped, and I was more afraid of being awake than I was of sleeping. Sooner or later, this all resulted in me becoming agoraphobic and antisocial, and all I ever wanted to do was stay home and away from the outside world.

Everything changed. I was still a teenager at that time and entering my senior year of high school, but my parents ended up having to hire a tutor to homeschool me so that I could graduate because I protested going back to my old school. And because I would never leave the house anymore, the tons of friends that I had gained over the three years of high school dwindled. Even the ones that I had kept from grade school.

It wasn't because they didn't want to be my friend. My post-traumatic brain convinced me that I couldn't trust them anymore. Or anyone in the entire world, for that matter.

Before all of this, I had tons of friends and led a pretty normal life. The night it happened—the night that changed my life—was at a party my friends threw for *me*, at the most popular teen nightclub on the beach strip at the time. I was fun and charismatic. Spontaneous and downright funny. Not to toot my own horn, but I was good people.

Now? Those friends were long gone from my life, and I was no longer that person I used to be. I chose to disassociate myself from everyone. Live a life to myself. Guarding myself from the world. From the unknown.

The present came tumbling back into focus when Aidan gently placed only his fingertips on my thigh. "Are you okay?" he whispered.

I nodded and forced a smile, trying my hardest not to show my worry. I could already imagine myself having a meltdown, alone, with no way of getting the support I needed from my therapist or my parents. I had made a promise to myself that this was going to be the weekend of new beginnings, one where I would leave my past in the past. But that declaration was made when I thought I would have the help I needed—*if* I needed it—to get through it.

No. This wasn't going to work. I could feel my cellphone inside my coat jacket, and I suddenly found myself fighting the urge to pull it out in front of everyone to make sure what Madame Clara was saying was true. If I had known I'd have no way of calling someone, I definitely would not have even booked this trip. The medicine wasn't wearing off already, but I could tell the anxiety was trying to reduce its effects by the slight quickening of my heartbeat.

Don't freak out, McCall. Do. Not. Freak. Out.

Chapter Four

After we waited for Tom and Ellen to explain to their kids why they would not be able to access the cartoon shows streaming on their tablet, I managed to build up the courage to speak.

"How are we supposed to call anyone if we need to?" I asked Madame Clara, my mouth dry. I wasn't at all prepared for something like this to happen. My therapist and my parents were always there for me when I needed them. Always just a phone call away.

Dr. Finn agreed to be available if I needed a few pep talks while I was away, and my parents promised not to send me straight to voicemail if they were in the middle of a golf game at the country club. I wasn't very close to my siblings, so the idea of calling them was completely out of the question. I was the baby of the bunch, and they all thought I was treated as so. None of them could ever understand why I needed special attention after the attack and felt like I should have gotten over it by now.

Fuck them. They'd never understand, because all that mattered to them was whether or not they were in my parents' will.

Mom, Dad, and Dr. Finn had all assured me that I would be completely okay on this trip to Maine, especially because what happened to me occurred so long ago and I'd be staying in a remote location. Chances of any hobos looking to kill someone this high in the mountains were very low, which made me feel slightly better.

Even with all that positive thinking, it was hard not to worry. Thankfully, I had let my nails grow long enough for me to bite them down again. I did that from time to time. Let them grow, then bit. Saved it for a dire situation.

"I am assuming that the reason you chose this destination for your vacation was to enjoy a weekend away from the hustle and bustle of wherever it is you came from," she said. Immediately, my eyes fell to my hands on my lap, trying to decide how to respond to her patronization. I could feel Aidan's eyes on me, watching as I kneaded my clammy palms on my knees.

"It is the reason," Aidan said. "And we are happy to be here. Thank you for having us. I think what some of us might be worried about is having to contact someone in the event of an emergency." I didn't know how, but Aidan knew exactly what I'd been thinking.

Madame Clara subtly rolled her eyes and shook her head. "There won't be one. And if necessary, the house landline will directly transfer a call to emergency services to the nearest town."

"Mommy, what's a *landline*?" Missy whispered.

"What about the hiking trails mentioned on your website? Are they easily accessible from here?" Preston asked.

"There is a trail that leads out to a small lake about two miles away. However, it seems the weather will prohibit anyone from hiking this weekend. A thunderstorm is expected to make landfall overnight. Those trails turn into a muddy mess after a good rain. I'm afraid it will not be wise or particularly safe to venture out there. And seeing as how the nearest town is an hour away down a steep mountain, I would prefer you not take any chances."

"So...basically, we're just stuck in a house where we can't touch anything for two days?" Gwen asked bravely. I suspected that she was getting on Madame Clara's last nerve.

"How you choose to spend your time within the walls of Hazelhurst Manor is entirely up to you. Our library has some very interesting books that you are more than welcome to read. You may be able to find some originals by Dickens and Austen. Although, we do have a stack of entertainment magazines in the study. They might be outdated, but I think the content will be better suited for you."

Gwen might not have noticed this as a jab at her intellect, but I did. It appeared Aidan did too when he raised an eyebrow and gave me a little smirk. And Preston assumed as much himself. "I think what my wife is saying is that we hadn't suspected there to be any issues with the weather this weekend, which is why we chose to come. We checked multiple weather apps and none of them suggested any rain in the forecast."

"If you haven't noticed, Mr. Prescott, the sky outside seems to contradict your...apps," Madame Clara said, the word *apps* falling from her mouth as if it tasted gross.

I felt kind of bad for these people. They booked a weekend at this bed-and-breakfast under the assumption that they were going to enjoy a nice vacation in an antique home and hike in the beautiful wilderness that surrounded it. But now, they would have to spend their time inside, confined within these walls. This might have been okay if we weren't prohibited to even *look* at certain things.

It didn't really affect me, though. I had plans all along to stay inside and tether myself to my laptop the whole weekend. As a matter of fact, that thought calmed me a bit. If I stayed to myself and worked on my writing, then I shouldn't need to speak to Dr. Finn or my parents. I should be safe. I should be protected from anything that would give me panic attacks.

Madame Clara's gaze landed on Tom and Ellen. "Just so you are aware, this house has been properly sanitized in accordance with government mandates. It is unnecessary for your children to be wearing face masks here."

"Oh, well...we weren't completely sure if anyone here has had their vaccinations," Ellen said.

"Preston and I actually had the virus," Gwen announced proudly, as if it was cool that she had an illness that could have killed her. "Caught it on our honeymoon in Italy, right when it all started. We were super sick for like...two weeks! It didn't stop us from consummating our marriage, though." She smiled wickedly and leaned into Preston, who giggled like a schoolboy. I swallowed a gag.

So the Prescotts weren't vaccinated because they'd already had the virus, which was acceptable being that it was a one-and-done deal. But I hadn't caught it, which meant I needed the vaccination. "I got the vaccine," I confirmed.

We all peered over at Aidan, who fidgeted in his seat when he realized we were awaiting a response from him. "I haven't had the virus or the shot. But in my defense," he followed quickly," I work mostly from home and don't get much contact with people." Hmm...another homebody like me. I wondered what his story was. PTSD? Phobias? Socially awkward?

"We don't trust the vaccinations," Ellen admitted. "We will protect our children any way we can, but if they happen to catch it, we'll deal with it then."

It was the same argument you'd hear on the news over and over again right when the vaccine became available. No one knew what the long-term side effects of it would be. The question was: protect ourselves now, or possibly risk illness later caused by the inoculation? What kind of long-term adverse effects or complications were we exposing ourselves to by getting the shot? I was usually a worrier of the now, which was why I chose to get the shot.

Kind of weird, though. I was the only one in the group who got the vaccination against a potentially deadly illness.

Madame Clara straightened. "I can assure you that none of our staff has come into contact with the virus. You all are the first guests we've had since quarantine was lifted. If your children continue to practice good hygiene, as well as everyone else here, I would presume the likelihood of catching it is very low."

Tom and Ellen glanced at each other then nodded as if to be on the same page. After a brief moment of understanding between the two, they each unhooked the masks behind their kids' ears. Max and Missy both inhaled and exhaled loudly, dramatically signifying that they could finally breathe normally again.

"Any more questions?" Madame Clara asked.

Missy leaned into her mother and whispered something so low, I wondered if Ellen could even hear her. Ellen giggled and nodded while Missy hid her head behind her mother's back. "Yes, Missy would like to know why you have purple eyes."

Madame Clara didn't glance their way. Staring straight ahead of her, as if to be so completely disinterested in this question and having to answer it that she just couldn't even look at anyone, she responded, "It is a rare optical condition that has run in our family for many years."

I hadn't noticed it before because I didn't usually pay much attention to the color of a woman's irises, but it was true. Madame Clara's eyes were a very unique and beautiful shade of purple. So light that I could even tell from where I sat a few feet away from her.

"Oh, wow," Preston blurted. "I thought those were contacts."

"They are not," Madame Clara said simply. "It's hereditary. Now, if you will all please bring your bags to your bedrooms. Feel free to explore the property, with the exception of the third floor and the cellar. Dinner will be served at six-thirty sharp. And please...dress appropriately." And with that, Madame Clara floated out of the parlor.

The group stood up simultaneously and we followed each other upstairs. I stopped at the second-floor landing while everyone else went ahead to pick their bedrooms, my eyes following the steps up to the third floor. It was dark. Nothing to light a pathway up the stairs. I could barely even see the locked door meant to keep guests out. There was no other sound besides the voices from my fellow travelers. It must have been where the manor's staff congregated. Or there could be bedrooms up there for staff members, which was rather unique. Considering the nearest town was an hour away down a winding mountain, the employees could very well live here, too.

The woman in the window from earlier. She could have been an employee. Madame Clara did mention her ancestors, so this was clearly a family-owned operation. Her staff could also be members of the family.

"Hey, are you okay?" Aidan called to me.

“Yeah, I’m okay,” I said, then pulled myself away from the curiosity above me. I was sure I’d find out who the woman was, eventually.

“Looks like there are two rooms left,” he said, and I wondered why this guy was still hanging around me.

“Uh...okay, you can go on.” I didn’t mean to sound salty, but I wasn’t interested in anything about this guy. Cute or not.

His lips formed a hard line, and I assumed he sensed the chill in my remark. Then he lifted my suitcase into the air. “I was just going to help bring this into your room for you.”

I’m an asshole.

“Oh, right,” I said and moved toward him. Avoiding eye contact—because I felt like a major jerk—I walked past him, down the hallway, and entered the first bedroom on the right with an open door. Aidan set my luggage down directly inside the doorway. “Thank you,” I said as I took the handle out of his hand.

“You’re welcome.” And that was all he muttered before stepping away, down the hall to claim his own room for the weekend. I shut the door quietly, locking myself into my “bedchamber.” The meds were still coursing through me, but it wasn’t suppressing the thought of that nerd-looking stranger somehow entering my room in the middle of the night while I slept.

This writing retreat might have been a bad idea. I wasn’t supposed to be having any scary thoughts at all while I was on the pharmaceutic. My mind should have been at ease. My heartbeat steady. But as I stood there, leaning back against the door, my eyes closed, my chin pointing toward the ceiling while I inhaled deeply, the air in the room started to thin.

What the fuck was I thinking? How could I travel so far away from home alone to a house with complete strangers? I wasn't ready for this. Anything could happen. My attacker could even be here. He could be either one of those three men traveling with me. Gray, menacing eyes or not. He could be wearing contacts. He could have been following me after all this time, nine years later, to finish what he started.

I reached into my jacket pocket for my phone, my shaking fingers swiping at the screen to open the contacts list. I had to call someone. My parents. I had to call my parents and tell them to come get me. They had tons of money. They could charter a plane and be here in just a few hours.

My fingers found my dad's name then pushed the button to start the call, but there was nothing. Not even ringing on the other end. I tried my mother's number next. Nothing. I pulled the phone away from my ear to investigate. No bars. No reception.

Dr. Finn. Dr. Finn would know what to do. She would tell me to breathe slowly. In and out, which was what I already knew how to do. But there was something different about it when Dr. Finn *told* me to do it. She had that calming therapist voice. The voice of rationale. The voice that could snap me back to reality and away from the foreboding thoughts that threatened to suffocate me.

She would completely understand what was happening to me right now. My therapy visits had increased over the past few weeks in preparation of this trip, mostly virtual because of the pandemic closures. I needed the extra talk time and the extra practice with the grounding techniques Dr. Finn had taught me to be able to even make it on the plane. And when I'd told my therapist about my decision to go on a writing retreat and that I'd chosen to leave the state—without anyone's influence—she first commended me on my bravery, and then expressed that it might trigger some unpleasant memories. So, she knew this would happen. That I would freak the hell out, which meant that she wouldn't be upset at me for contacting her.

I opened my text messages and found Dr. Finn's name instantly. She was my most recent and frequent correspondent.'

Hi, Dr. Finn. It's me. Please call me back as soon as you get this. I am in need of some encouragement at the moment.

Sent.

But almost immediately, I received a notification saying that the text message could not be sent. I tried again right away, even though my irrational brain knew it wouldn't go through.

If you can't get through to me on here, please try sending an email instead.

Sent. Failed notification.

But then I remembered there was no Internet available for me to check my emails. I sent another message.

You might not be able to get in touch with me through email either. Can you please just keep trying until you do?

Sent. Failed notification.

As I stood there typing, my own words began to calm me down. Now I had to apologize because I absolutely knew how ridiculous all this was and I felt like an idiot.

I'm so sorry to bother you, Dr. Finn.

Sent. Failed notification.

That was the thing about anxiety. Sometimes it would be over in a flash, but no matter how long or short, it was always an inconvenience either to myself or someone else.

I sent three more messages, two to Dr. Finn and one to my dad who was much more technically inclined to figure out how to read a text message than my mother, just to say that I made it to the B&B and that I was okay. Eventually, I talked myself down, which takes a lot more effort, but it can be done. I kept reciting to myself that I needed this place. Not only because I required the inspiration to write another book, but because I knew that it was time. It was time for me to take the proverbial giant leap of faith into once and for all putting my past behind me. I was so exhausted from all the energy it took at being fearful of the world around me. That fear controlled my life for so many years, and if I didn't do anything about it, it would eventually swallow me whole. It would leave me lost and forgotten. Left alone to drown in my own sea of regret and sorrow.

When I finally felt relaxed enough to step away from the door, I settled into my bedroom and focused on something other than trying to get through to someone on my phone. I glanced around the room and was once again taken back to being a kid and visiting a Louisiana plantation. That canopy bed that I so desperately wanted to jump on when I was younger was going to be where I would sleep for a couple of days, with no dumb rope blocking me from it. Its fat sculpted mahogany bedposts nearly reached the coffered ceiling, and sheer, beige curtains were tied back neatly by braided fabric. Matching mahogany nightstands aligned the bedsides, with two colorfully stained Tiffany lamps dully lighting the room in a jaundiced glow sitting on each one. A small writing desk was situated right in front of the only window and a massive, beautiful armoire stood all alone on the other side of the room.

I spun around slowly to take in all the details. But once I realized there was just one door, which led to the hallway, anxiety threatened again to overpower the medication that was supposed to be containing it. This must mean I didn't have my own bathroom. *Fuck me.* Having to share a bathroom with total strangers only added another layer of panic. There had to be more than one bathroom on this floor.

At the moment, I didn't have to use the restroom, so instead of freaking out about it now, I decided that maybe I should take a nap. Or at least lie down to relax and mellow out. Allow the meds to do its job.

One look at the modest, queen-sized bed draped in maroon silk sheets and suddenly, exhaustion from all the traveling had finally consumed me. I shrugged my coat off and hopped onto the firm mattress, its coil springing me up and down and into my bottom. It was unfortunate. I preferred a softer memory foam or pillow top. But I had to expect that an old house with old things would have old beds.

Anyway, I was tired, and the weight of my worries forced my eyelids shut.

The catnap only lasted about twenty minutes, but it was exactly what I needed to regroup and refresh. I awoke with a sense of relaxed assuredness. It took me a moment to remember where I was, but the odd aromatic mixture of moth balls and cooked meat reminded me that I wasn't home. And immediately, an inner voice told me that I would be strong enough to get through this weekend alone and motivated to write.

It might have been the drugs giving me the courage to think this way, but it was how my brain worked anyway. The nervousness was either full on or not there at all. Before I started therapy and pills, the anxiety just kind of lingered around every second of every day. Waiting for something to *almost* happen or *maybe* happen to rear its ugly head. Now, I usually just went from zero to sixty, sixty being the number when I needed to pop a pill.

The nap seemed to have slowed my heart rate down enough to calm me, and I wanted to take advantage of finally feeling a sense of calm before something made me panic again. It was time to explore the estate and begin the process of brainstorming ideas for my new book.

I opened my suitcase in search of a knit cardigan. It wasn't nearly as cool as it was outside, but there was a draft coming from somewhere. Either the house wasn't properly insulated, or Madame Clara and her staff deliberately set the temperature colder.

After pulling on my sweater, I checked to make sure my pen and notepad were inside my bag before slinging the strap over my shoulder. But before I could make it to the door, a faint humming sound stopped me. Or was it singing? My ears perked up and I searched the room, tracing the ceiling as if it would raise the volume enough for me to decipher what the sound was.

I spotted a brass vent in the far corner of the room and inched toward it, the soft hums growing louder with every step. It was harmonic, entrancing even. The sound resonated softly, encasing me in a kind of mesmeric state. The melody...it was sultry. The kind of sound that could only come from a very sensual woman. Deep and raspy. It commanded me to keep stepping closer and closer to the vent until I was practically hugging the wall. My body wanted to resist, but part of it couldn't. As if I barely had control over my own legs. But my brain was fully aware of what was happening.

Then the humming stopped abruptly, and I was able to take control over the pull it had on me. I backed away from the wall and glanced around the room, dumbstruck.

What the hell was that?

Chapter Five

I wasn't going to let whatever just happened in the bedroom hinder my plans. It was probably some weird, old timey music that I'd never heard before. Besides, the anxiety was lying dormant just below the surface and I should take advantage of that while I could.

I stepped out into the hallway lined with doors and glossy paneled walls. I was too busy trying to escape Aidan before to notice that the walls were heavily decorated with framed black-and-white photos. The entire span of the corridor, which seemed to go in only one direction from the spiral staircase, was darkened. If it weren't for the tiny amber flames dancing off the candles encased in glass on the walls—a very authentic throwback to life without electricity—that emitted just enough light to see a couple of feet ahead, it would have been pitch-black. The muffled sounds of the manor's new guests seeped through the thin cracks of each closed door, and a sense of relief washed over me. As much as I preferred to be alone, I was glad not to be the only guest in this house.

The dusky glow from the candles cast a light bright enough for me to observe the pictures as I slowly strolled down the hallway. The images were of people. People seemingly just posing to take a picture. In one, a man and a woman sat side by side, their posture near perfect, clothed in what looked to me like fancy attire—the man in a dark three-piece suit and the woman donning a black, long-sleeved gown. Their eyes were relaxed, blankly staring back at the camera. They didn't look particularly happy to be taking a picture. They weren't smiling or showing any teeth, but I wouldn't necessarily say it was a frown, either. The couple just looked to be there, as if sitting in front of a camera wasn't all that important. As if they were bored.

Between the couple sat a toddler, a little blonde-haired girl in a brilliantly white dress that practically gleamed in contrast to the colorless, aged quality of the picture. She rested back against the man and the woman whom I assumed to be her parents, her eyes closed and mouth agape. The poor little girl had to have been so tired, she couldn't keep her eyes open. I chuckled.

"What's so funny?" a voice asked. The timbre startled me, and I jumped when Aidan's face appeared from the shadows of the hallway. He stepped next to me, and a sudden wave of annoyance flushed me. I wondered if I was going to have to actively avoid this guy over the entire weekend.

"This one," I said, pointing to the little girl in the photo. "She looks like she couldn't stay awake." Aidan stared at where my finger had landed.

"Ha! That is funny. You know, I've read that taking a picture back in those days wasn't easy. The exposure time was a lot longer than it is now, which meant people had to sit still for long periods of time in front of the camera," he said.

"Well, that explains why she's passed out. I feel sleepy just imagining myself having to wait, too," I mused. Without even thinking about it, I retrieved my notebook from my bag, opened it, and began writing some notes. It was a little difficult to do in the poorly lit hallway, but there was just enough glow for me to scribble down what Aidan had just said. I would check the authenticity of the information whenever I could get online. Though, it did sound like he knew what he was talking about.

"Whatcha got there?" he asked, leaning in a little too close for comfort. I slammed my notebook shut and stepped back, continuing my walk down the hall.

"It's a notebook," I stated plainly.

He chortled. "Uh, yeah. I know. What are you writing in it?"

Jesus. Was this guy going to let up? Clearly not, because he continued to follow me down the hallway. "Just stuff."

My eyes drifted to the next image, which was stoically similar to the last. Only this one displayed a photo of six children, all lined up from tallest to shortest. Again, no one was smiling, and despite the pigtails and bows in the little girls' hair and adorable young boys wearing tiny suits that were shorts instead of pants, there was something unsettling about this particular photo. The chubby-faced child with perfect fat curls in her hair standing at the very end—the youngest of the group, I would assume—appeared to be asleep. Or half asleep. Her eyes were partially closed, and although she was standing straight up like the rest of children, her head was slightly tilted, as if it were too heavy to keep upright.

I squinted at the photograph, shifting positions to block the glare reflecting on the glass from the sconce on the wall. "What do you think is going on in this photo?"

Aidan sidled next to me to examine what I was talking about, sliding his glasses up the bridge of his nose. “Just looks like a few kids posing for a picture. I wonder how hard it was to get them to keep still for so long.”

“No, there’s something...off. Look at the little girl at the far end.”

Aidan leaned in closer until his face was just inches away from the portrait. “Oh, you know what this is? It’s post-mortem photography.”

“Post-mortem?”

“Yup. Back in those days, death was extremely common. People died all the time from epidemics like cholera and even just the flu. Then when photography became popular, people started using it as a way to remember their recently deceased loved ones.”

“Why would you want to remember the way someone looked when they were dead?” I asked, shocked that something like that was even a thing. My grandmother came to mind, who died when I was thirteen. It was horrifying to even imagine posing next to her cold, lifeless body for a family photo.

“I guess people were just more comfortable with death back then. If you think about it, why shouldn’t we be? It’s just a part of life,” Aidan said, completely unperturbed by the whole thing. I, on the other hand, didn’t feel the same way about death. There was a time when I’d never contemplate about death or dying. It never even crossed my mind. But when a person was put in a situation where death could very much be the outcome, your whole view of it changed.

Dr. Finn and I had spent countless hours discussing death. After I’d fully accepted what happened to me, the what-ifs began, which was basically where my anxiety got its fuel. What if things had happened differently that night? What if my friends hadn't thrown that party at the teen club in my honor? What if I hadn't decided to bring a load of my gifts to my friend's car alone? What if I hadn't decided to exit through the back door of the club into the alley as a shortcut? What if the hobo had attacked me from behind, instead of the front? What if I hadn't remembered that one move I'd learned in the self-defense class our school had provided for the girls in P.E., the one that disengaged an attackee from their attacker? What if the hobo had a weapon? A knife? A gun? What if he had killed me?

The what-ifs could really fuck with your mind. Play on your emotions. Make you begin to question whether or not something different actually *did* happen. It took a lot of cognitive behavioral therapy and a lot of medication to get a handle on the what-ifs, but in the end, I learned to stop creating scenarios in my head and appreciate the fact that I DID NOT die. I was still breathing. Still alive.

I was only human, though, and it was hard to get rid of those pesky what-ifs altogether.

It certainly didn't help that over the past few months, the global pandemic claimed many, many lives. I hadn't been able to read a news article or watch TV without being notified of the death counts all over the world. But usually, I tended to steer clear of conversations about death in order to keep the what-if questions at bay. Even in the books that I've written. All three starring a timid heroine who finds herself in a crappy situation that she must fight her way out of:

A nerdy college coed who successfully defeats a maniacal serial killer.

A sheepish kindergarten teacher who survives an apocalypse caused by a flesh-eating virus.

A docile housewife who runs away from an insane cult that tries in vain to convert her.

Every single story portrayed heroism and female empowerment. A woman learning to overcome her worst fears. Something that I often felt I could not do, which was apparent to my shrink, too, when she read my books. I hadn't realized I was subconsciously writing about myself until she pointed it out.

Regardless, the main characters were all placed in horrible situations, their strength and courage tested to the max. They were all put in a position that could have very well taken their lives, except they fought to stay alive, beating the odds in the end. They were heroes. *My* heroes, and I envied how fierce they were. They never died. None of my books ended in casualty. They all survived somehow.

And now, I seemed to be completely surrounded by the deceased. I took a step into the center of the hallway and spun around, peering into both directions. The walls in the narrow corridor were covered in an assortment of "death" photos, almost every picture containing at least one person whose eyes were shut. Some of the snapshots were apparent and the deceased individual wasn't hard to miss. The dead bodies were either lying in a bed or in a coffin surrounded by people—the mourners' expressions unemotional and unnerving. But some of the images took second or third glances, or even a full-on examination to determine who the dead person was. Somehow, their bodies were propped up, sitting upright or even standing. If it wasn't for the morbidity of it all, I would actually commend the photographer for their creativity.

The most disturbing ones were the children. The babies and toddlers looked like they could have been mistaken for porcelain dolls.

What was I saying? It was all disturbing!

"All of these pictures have dead people in them," I stated.

Aidan stroked the glass of one of the framed photographs. "It's kind of fascinating, isn't it?" he asked dreamily.

"Fascinating?" I countered.

"Yeah, I think so. I mean, isn't there something real and pure about it all? That our bodies are capable of working on its own for an X amount of time, and then it shuts down when it feels like it's had enough. That's presuming we die of natural causes. But even if we were brutally murdered or crushed by a car or something, death is still a natural thing. It happens to all of us. Every single individual on this planet, no matter their beliefs or color, shape or size, shares that one thing in common. Isn't that special?"

I never considered his point of view before. "Sure...I guess."

Aidan moved away from admiring the photographs and walked toward me, shoving his hands into the pockets of his jeans. "Besides, no one truly knows what happens when we die. It doesn't have to be scary. Maybe we even come back as something better," he said.

I squinted at him, suddenly curious as to why he was even here, vacationing in the mountains alone. But before I could ask him, one of the doors in the hallway swung open and the piercing cries of a little girl stung my eardrums.

"Shh...Missy. It'll be okay," Tom said, one arm wrapped around his daughter's back. Missy was clinging to his leg, her face bright red and soaked with tears. Hair matted and sticking to her skin. Tom saw us and asked, "Hey, do you guys know where the bathroom is?"

"I haven't seen one yet," I said.

"There's gotta be one up here somewhere, though," Aidan added. "Everything okay?"

"Oh, yeah. She just got sick all over the bedspread," Tom explained. I leaned over and peeked into the room behind Tom and Missy, spotting Ellen stripping the bed sheets off the bed and rolling them into a ball. "I take it Madame Clara won't be too happy about this."

"I'm sure it was only an accident," I said, fighting the urge to take a few steps back away from Missy. I'd had my vaccination, but I still didn't want to take any chances. Besides, I had to make sure I was good and healthy to get some writing done.

"Well, she ate a bunch of candy on the bus ride here, so I don't know how much of it was an accident. Mostly my fault. It was the only way to keep them in their seats for an hour straight. Sometimes you just have to bribe them," Tom said.

"Wouldn't candy keep them hyped up?"

"Sugar-free," Tom whispered, as if that would make a difference to young Missy. Candy was candy to her.

"Tom, please get her cleaned up," Ellen called out. She had tossed the bundle of sheets on the floor and was now pulling clothes out their suitcases.

"Mom, can I have some juice?" Max asked his mom, waving a green box of apple juice and a straw wrapped in plastic directly across her face.

"Yes, Max. Tom, we need to ask for more sheets."

Tom shut his eyes and took a long breath in. "Okay, Ellen. I'll ask someone when I see them."

"Do you guys only have one bed in there?" I wondered out loud.

"Apparently, none of these rooms have double beds. You'd think they would be prepared for larger families if they're using it for lodging, you know?"

"I'm sure they'll give you a cot," Aidan said sympathetically. "If I come across Madame Clara or someone, I'll ask them."

"Thank you." Tom shut the door to his bedroom behind him then ventured out into the hallway in search of the bathroom. It felt like we watched Tom and Missy's backs as they padded down the hallway side by side for twenty long minutes before they finally hooked a right and disappeared, the sound of a closing door echoing down the corridor a second after. It was good to know that there was a bathroom at all on the second floor, but it still sucked that we all had to share it. Aidan glanced over at me.

"Do you have any kids?"

The giggle escaped my throat before I could stop it. "Um, definitely not."

He smirked, his brows knitting together and looking like he didn't get the joke. "Why is that funny?"

I didn't have the time to indulge this complete stranger with the woes of my life. The nine years of therapy and the ups and downs of having to deal with my mental health. The agoraphobic tendencies. The distrust for the general public. The obsession with checking men's eyes. All these factors played into not being able to find friends and a boyfriend. My peers from high school were all very supportive when the incident happened at my birthday party, but then I stopped going out to places with them and became a recluse. Once we all graduated, they moved on to bigger and better things. Probably making friends with people who weren't weighed down with such baggage and could reciprocate the friendship. And as far as the opposite sex went, I didn't put myself out there enough for guys to even notice me.

Over the years, my mental health had improved, but certainly not enough to meet someone, marry them, and have babies. Those milestones seemed so far out of my reach, though Dr. Finn swore that it would eventually happen for me. According to her, I was still young. Still had all the time in the world to get out there. But I didn't feel like that sometimes. It was very apparent to me that anything could happen. That my life could be snuffed away at any given time.

"Do you have any kids?" I asked, initiating the continuation of our walk down the hallway.

"I don't. But I want them. Someday."

Although this guy was proving to be a bit annoying with his weird beliefs in death and fixation on making small talk with me, I was still interested in him. There was a certain appeal to him, and as much as I wanted to be alone so my writer brain could start doing its thing, it was kind of nice to be exploring the manor with someone. Especially if he was offering up knowledge that could help inspire some book ideas.

My next question was obvious. "Are you married?"

"No," he responded. "I'm very single."

Heat spread through my cheeks. Why did he have to add the *very* in there? Oh God. I hoped he didn't plan to hit on me. I wasn't at all prepared for something like that. This weekend was only supposed to be about writing, which was why I chose a place so secluded in the first place. Dr. Finn and I hadn't discussed the possibly of meeting a guy. Other people, sure. We expected that other people would be around and that I would have to communicate with them. She helped sharpen my social skills after not having exercised them in so long. But we did not talk about there being a *very* single cute guy with an adorable mole on his face. I was only beginning to turn my life around. I was far from feeling comfortable enough to trust a complete and total stranger from who knew where, on a vacation for who knew what.

I finally spotted an open door at the end of this ridiculously long hallway, but the sound of something stopped me in my tracks. Aidan paused when he noticed I wasn't moving anymore.

"What is it?" he asked.

I brought my finger to my lips, indicating for him to be quiet. My ears twitched at the muffled noises coming through the wall to my left, and I examined it as if it was going to reveal what the sound was. All the doors to the bedrooms were closed, so I couldn't tell exactly where the source was coming from.

"Do you hear that?" I asked him. Aidan stood perfectly still, his eyebrows raised into a curious arch. I couldn't tell if he was really hearing the same thing I was or just humoring me. But it was unmistakable. There were muted hums vibrating through somewhere. Not like the humming I thought I heard earlier in my bedroom, which had more of a harmonic tune. These hums were reminiscent of moans. Erratic. Erotic, maybe? Pleasing moans. Moans sexual in nature.

Aidan's eyes widened when it finally registered. "Is that...?"

I shushed him, listening harder to what my mind had already put together. There was no denying it. It was two people having sex.

"It's gotta be Gwen and Preston," Aidan said. He was right. It couldn't be Tom and Ellen. Aidan smirked. "They really didn't waste any time."

To Gwen and Preston's defense, they did say this was a romantic getaway. But wow. Were they that horny that they couldn't wait until after dinner, later tonight when everyone else was asleep? I couldn't decide whether to be grossed out or jealous.

Aidan's eyes found mine and we both stood still for another moment, listening to the long, soft purrs of Gwen's feminine tone and the short, deep grunts from Preston melding together in unison. The combined intimate sounds swirled between Aidan and me until suddenly, something in Aidan's eyes changed. He bit his bottom lip and narrowed his gaze at me, charging the air around us with desire. His stare moved from my eyes to my mouth, his chest rising and falling faster and faster. It was as if something switched inside of him and he became hungry... starving, and I was a juicy hamburger dangling on a hook right in front of him.

I was just about to move away from him when he placed a hand on my cheek and cradled my head, then his fingertips dropped down to my neck, grazing my collarbone. The softness of his touch immediately sent tingles all throughout my body, forcing me to freeze. What the hell was this guy doing? He was a total stranger. I had no idea who he was and yet, his brown eyes pierced into mine as if he'd never seen a woman before.

Right as I'd made the decision to take a step back, his hand fell from my collarbone and onto my breast, palming it into his hand. Instinctively, I stiffened, and my brain screamed at him to let me go, but my body wouldn't move. It couldn't move, and I wondered if it was because I was too shocked by what was happening...or was it because I actually didn't *want* to move?

A very foreign sensation ignited from his hand on my boob to another private part of my anatomy, something someone hadn't been responsible for ever since my high school boyfriend made it to second base on our third date. Well, we ended up making it farther than that, but it had been a long time since anyone had awakened that part of me.

The moans and groans of Gwen and Preston grew louder, and Aidan moved closer to me. After a gentle squeeze of my right bosom, he picked me up and maneuvered me against the wall, my body slightly slamming against the paneling. His head hovered over mine now, his hand finding my face again. I flattened myself against the wall, still trying to find the strength to push him off me, but for some reason the muscles in my body wouldn't budge. Like they somehow forgot how to work. All I could do was stare up at him and allow what was about to happen, to happen.

His eyes watched my lips very carefully before he leaned down and kissed me. Softly and slowly his lips met mine, and when they parted he took in my bottom lip, gently sucking on it. I couldn't breathe. I couldn't speak. I couldn't move. All I could do, all I actually *wanted* to do was kiss him back. Kiss this complete and total stranger whom I'd just met.

So, I did. I kissed him back, that charge of desire in the air finding its way into my lungs. My muscles could finally move, and I wrapped my arms around Aidan's neck. He wrapped his around my torso, squeezing me into him. It was then that I realized just how serious he was about wanting me. Because I could feel him. *It*. His erection rubbing on the outside of my jeans.

We full-on made out, our tongues twisting and twirling around in each other's mouths, his stabbing at my teeth and the inside of my cheek as if he'd never kissed another woman before in his life. As if he were some kind of teenage novice. I couldn't accept that. He had to have kissed a woman before. It had to have been because we were moving so fast.

The sounds of Gwen and Preston continued and with each passionate grunt of theirs, our movements sped up. I didn't know this man but what we were doing, ravaging each other in the middle of this dark hallway, felt right. Felt necessary. My mind had gone completely blank. No bad memories. No anxiety. No nervous ticks. Not even one qualm over practically having sex in a hallway surrounded by pictures of dead people. We were animals. Two species of the same kind that were famished and in need of each other in order to live.

And then the sounds stopped. And when it stopped, we stopped. Aidan released me, I released him, and the hallway became completely quiet. No more sex noises percolating through the paper-thin walls. We stood in front of each other, Aidan's expression contorted into a look of shock and bewilderment. I knew I must have pulled the same face.

"I'm...I'm so sorry," he apologized, his eyes sincere. "I truly didn't...I don't know why I did that." His remorseful words hit me hard. What did he mean, he didn't know why he did that? Because I kind of felt like I didn't have control over myself either. Regardless, it felt really, really good.

But I didn't want to show my vulnerability, so I acted stunned as well. "No, I'm sorry. I don't...what was that?"

"I don't know," he said. "I couldn't help myself. I couldn't stop. But please don't think I do that to just anyone." He seemed genuinely remorseful. On the edge of running away from me. He rapidly rubbed the back of his neck and kept his eyes lowered to his feet, switching his weight from one side to the other.

"No, I don't either. I mean, I don't just kiss people I don't know," I said, trying to the giggle the awkwardness away.

The sound of running water and a toilet flushing paused our incessant apologies. Missy's little voice floated out into the hallway. "Daddy, I don't feel sick anymore. Can I have some more candy?"

"Maybe after dinner, honey. Right now, we have to go help Mommy out with our clothes. Then maybe we'll do some exploring and then—oh..."

Aidan inserted his hands into his pockets and backed away as nonchalantly as he could. I tried to casually pat my hair down and straighten my shirt, but the rise in Tom's eyebrows proved that he could tell something was going on. "Yeah, uh...sorry. We didn't mean to—"

"Oh, no. You didn't. It's okay." I switched my attention to Missy. "How are you feeling?"

Missy's big green eyes—just like her dad's—drifted from me to Aidan, and then she took a step back and hid her face behind her dad's leg.

"Sorry, she gets a little shy," Tom said.

Aidan finally spoke, but his voice was shaky. "I was like that, too, as a kid."

Tom nodded then walked around us. "We'll see you guys at dinner," he said, making his way back to their room.

There was another second of silence between Aidan and me before he simply turned around and disappeared into the shadows of the hallway, leaving me standing there. Alone and completely confused about what had just occurred between us.

Chapter Six

I stood motionless for a few more minutes, completely baffled by what had just transpired between Aidan and me. After trying my hardest not to feel like I was being judged by the dead people on the walls, I was finally able to move and head for that open door at the end of the seemingly never-ending hallway. As much as I wanted to hide away in my bedroom and obsess about what just happened, I couldn't do it. I HAD to focus on my writing. Because...sometimes, things just spontaneously happened, like what occurred on my sixteenth birthday. Sometimes, there was no reason to worry about it and no reason to be overcome by the what-ifs.

It was perfectly okay not to have all the answers. It was perfectly okay not to question every single little thing!

My breath quickened. The walls were caving in, and the floor of the corridor began to warp. My eyes crisscrossed, and I tried unsuccessfully to straighten them out. The dizziness had come on strong, forcing me to stumble before I finally stopped trying to walk. I concentrated deeply on the air entering and leaving my lungs, trying in vain to prevent a panic attack from happening despite the benzodiazepine still doing what it was supposed to do.

It was okay. It was all okay. I mean, it was really damn weird how Aidan just smashed against my body and kissed me. Kissed me passionately, like I'd never been kissed before. That was strange, right? People didn't normally do that to people they'd just met. And what really had my mind spinning was how I didn't stop it.

Obviously, Aidan fancied me. But...wait, did he? He seemed pretty freaked out by his own actions. What if he just lost his mind for a moment? What if he was having a stroke and really *didn't* like me at all? And why didn't I freak out as much as he did? I was traumatized by a stranger having attacked me nine years ago. Completely screwed in the head by it.

I could still smell the putrid scent of his skin. I could still feel the forceful way he grabbed my wrists and held me in place. I could still see those gray, empty, menacing eyes boring into mine right before he broke my arm and buried his teeth into my neck.

So why didn't I stop Aidan? Was it because I actually *wanted* him to kiss me?

If I was being honest, the sound of Gwen and Preston... As much as it activated my gag reflex to think about being with a much older man, it was pretty hot. Those moans and groans awakened my pleasure zones, and it just so happened that a good-looking guy was standing right beside me. I must have been desperate and just didn't even know it because this was the first time in what felt like eons that I had even been that close to a man.

I doubled over and lowered my head down to my knees, trying to recall and utilize those stress-reducing yoga moves I'd learned years ago. Okay, enough. It was over. I was in control of my body and my mind and what happened had already passed. There was no sense in dwelling. No sense in making it out to be more than it was, especially if it happened to be that he was stroking out or something.

When I felt I'd regained my composure and could walk steadily again, I proceeded down to the open door. Once I entered, there was no mistaking what the room was, and any residual anxieties I just had immediately dissolved. It was Hazelhurst Manor's library—a bibliophile's dream.

My jaw dropped when I stepped inside, all of my wildest fantasies as a writer and reader coming true. The large room was filled to the absolute brim with books. My heart fluttered at the sight of the floor-to-ceiling wooden bookshelves that aligned every single inch of space along the walls, the height of each bookcase soaring several feet above my head. There had to be hundreds and hundreds of books, their colorful spines of various sizes breaking up the intense, dark hue of the mahogany shelving and crown molding. The entire room was carpeted by a giant vintage Persian rug, with ample seating to relax in and get lost in a story. The faint scent of vanilla filled my nostrils, and I seriously considered making this my "bedchamber" for the rest of the weekend.

The thought of ditching my writing to bury my head in an epic fantasy or a timeless romance sounded like heaven. It might not have been my go-to genre, but I could still appreciate the classics, written by the trailblazers of the literary world. Given the age of the house, I wondered what time-honored tales could be just within arm's reach. There had to be first editions in here like *Great Expectations* and *Wuthering Heights*. Better yet, murder mysteries by Agatha Christie and Alfred Hitchcock.

Madame Clara had already hinted at the library's impressive collection when she passively insulted Gwen.

I spun around like I was some kind of Disney character, my eyes following the rows and rows of books. I even squealed like a kid when I noticed the ladders affixed to shelves and skipped to one of them, gently grazing the texture. It looked like it was carved right out of one of the trees outside. I pushed it and smiled wide when it glided across effortlessly. There was no stopping me. I just had to climb up and pick out a book.

I grabbed hold of the edges of the wooden ladder and glanced up. The ceiling was easily ten feet high, and I was determined to reach the highest row of shelves to find a book. But before my boot could make it up past the third rung, the wood cracked beneath my weight, and I lost my footing. My Doc Martens slid off the ladder and I held on for dear life to the sides, but gravity didn't care about my semi-quick reflexes. I fell off the ladder and, surprisingly, landed on my feet.

It wasn't a clean dismount, though. The misaligned weight from my clumsy descent caused me to stumble backwards and knock into some kind of pedestal, which prevented me from falling on my ass. The pedestal didn't budge, but the vase filled with flowers and the decorative velvet sheath covering the pedestal slid off. The glass vase plunged to the floor. Thankfully, the fabric from the sheath and the carpeted floor protected the vase from shattering into pieces, but there was still a loud thud and the contents of the vase spilled right out of it.

"Shh," I hissed at the mess I'd made, worried that the noise might alert Madame Clara to come in here and lose her shit. But my concern over the wreck immediately faded when what had been hidden underneath that vase and decorative sheath caught my eye.

It was a glass display case. Anything inside of a glass display case had to mean that it was valuable. I reached out and placed my fingers on the edges of the square translucent box. A giant, thick book was positioned upright and open, showing its discolored pages. The trim of the paper was timeworn and very fragile-looking, the writing faded and barely eligible.

I leaned in closer, careful not to fog the glass with my eager breath. I couldn't read the words even if the ink weren't disappearing. It was in another language, the font very similar to Old English. I'd taken both Spanish and French in high school, but this looked nothing like that. The strange letters were mixed with numbers and symbols I had never seen before, and it instantly reminded me of the cryptograms my friends and I used to make up as a way to pass notes in class. We were the only ones who could decode them. That way, if we were caught, our teachers would have no idea what we were talking about. It might have been a little dramatic. It wasn't like we were passing around classified secrets. I think the thrill of it came from creating the ciphers.

However, I was pretty positive that this clearly antique, leather-bound book didn't contain a melodramatic retelling of how my mom and dad grounded me over sneaking in late on a school night or about how my best friend thought the new boy in school was hot. No, there was something special about this book. I could feel it. And the way it was hanging out in its case... As if it were its very own exhibit in a museum or something.

"It's from the Middle Ages," a voice behind me started. I flinched at the sound of the masculine voice intruding the quiet library. For a moment, I considered huffing loudly in agitation over Aidan encroaching upon my personal space yet again, but when I turned around, I realized it wasn't him.

"It's a family heirloom. Passed down from many generations." The very tall man stood erect in the doorframe of the library with perfect posture, his hands behind his back. I eyed him sideways, taking in his ebony, neck-length waves parted down the side, combed over and tucked behind his ears. The milky skin on his face was cleanly shaven, not even one single stub. Cheekbones sharp and chin pointy, like a male supermodel. My eyes drifted down his body; shoulders broad and legs long. He wasn't muscular, but he wasn't lanky either. Undoubtedly, this man was very attractive. A mysteriously good-looking man wearing a...bowtie, waistcoat, and trousers? *Oh, shit.* That attire wasn't something people of this millennium wore unless they were trying to be an ironic hipster. He must be one of the B&B employees.

I glanced at the big water spot in the carpet and red roses strewn all about then back to him in a panic. "I-I'm sorry. It was an accident. I didn't mean to—"

The man shook his head. "No worries. But I see that you uncovered something very special."

Well, it didn't seem like he was upset about it. Something told me if it was Madame Clara who had walked in here, she wouldn't be so cool about it.

"And don't worry, I won't tell Madame Clara about this little mishap," he said, winking at me. "You're right to be worried. She would most certainly go berserk if she saw this." It said a lot about Madame Clara if her own employee was admitting to her rough edges.

A moment of silent gratitude passed before I chose to speak. "Did you say Middle Ages? As in, medieval times?" I asked, stunned. That meant that I was standing next to a book that had been around for over a thousand years! I spun back around and mentally cursed at the glass preventing me from picking up the rare piece of literary art. I wanted to touch the cover, smell the paper, sit down with it and try to figure out the language myself. Decode the cipher. If this guy was right and the book was really from the Middle Ages, it didn't matter what it said inside. It would be nothing short of special. But I really wanted to know. "What language is this?" I asked, turning to face the man again. "And what's the book abo—"

I gasped and shuffled backward as my arms involuntarily swung up to protect my face. The man must have moved from the threshold of the door directly behind me while I was admiring the book in the case. I didn't even hear his footsteps.

"I'm so sorry," he said softly, peering down at me. "I didn't mean to frighten you."

"I...it's okay," I said, wrapping my arms around myself, suddenly feeling a draft of cool air find its way up my sweater sleeve. This guy was standing too close for comfort.

But before I could step away from him, I took a gander at his eyes. It stopped me cold. His eyes. They were... They were... purple. Not like a bright, neon purple. But a light purple. Just like Madame Clara's. The hue reminded me of the dying lavender plant sitting on the windowsill in my apartment. Or what it looked like before my mother made the mistake of bringing it to my place. A pang of guilt shot through me. My poor plants.

Madame Clara claimed that her eye color was genetic, but there was no way. I had never seen another person with eyeballs like this. They had to be wearing contacts. What were the odds that two people who had the same rare genetic eye condition knew each other? Unless...

"Are you finding your accommodations to be suitable for your weekend stay, Miss Harris?" he asked, not moving an inch from where he stood. It was obvious now that he worked here and had access to the guest reservations; otherwise, he wouldn't have known my last name. Considering all the information we had to give before booking a stay, I wouldn't be surprised if the man even knew my blood type.

"Yes, thank you for asking. The bed is quite comfortable," I lied.

"Good." He finally moved and took a short stroll toward the book in the glass case, studying it. I got the feeling that maybe he suspected I might have been trying to get inside by the way he inspected it, but I would never do something like that to an object that was so clearly valuable, it had to be stored inside a sealed glass case.

"I wasn't trying to open it," I said. "You walked in right after I had knocked into it."

He ignored my attempt at defending my innocence. "Have you ever read the Bible, Miss Harris?"

What an odd question. Something that I hadn't really thought about since I was a child. My parents raised me Catholic. As a kid, they enrolled me into Sunday school, which was, I think, the last time I'd ever read anything from the Bible. When I got older, worshiping a Deity wasn't exactly on my list of things to do anymore. Especially after what happened on my sixteenth birthday. I became angry with God for a while for making me have to experience such a horrible event that had altered my life so dramatically. If that hadn't happened to me, if my mental health hadn't endured such debilitating effects from it, I could be a totally different person. I could be able to have friends and date. Trust people. I could be a world traveler. An adventure-seeking wanderer who stayed in unique hotels and met unique people then wrote bestselling novels based on her experiences. I'd be anxiety-free and completely normal.

The man's expecting eyes were awaiting an answer from

me. I said, "Um...when I was younger. But I don't really remember much of it. Is that a Bible?"

He chuckled. "Not one that you are familiar with. But it is a bible, of sorts."

Of sorts? I was perfectly aware that the people of the world believed in many different gods. There were many different books of scriptures and sacred texts in many different languages about each of those gods. But I wasn't sure what kind of bible there was in medieval times. And even though I didn't really remember what was in the New Testament, the words displayed inside that protective shield of glass didn't look like any letters or symbols I have ever seen before. Not even close to Hebrew.

The handsome man continued, "It is a collection of stories and beliefs written by powerful entities of the past. But we don't necessarily call it a bible. It's more of a handbook."

"A handbook for what?" I asked, my curiosity growing rapidly for what this book was about and where it came from.

"What is *that* book for?" he countered, shooting his chin toward my notebook of story ideas. I hadn't noticed that it was in my hands. I must have instinctively pulled it out of my bag when he started talking about the "handbook." I still didn't have any idea what my next book would be about but noting all of these interesting facts I was finding around the house could definitely lead somewhere.

I self-consciously placed the notebook back into my satchel. "Oh, it's nothing. I just like to record unusual and interesting things."

The man's expression changed, a sudden unease flashing through his mystical eyes. "Are you a reporter?"

"Um, no. I'm a writer. Of books."

He nodded slowly. "Your online application didn't mention anything about being an author."

It was true. When I'd filled out the application, under *Employment* I typed *Receptionist*. Sure, I was a writer and technically an author because my books were published. Albeit self-published, but published, nonetheless. Honestly, though, I never truly felt like an author. And no one I knew treated me as such. My parents hadn't even read any of my books, and I didn't personally know anyone who did besides my therapist, which I assumed had to have been a type of homework for her to get to know her patient better. I believed it might have had to do with validation. People around the world bought and read my books online, but they could essentially buy and read absolutely ANY book online. But not just ANY book was in bookstores or published through a large and well-known publishing house. Once I succeeded in that, then I'd feel like an author. Validated.

"Is that a problem?" I asked skeptically.

"No," he answered. "It's just that my mother would prefer she gets to know the guests before they are selected to stay at the manor."

"And why is that?" Now I sounded like a reporter, but I did find it odd that I had to fill out an application to stay at a B&B. At first, I'd thought I was filling one out to work here. But when I realized it was to *stay* here, I'd admit it was part of what intrigued me.

The man waved his hand out in front of the glass display case, as if showcasing a prize on a game show. "In a house full of historical and valuable artifacts, wouldn't you want to know exactly who is going to be staying on your property?"

He had a point. A very good one, too. I nodded in understanding. "So, your mother is Madame Clara?" It had just dawned on me that he had said 'his mother,' but I wasn't surprised. Those eyes gave it away.

"Yes. She is my mother."

Without even taking the color of their eyes into account, I could see the resemblance now. He was just as pasty as his mother, his features just as mystically striking.

I felt like an apology was warranted. But I didn't want to insult the man. He strolled past me toward the door, arms still behind his back. He was playing the character of an 1800s gentleman very well. "I know she could be a bit...intimidating."

Scary was a better word.

"But I assure you it's just because she is old and grumpy and cares very deeply for this house."

"How old are you?" I asked, adding, "If you don't mind me asking." I didn't want to be rude, but judging by how young Madame Clara looked, this guy couldn't be that much older than me.

A charming grin crept up his face. "How old do I look?" he questioned me, one eyebrow popping up.

I didn't want to play this game. I wasn't very good at it. Once on a rare, anxiety-free day, I had approached my neighbor's kid and offered her the extra cookie with cartoon-inspired icing I'd gotten at Starbucks. The girl had looked me dead in the eyes and said in the most adult, sophisticated voice I'd ever heard, "Do I look like a child?" Turned out she was only thirteen years old, which to me was still a child. But apparently, the tweens in Miami didn't think so.

I shrugged. "Twenty-six-ish?"

He bowed his head. "That's flattering. Thank you. You should be getting ready for dinner soon. My mother isn't too keen on tardiness. Also, the haggis is best served piping hot."

"Haggis?"

He stepped aside, gesturing for me to come out into the hallway with him. "Oh, you'll enjoy it. Winston, our chef, does an amazing job preparing it."

I had no idea what haggis was, but I assumed it was something people ate in the 1800s. This meant that it was probably not going to be appetizing to me. I was no foodie. My parents always teased me about being so thin and advising that I eat more food to gain weight. My intentions weren't to be skinny—I just didn't indulge myself. I ate only when I was hungry, and it was never an amount that exceeded what my stomach could handle. Feeling full and bloated because of overeating just wasn't appealing to me. I ate to survive, with the occasional chocolate cake and vanilla ice cream with Hershey's syrup fix.

I was open to trying new foods, though. Especially if the B&B was maintaining authenticity to its era. Personal experience was very good for writers, and if it was something that wouldn't necessarily trigger my anxiety, then I was all about it.

Madame Clara's son waited for me to exit the library. Once I reached him, he ushered me out into the hallway, and we walked side by side until we made it to my room.

"I'm really sorry about the vase," I said.

"It's quite all right. I'll have it cleaned up before my mother sees it. Oh, here." He held out his hand. "I'm sorry it's so worn. I have not been very kind to it."

Out of nowhere—he must have been carrying it behind his back and I didn't notice—he placed an aged book into the palm of my hand. My arm dipped under the weight of it. It was very thick, looked to be roughly a thousand pages or so. I swiped my hand over the cover, the leather smooth against my skin. There was no title. No author name. No cover art.

The book was shut tight with a thin piece of fabric wrapped around it several times over. I unwrapped it carefully then flipped through the rough-cut paper with distressed edges. As I skimmed each page, I realized the words were handwritten and in English. But there were no paragraphs or breaks between, just consistent sentences. The binding was unusual too—the pages unevenly stitched together by black thread. It seemed to be more like a handmade journal than an actual, traditional book.

"It's something that I have been working on for a very long time," he explained. "I wonder, since you are a writer, if you'd give it a read-through?"

Here we go...my least favorite part about telling people I was a writer. For some reason, aspiring writers tended to think that ALL writers were professional editors and proofreaders, too. As if we had all this time on our hands to read their half-assed stories. Sure, let me just put my own writing on hold, along with everything else that came with being a writer such as researching and reading other books that were traditionally published in order to hone my skills, so that I could read the sloppy first draft of a story in a genre that I was the least bit interested in.

Granted, only about three people have asked me to read their unfinished novels—two at the animal clinic and a barista at the coffee shop I frequented. But each time I was asked, I felt this incredible, uncomfortable weight of moral obligation right on my chest. I didn't want to be an asshole, so I agreed to read them. And each one was just as terrible as the next. Romance and erotica...of course. One of the stories was even too cringy to finish. The amount of raunch was just too overwhelming.

The people who wrote these stories weren't truly passionate about them or writing in general. It was abundantly clear when I'd given them constructive feedback and they didn't ask questions at all, and never again did I hear a thing about how their "books" were progressing. It was barely a hobby for them. Something they wanted to try out because of the release of a couple erotica novels that skyrocketed to the bestsellers list. *Oh, those authors wrote about sex? I'm human. I've had sex. I can write about it, too.* They liked the idea of being a writer, but just didn't want to take it seriously enough and dropped it completely when they realized how much work they'd actually have to do.

Now this man, who still hadn't told me his name, was towering over me in the darkened hallway full of deceased people, waiting for me to agree to read this monstrosity. I opened my mouth to answer, but he cut me off.

"Please, don't feel obligated. I understand that you are here on a vacation."

"No, it's okay," I interjected, forcing a smile. I had no idea why I couldn't tell this man no. "If anything, I'll just read a few chapters. How's that?"

He smirked. "Perfect. That's all I ask. Thank you. Do you happen to have any of your books on hand?"

I only brought a few copies of my second novel and had one stuffed inside my bag with my laptop. I retrieved it along with my business card that had my website and the names of my other novels so he could purchase one if interested. I didn't mind giving one book away for free. Most of the time, it was a helpful marketing gimmick that sort of coaxed the reader into buying more of my work...if they enjoyed the free one.

I passed my book into his hands. He smiled. "How lovely! I look forward to reading your work. I'm Landon, by the way. Landon Hazelhurst."

"It's nice to meet you, Landon. I'm going to get ready for dinner now."

Landon bowed his head then disappeared into the shadows of the corridor. I finally entered my room, locking the door behind me and realizing that Landon never did tell me how old he was.

Chapter Seven

For some odd reason, I'd had the gut feeling to pack at least one semi-dressy outfit. Although I planned to stay in to write, I haphazardly stuffed it into my suitcase as a just-in-case. Just in case I felt like wearing something other than the usual oversized T-shirt tucked into denim overalls or jeans—my idea of comfortable. But I was stressing out. Madame Clara distinctly said to dress appropriately, which was a bit vague. I hadn't the slightest clue what the appropriate attire would be for a bed-and-breakfast dinner.

I had been to semi-formal occasions at my parents' country club—social mixers that my mother insisted I attend in order to make friends and find a suitor. I had to pop a benzo every single time I went, but it still didn't ease the tension enough to pull me away from sitting at the farthest table in the corner, away from every other desperate twenty-something trying to find love. And, anyway, I wasn't the best at transforming myself from chill to glamorous. You'd think my fashion and makeup situation would be on point considering I had rich parents who always dressed to the nines, but I honestly didn't give a rat's ass about that stuff. When someone suffered from anxiety and depression, sometimes self-care tended to take a backseat to everything else.

Speaking of benzos, the muscles in my body were going rigid again. My feel-good meds were wearing off, the anxiety hitting me with a new wave of worry over being alone and so far away from home. But now there was the added anticipation of seeing Aidan's face after that spontaneous make-out session in the hallway and uncertainty about what I might have to eat for dinner and Landon's million-page manuscript glaring at me from where I had set it down next to my laptop on the writing desk. That nauseating churn was starting in the pit of my stomach, and I switched my attention from unloading my suitcase to the satchel sitting right next to it on the bed. The orange bottle of pills rested right on top of everything else. My very own IN CASE OF EMERGENCY box.

I wasn't addicted to these anti-anxiety pills. In all honesty, I only ever really used them when I knew I was going to be in a situation that would heighten the possibility of a panic attack. When I was writing in my apartment, I didn't need them. And when I was doing mundane, routine things like working or shopping for groceries, they weren't particularly necessary. Those were places I frequented all the time. I knew what to expect when I had to go. But if I knew I was going to be stuck somewhere and couldn't leave right away—when my *options* were limited—then I would take one.

Again, I began to wonder why I was even here in the first place. While going to the mountains in Maine wasn't my first choice, especially because I had never even been before and traveling alone wasn't exactly the best thing for my mental stability, staying in my apartment and stressing over coming up with a story idea for a new book might have been worse.

I needed a different setting. And after careful consideration and making an enormous list of pros and cons—where the cons outweighed the pros, but I left that sheet of paper at home—I decided to just go for it. While this decision was going to test whether or not the many years of therapy had been a total waste of money, it had to be done to find out. My heart felt like it was ready to finally put the past behind me, but my mind was doing that thing where it made me second guess my choices over and over again until I finally gave up and chose to quit altogether. But then there was the creative part of my brain that craved inspiration. Scratch that. It was in NEED of some. Something to ignite that fire under my ass to get words down on paper.

You had to do this, McCall.

I eyed the bottle of pills thoughtfully, considering what the consequences would be if I decided against taking one right now. Dr. Finn constantly reminded me that while I was too busy searching for actual exit doors and coming up with ways to make sure I could get to my safe zone—otherwise known as my home—as quickly as possible, that I forget no matter what was going on, no matter where I was, I always had an escape. The benzodiazepines. They were always with me. A tiny tablet and a sip of water could douse those irrational little wildfires that sprung up at the most inopportune times. All I had to do was reach into my purse, swallow one, and it would be over.

Now if I didn't take one, what was the worst that could happen? I'd have to excuse myself from dinner to run up to my bedroom for a pill? Better yet, why didn't I just bring them down with me? Stick a tablet inside my bra?

It was a new beginning for me. Deciding to leave Florida alone was just the first step to getting my life back after all these years. It was time that hobo son of a bitch stopped controlling me. I lifted the bottle up to get a good view, shook it once to hear the clamor of the pills, then shoved them back into my bag.

You can do this, McCall.

I walked away from that bag and unzipped the other, pulling out my sweater dress and laying it out on the bed. In only my bra and panties, I spun around in search of a mirror to apply the little bit of makeup that I owned. The bathroom a few doors down was sure to have one, but it would be a miracle if it was empty, especially if all the guests were getting ready for dinner at the same time.

My short quest to finding a mirror in this room had failed. Not one in sight. There were only four framed crotchet squares hanging near the desk and a portrait on the wall in front of the bed. It was of a woman, posing head on from the waist up. It didn't quite stick out to me when I'd entered my room for the first time. Sort of blended in with the wallpaper. I padded closer to it, grazing the ornate, tarnished gold frame with my fingertips. The colorized photo was old and faded, but the woman in the picture was still very much visible. A familiar-looking lady sporting the same Edwardian hairstyle as Madame Clara. She stared back at me, and I realized that she very much resembled Madame Clara in physical features as well. They had the same steely glare, as if to be mentally scolding anything and everything. I wondered if maybe there was some relation. It would only make sense to have pictures of loved ones hanging up inside a house that had been in the family for generations. If she was kin to Madame Clara, she had to have been a great-great-great aunt or something because clearly the portrait dated back way before any of our times, and then some. Her outfit alone was proof of that. Buttons. So many buttons running vertically up the front of her garment, along her stomach and chest. The lace from her dress rose all the way up her neck, practically strangling her. Giant pearl earrings dotted her earlobes, and an elegant barrette was planted right on top of her head. Madame Clara did do a pretty good job of replicating the outfits from that time in history.

I turned away from the portrait to fetch my compact mirror in my luggage, but an odd sensation pricked at the peach fuzz on the back of my neck. The sound in the room changed, stimulating my eardrums. There was a strange phantom feeling, like one would get when they were alone in a room, and then suddenly, they felt an empty presence. A space in the air that was being filled by something they couldn't see. The many horror movies I'd seen where clueless characters approached something frightening by slowly walking toward it crossed my mind. If only they understood that they were just giving the villain enough time to get to them, they might live through to the end.

I quickly twisted myself in all directions of the room, scanning every inch for something or someone. There was nothing except myself and my own ragged breaths. But even still, there was an invisible presence somewhere near me. The portrait of the lady on the wall caught my attention again, and I studied it.

Once more, I stepped closer to the frame, analyzing it thoroughly. Every outline of her face. The way the ashen color of the picture made her skin look so smooth. Not a single blemish across her defined cheekbones. Fly-aways from her elegant hairstyle delicately framed her eyes, her dark, thick eyebrows arched just above them. Long eyelashes outlined her irises and pupils. And her eyes... They were red. Almost glowing. Certainly a red-eye effect that usually occurred when using a photographic flash. However, upon deeper inspection, I couldn't tell if this was a photograph or maybe a painting.

I leaned in even closer. Those eyes were so hypnotizing. Mysterious. I almost wanted to—

Blink

What?! What just happened? She blinked. The woman in the portrait blinked right in front of me. Her eyelids literally just shut then opened again!

I shuffled backward until my ass hit the edge of the bed. *Holy shit!* I stared at the woman in the portrait and the woman stared back at me, her eyes open and regular and red and just the way they were before she blinked, but she most certainly just fucking blinked! My heart thumped inside my chest and my hands began to tremble. What the hell was that?

A light rapping at my door practically threw my already frightened body on top of the bed and under the covers, but I was quickly able to determine that someone must have been knocking from the other side. I rushed for the doorknob and swung the door to my room wide open.

Aidan's eyes expanded into saucers as they swept over my half-naked body. Too many seconds passed before I realized what he was gawking at. I threw my arms over as much bare skin as I could.

"Shit!" I blurted, and then slammed the door in Aidan's face.

"I'll...uh...I'll just see you at dinner," he muttered through the door.

I facepalmed myself, shaking my head at my stupidity. My encounters with this guy were getting strangely out of hand. I huffed a few breaths of embarrassment away before glancing back at the woman on the wall. She was there in the same spot I'd left her, with the same facial expression. Glowing, crimson eyes open. Stony glare. Motionless. Did I imagine her eyes blinking? I must have. There was no way a picture could have done that.

To avoid making physical contact with the portrait, I maneuvered around the edge of the bed and back to my bags to continue getting ready for dinner. It wasn't that I was afraid of it. I just didn't trust it. Or myself. There was an annoying itch to pull that sucker off the wall to investigate. Examine the back of it for some kind of string or mechanism that could have manipulated the woman's eyes. But I didn't want to do it because...I had to have been wrong.

The bottle of medication inside my bag caught my eye. Was I having some kind of weird side effect from not taking one? Or was it stress? Or anxiety? Or paranoia? All of those things could cause hallucinations. Induce a multitude of bizarre psychoses. Or it could have just been that my brain was coming down from the medication and not responding well to it leaving my body, something that I'd never experienced before in the nine years I'd been taking it.

I attempted to focus on getting my outfit together, but my gaze slowly shifted from the clothes to the woman in the portrait on the wall of my room. "You totally blinked at me, bitch," I mumbled, wondering if she could hear me.

Chapter Eight

I stepped out into the hallway backwards, the front of my body facing the bedroom door. I shut it then ran my fingers along the wire of my bra to make sure one last time that the emergency pill was there. There was a brief moment of bravery when I considered not taking it with me and placing the entire bottle inside the safe underneath the desk, where I had placed my laptop and purse. But I couldn't quite get up the nerve. The irrational what-ifs invaded all other thoughts. What if I needed to get to it, but couldn't in time? What if I lost the key to the safe?

The rational portion of my brain tried to challenge my own question: why would I need the whole bottle? I only ever took one tablet at a time if I needed to. That was when I decided to compromise with myself and plucked one tablet from the bottle, stuffed it into my bra, and left the rest inside my travel bag.

My fingers found the round outline of the pill. This dress didn't have pockets, but thankfully, the cup of my bra was large enough to hold things securely. I thought about stuffing my notebook of story ideas in there, too. While my breasts were large for my petite size, they weren't *that* big. Trust me, I'd tried.

"Ugh! Can you believe we don't have a way to lock our rooms?" Gwen scoffed behind me. I turned around to spot her screwed-up expression a few doors down the hallway. She and Preston were engaged in their own conversation and hadn't noticed me yet.

"Honey, it'll be okay. We've placed some of our valuables in the safe," Preston said.

"Yeah, *some*. What about the rest that couldn't fit? Like my Chanel poncho? It's vintage!"

Gwen pouted and sucked in a breath of air, a squeal escaping her mouth. Preston consoled her by rubbing her back, and she leaned into him as though her world was crumbling around her and she needed his support. I dropped my head and began to walk down the hallway toward the stairs, trying my damnedest to go unseen, but Gwen was set on inviting me to her pity party.

"McCall!" she cried out.

I stopped, closed my eyes for a brief moment, then plastered a smile on my face and swung around. I had only known Gwen for approximately four and a half hours, but I already knew she was a handful.

"McCall," she howled, waving off Preston's aged, comforting hands. She staggered over to me, stopping just inches from my face. I couldn't help but gape at her ample bosoms, both of which were practically spilling over the front of an extremely low-cut, shiny gold dress. The hemline stole my attention, and I couldn't keep my eyes from wandering down to her tanned thighs. One wrong move and Gwen's crotch would be on full display. Here's hoping she was actually wearing underwear. I couldn't wait to see Madame Clara's reaction to Gwen's *appropriate* dinner attire.

"McCall, can you believe this place? How are we supposed to have any fun if we're all worried about who's going into our bedroom and stealing our things?"

Preston leaned in and whispered, "Sweetie, I don't think anyone will—"

Gwen raised her voice over his, tossing a long, untamed strand of platinum hair over her shoulder. Her mane seemed more voluminous than it did before, and I assumed half of it wasn't even real. She most definitely added extensions for this dinner. "What kind of hotel doesn't have key cards?"

Ah ha! She didn't know exactly what a bed-and-breakfast was, either. Although, now I wasn't too proud to be in the same club as Gwen. Subtly, I glanced at my watch, noting that we had exactly fifteen minutes to get downstairs to the dining room. This was a reservation I didn't want to be late for, seeing as the consequence might just be Madame Clara refusing to serve me dinner if I was. Without interrupting Gwen's rant about the lack of "hotel" security, I turned back toward the stairs and continued walking. Gwen and Preston followed suit, but the tirade didn't let up.

"The only reason I'm even on this trip is because every other one of our favorite resorts was booked! People just couldn't wait to take their vacations after quarantine was finally lifted."

"Well, we liked the idea of being in a place with so much history, though," Preston added, clearly desperate for Gwen's approval.

Gwen leaned in close to my ear. "I would much rather be getting a massage on the beach at St. Regis."

"What was that, darling?"

"Oh, nothing, Puddin'. I was just saying how it sucks we won't even be able to go hiking!" she said over her shoulder to Preston, but then her big, crimson lips mouthed *no* at me. A pang of pity struck my heart for Preston. Poor guy probably never got to do anything he wanted to do. They were only here because of a technicality.

Gwen's fretting carried on as we descended the stairs to the foyer, right up until we entered the dining room and gathered around the massive dining room table. As much as I didn't really care about her rich-girl problems, people like Gwen sometimes made interesting characters in a book. Secondary characters, though. They were never the main. Too egocentric to be the hero. People like her were deemed useless in just the first few chapters.

The varnished, wooden dining table nearly took up the entire room. On it, an elaborate spread of china and silverware and etched water glasses adorned almost every inch, reflections from candles in the giant brass candelabra set right in the middle of the table flickering a tawny gleam all over everything. Ellen and her two kids were already seated on one side of the table, Aidan sitting next to Max on the end. Tom sat across from Ellen on the other side, and Preston and Gwen took their seats next to him. This meant that the last chair available was directly across from Aidan.

There were two ways I could approach this situation. I could lift my head up, straighten my back out, and confidently saunter over to my seat. Just act like Aidan didn't on purpose/accidentally make out with me, and then get an eyeful of my undergarments, which was basically a bikini anyway. Random people on the beach have seen me in a bikini, which practically never happened because I practically never went to the beach.

Or I could cower and shamefully drag my heeled boots in his direction, never making eye contact with him once throughout dinner. I hadn't been involved with a guy in so long, I forgot about the protocols—if there even were any. The benzo was no longer actively coursing through my bloodstream, which most definitely would have made this a whole lot easier. Its job was to make me care less, and the less I cared, the less my mind would overthink things. But I was on a journey of healing. It had been nine whole years since some asshole ruined my life. I'd taken this gigantic step forward when I decided to even come on this writing retreat alone. And now I was here, and I wasn't going to let—

"Miss Harris!" Madame Clara barked. "If you could please take your seat so Chef Winston can serve your appetizers."

My eyes darted between everyone sitting at the table, all of whom were staring back at me, confused as to why I had just been standing there motionless. I nodded at Madame Clara and lowered my gaze, then began my walk of embarrassment toward the seat in front of Aidan. Too late to choose the audacious McCall with no fucks given. Aidan probably already understood why I had hesitated before sitting down, but I was sure everyone else just thought I was an idiot.

I pulled my chair out and yanked the hem of my sweater dress down, self-conscious that Aidan might see too much leg, which was ridiculous. He'd already seen a lot more than I'd wanted. My elbow made contact with the silverware as I sat, sliding it against the porcelain china plates and generating an obnoxious clank, which sounded ten times louder echoing throughout the quiet room. Everyone's eyes were on me, waiting for me to get settled.

Don't care, McCall. Just don't care about it.

Madame Clara's attention went straight to Gwen, her expressionless face morphing into a scowl. "Mrs. Prescott, at Hazelhurst Manor, we prefer our guests to dress in a more appropriate manner. This is not a brothel."

"Excuse me?" Gwen asked, bringing her hand up to her chest as if surprised by Madame Clara's brazen comment.

"Your smock is far too revealing for dinner, and I will not tolerate such a lewd attempt at getting attention."

Gwen gasped. "Getting attention?"

Madame Clara did not waver. "Dinner may not be served until Mrs. Prescott either changes her dress or covers herself up."

I was thankful to no longer be the prime focus in the room, but what was happening to Gwen seemed far worse than clumsily drawing unwanted awareness to myself. The rest of the group sat still and silent. Even Preston didn't know what to say when his wife stared at him, waiting for him to say something to defend her. Finally, she spoke. "I don't remember seeing anything about mandatory dress attire on the application," she said, sass dripping from every word. I questioned whether or not she even had a hand at filling out the application. Preston probably did it all.

"I'd like to give our guests the benefit of the doubt when it comes to comprehending what is considered class and what is not."

Oh snap! Madame Clara was extracting her claws and digging straight into Gwen. I wrung my fingers under the table, holding my breath and fighting to swallow the lump in my throat. Madame Clara looked on and Gwen stared at her. I presumed she was desperately searching every corner of her brain for some kind of cheeky comeback. One to match Madame Clara's shameless remarks. But the tension in the dining room was devastating. Between Gwen and Madame Clara and me and Aidan, I didn't know what was about to happen and the shadow of my anxiety monster was there. It was ready to reveal itself.

To everyone's surprise—and I knew this because three people at the table audibly gasped, including myself—Gwen promptly stood up from her chair, scraping the legs on the Persian rug underneath. She slammed her cloth napkin down on her plate, let out a whiny groan, then stomped away, around Madame Clara and up the stairs, her heels pounding with every step.

It could have been that I was seeing things, but Madame Clara's lips curled up for only a split second—a unit of time short enough to miss by a mere blink—before returning to its usual angry frown.

Chapter Nine

Not a single word was uttered at the table in Gwen's absence. Even the children looked to be too afraid to move. Long, agonizingly uncomfortable minutes passed before the rumble of Gwen's heels vibrated through the floor above us, making their way down the hallway, then the stairs, and back into the dining room. With her chest now shrouded by a glittery shawl, she plopped down in her chair and aggressively placed her cloth napkin back on her lap. The shawl was completely sheer, her cleavage still commanding the spotlight. Gwen's rebellion against Madame Clara's house rules. But it seemed to satisfy the lady enough for us to finally move on from the whole debacle that was Gwen's boobs.

"Now that everyone has arrived..." Madame Clara announced.

"Bitch," Gwen whispered only loud enough for me to hear.

"...dinner may begin." Right on cue, the door that led to the kitchen swung open and a metal cart filled with plates of food rolled out of it. A very small, old man wearing a white chef's jacket two sizes too big and an almost comically tall chef's hat was hunched over the handle, operating it from behind. He wheeled the cart to Aidan's side of the table first, moving at a snail's pace, then began to distribute the appetizers to each person.

"Your first course is jellied eels," Madame Clara said from where she stood at the head of the table. It seemed she wasn't going to be having dinner with us, which was perfectly fine with me. She, along with her employees, probably waited until the guests were done to have their meals. "These particular eels have been imported from England, the recipe loaned to us by Winston, the Hazelhurst Manor chef."

Madame Clara gestured at Chef Winston as he set plates down in front of Missy and Max. The kids didn't for a second hide their horrified expressions at the jiggling serving of seafood before them. Madame Clara watched them carefully. "Many people like to add a splash of vinegar or a pat of butter to elevate the flavor," she suggested.

Chef Winston finally made his way to me, placing the plate of exotic fish in front of me. I wasn't sure if eels were considered exotic or not, but they certainly were to me. Even growing up with parents who had expensive taste, I had never in my life eaten this. Caviar was a staple at the country club, but I didn't dare touch it. Disgusting.

The chef gave me a crooked smiled, the deep pockmarks in his blanched skin stretching with his chapped lips. His spaced-out teeth brown and yellow against the glow of the candles. A few strings of gray hair had found their way out of the chef's hat. His white eyebrows were as bushy and wild as those of a teenaged girl who had never plucked before. I smiled at him weakly, carefully checking his eyes. Chef Winston looked like he could have been a homeless man Madame Clara had picked up just that morning. My heartbeat quickened at the memories of that horrible night...

But the color of Chef Winston's pupils was, remarkably, the same unique purplish hue as Landon's and Madame Clara's. I had to remind myself that this was a family-owned operation. Therefore, the chef could very much be related to Landon and Madame Clara and have that same rare genetic eye condition.

I glanced down at my eels. Thankfully, they were chopped up into small pieces, but encased in some kind of clear, gelatinous substance—hence the name *jellied* eels. It didn't even look close to appetizing. When Chef Winston finished distributing the first course and disappeared back into the kitchen, I poked at the texture with my fork, wondering how the hell I was going to swallow a bite of it. Dread began to bubble in the pit of my stomach over the idea of chewing through the gray outer layer. I could somehow taste the potent fishy odor exuding from the plate.

The din of cutlery making contact with glass came from the rest of the table, and I glanced at Aidan first. He was slapping pats of butter onto his eels, then stirring the jelly and the eels and the butter to mix them all together into a mushy mess. Tom and Ellen took turns pouring an obscene amount of vinegar over their dish until the eels were swimming in it. The kids steadily glared at their food; their backs pushed against their chairs as they stabbed at their dishes with a fork a safe distance away.

Gwen, who sat next to me, braved the originality of the eels without adding anything to it. A chunk rested on her fork, which she held up in front of her face and thoroughly inspected. She smelled it then stuck her tongue out and allowed only the tiniest tip of it to make contact. When it did, she scrunched her face and reached out for her water glass, frantically taking a huge gulp.

Strangely, the sound of chewing drew everyone's eyes in the same direction. We all watched Preston, who was seated at the far end of the table, casually slicing smaller pieces of his eel and placing it into his mouth. He nodded his head and raised his brows in satisfaction, swallowing then going for more. When he finally realized the only noise in the room was coming from himself, he met all of our gazes.

"This is so interesting," he said between bites, completely clueless that we were all gawking at him in sickened amazement. "Quite delicious. Madame Clara, is this a meal that was frequently served in the eighteen hundreds?"

Preston's delight over the jellied eels was unexpected and gag-inducing. But the fact that Madame Clara was still standing near the table, watching over all of us, was downright creepy. It was almost like she was trying to make sure we ate the food in front of us.

"Jellied eels were considered a snack and sold from street carts in London in the Victorian era," she explained.

"Um, can we please have some cocktails or something?" Gwen rasped.

"Wine and spirits will be served in the parlor after dinner," Madame Clara answered. That was unfortunate. Having something to drink other than water would definitely help choke down the rest of this meal.

Each of us managed to take at least one bite of the vile appetizer, and I wasn't even exaggerating. It was absolutely, positively the most vile thing I had put in my mouth. The way the fish squished and popped open between my teeth and the salty, clear Jello substance filled my cheeks and found its way into every crevice. It was almost traumatizing.

Madame Clara—clearly displeased by the amount of leftovers on everyone's plates, except Preston's—helped Chef Winston clear the half-eaten dishes from the table. This was immediately followed by the distribution of the main course.

As Chef Winston was busy placing entrees in front of everyone, and Madame Clara stood back and watched, waiting for him to finish so that she could explain what we were about to eat, the kitchen door swung open and a younger woman carrying a glass pitcher of water appeared. Her long, charcoal hair was parted down the middle and outlined her pale, narrow face, the length of it reaching all the way down to her butt. The features of her face were colorless. No makeup. Lips nearly white. Overall, she just looked washed out and sickly. Like she was severely anemic.

The girl wore a white, long-sleeved blouse with buttons for days, which tucked into a floor-length, ruffled red skirt that swooshed as she walked. She made it to Aidan first, reaching around him from behind to fill his water glass. Without looking up from what she was doing, without uttering a single word even when someone thanked her, she replenished the water glasses around the table.

When she reached over me with the pitcher to refill my glass, a touch of her scent found its way into my nose. It was a hint of foul familiarity that struck me. An odor that I'd only smelled once before, nine years ago. My pulse immediately revved up, and I became frozen in my seat, especially when she turned to me and our eyes met. Her eyes. They were not that unique purple shade that Landon and Chef Winston and Madame Clara had. They weren't anything like the seven other people who were sitting at this table.

They were gray. Gray and empty and menacing.

For some reason, she seemed to be enraged by my presence as she narrowed her gaze at me before retracting her arm from my water glass. Then she scampered out of the room with her head down, her long, obsidian hair hiding her face. I glanced around at the other guests sitting at the table, trying to see if anyone else had caught a glimpse of the way she stared me down like she wanted to bite me or something, but everyone was preoccupied with other things.

On top of the incredibly unsettling resemblance of her eyes to the man that could have killed me so long ago, it was apparent that she was, indeed, the woman with milky-white skin and raven-colored hair from the third-story window I'd spotted upon entering Hazelhurst Manor earlier. I was happy to learn that I hadn't imagined her, but now I was rattled.

It had never occurred to me to consider that maybe the "man" who attacked me at my sixteenth birthday party was actually a woman. All these years, all of the many eyeballs belonging to men that I had examined—every hobo on the street corner or under a bridge that I thought could possibly be the asshole who ruined my life. Any male who looked like he could even remotely be capable of fitting the bill of the stinky man with silver eyes, I questioned. But the idea of it being a female... I just never thought of that.

The smell of the entree snapped me back into the now, which was much better than the jellied eels and rank odor of the long-haired girl. It actually even looked appealing enough to enjoy. A round meat patty on a bed of lettuce surrounded by vegetables. My mouth watered, the hunger beginning to take over. I hadn't eaten a single thing since before my trip, and that seafood atrocity currently trying to digest in my stomach wasn't enough food for me. My guts bubbled, and I wondered if it was just hunger or that my belly was offended by what I fed it. It could also very well be the new unnerving suspicion that just about ANYONE, male or female, could have attacked me many years ago.

"The main course before you is haggis," Madame Clara declared. I had no idea what haggis was, but that name worried me.

"Ah, yes!" Preston enthused. "I've heard of this but have never had it." Of course he had heard of it. He was older than my parents. "If my memory serves me right, I believe it's sheep."

"That is correct, Mr. Prescott. But more specifically, it's the heart, liver, and lungs of the sheep."

And there it went. My appetite had completely vanished. Aidan's eyes widened as he glanced down at his plate in distaste. Ellen's shoulders slumped, as if she'd just been let down. And Gwen whispered near my ear, "What would it take to get a damn Caesar salad around here?"

My sympathy truly lay with the kids. Missy and Max simply looked defeated. Max tilted his head and huffed a breath like he'd just had the longest day at work. Missy almost looked green. She leaned over to her mother, who sat next to her, and whispered something.

"It's okay, sweetie. It's meat. You like meat," Ellen said in a soothing tone.

Madame Clara glared at the kid. "It will not harm you, child."

"I don't want to eat sheep," Missy mumbled.

"What was that?" Madame Clara asked, rushing over to Missy's chair.

"I said, I don't want to eat sheep!" Missy picked up the haggis patty and tossed it to the middle of the table. The meat collided with a water glass, knocking it against another water glass, cracking them both. I had never really been around a kid who was having one, but I assumed this was what they called a tantrum.

"Melissa!" Tom and Ellen both exclaimed.

But out of the blue, Madame Clara pulled Missy's arm and yanked her out of her seat and away from the table. Gripping the little girl's forearm, so tight that I could see Madame Clara's fingertips dip into her skin, she leaned down and pointed a finger in Missy's face.

"You are not to throw things in this house! You have broken my glasses and for that you should be punished!"

Tom and Ellen both stood up, their expressions clearly stunned by the way Madame Clara was treating Missy. Ellen quickly moved to her daughter's aid, picking her up and snatching her out of Madame Clara's clenched fist. Missy yelped, and I prayed that it was only out of fright and not because Madame Clara actually hurt the kid.

Tom threw himself in front of Madame Clara and his family. "How dare you touch my child! What's wrong with you, lady?"

Madame Clara straightened up, crossed one hand over the other and rested them in front of her groin. Suddenly, she was cool, calm, and collected. "That *child* needs to be disciplined. We do not tolerate such behavior at Hazelhurst Manor."

"She's angry because of this ridiculous food!" he yelled, the veins in his neck protruding as he spoke. "You expect a kid to eat this? If you're going to invite children into your home, then you should be prepared to cater to them. We are paying you, after all."

"I expect your children to have manners," she retorted.

"Well, you can take your manners and shove them up your ass." Tom leaned into Madame Clara, his face so close to her, I was afraid he might headbutt her. "We're leaving first thing in the morning. Come on, Max."

Max hopped off his chair and the entire family shuffled out of the dining room and up the stairs, the sounds of little Missy's soft weeps lingering behind.

I hadn't realized it, but my hands had been covering my mouth the entire time this was unfolding in front of me. The rest of us peered into one another's bewildered eyes. Silent and completely at a loss for words. Only the heavy ticktocks of the grandfather clock echoed from another room. Madame Clara smoothed out her gown and attempted to smile by pressing her lips into a hard line. "Let's finish up dinner, shall we? Dessert is waiting."

What the shit just happened?

Chapter Ten

The rest of dinner, food-wise, turned out to be not so bad. I wasn't sure if maybe my hunger had overpowered everything else, but I managed to get down most of the haggis. Once I got past the weird crumbly layer and faint bitterness of what a dirty gym sock might taste like, the "meat" kind of hit the spot. And dessert was surprisingly delicious. I had heard of baked Alaska before, but never tried it. The cake part was spongy, the ice cream was creamy, and the toasted meringue on top was the perfect crunchy texture to bring it all together. Chef Winston even made a whole display of it, splashing a bit of rum over the top and igniting it, creating a mesmerizing burst of blue-tinged flames. I nearly giggled with excitement when it happened and wished he could do it over and over again.

However, after the incident with Tom, Ellen, and their kids, the rest of us were still at a loss for words. As I took bites of the strange 19th-century supper and chewed quietly, I replayed the whole thing from start to finish in my brain. How shit just hit the fan seemingly out of nowhere. Madame Clara's stern voice. The way she gripped Missy's little arm, her nails, polished black, digging into the kid's skin. How irate Tom had become, practically leaping out of his seat and lurching at Madame Clara. There was a split second where I thought he was going to reach out and wrap his hands around her throat; he was so mad. I had never seen anything like it before, and I couldn't wait to get upstairs to write it all down. Not that I would exploit the way Missy was treated. She was clearly freaked out by this woman she barely even knew handling her as if she were some orphaned troublemaker. But a good book, in my opinion, required a healthy dose of shock and awe. And this...was shocking.

As I mulled over the events that had just taken place, thoughts of the girl with long, black hair and evil gray eyes pouring me water crept in. I was trying to convince myself that there was no way the girl, who looked to be a few years younger than me, could have had anything to do with my attack so long ago. It would have been biologically impossible.

My irrational brain was fighting me on it, though. Just more of a reason for me to get my ass upstairs to start writing. To focus all my efforts on something else other than my past. Besides, Dr. Finn and I had discussed on many occasions the possibility of my anxiety and paranoia causing delusions, which is partially why I was pretty positive the blinking portrait in my bedroom didn't actually blink at me. I could just be imagining that girl having the same eyes as my attacker.

As much as I wanted to run up to my room and get started on writing something epic, it would have to wait. Dinner was done, and Madame Clara insisted that we move our little party into the parlor for after-dinner drinks and mingling.

"The whole point of a bed-and-breakfast, and why it stands out against a corporately run hotel, is for the guests to create a genuine experience *together*," she'd said before corralling us into the other room.

I finally got the definition of a B&B. But had I known that I was going to have to share my day with perfect strangers, I would have chosen a damn Motel 6. My plans were to spend the entire weekend holed up in my room, writing and eating takeout from a local IHOP or chips and chocolate bars from a vending machine. I even brought the change and loose dollar bills I kept in a velvet Crown Royal bag from under my bed back home. Getting to know random people and having to attend dinner with them was never even a thought that crossed my mind.

But I was here. In my sweater dress. Wearing minimal makeup and heeled boots and currently fighting back the anxiety demons that were hanging off the ledge of my sanity. They wanted to fall into my limbs to make them tremble and into my stomach to make me nauseous, but I was managing to keep them at bay. Mentally talk them down.

You have options, McCall. You have your pill in your bra and you can go back upstairs at any time.

A silver tray of alcoholic beverages sat in the middle of the coffee table in the parlor. I picked up a glass of champagne and strolled over to the extravagant fireplace in search of warmth. The entire house was drafty, and I wished I had my coat.

"You look really nice tonight," Aidan said as he approached me, one hand in the pocket of his slacks and the other holding a cocktail. We stood next to the fireplace together, the red-orange incandescence brightening the amber liquid in his glass. I shifted my weight from one foot to the other and took a sip from my champagne flute. The bubbles tickled the back of my throat and I coughed deliberately, trying to buy myself time to figure out what to say. We were both guilty of avoiding eye contact during dinner. We were both clearly embarrassed and confused by what happened in the hallway earlier. But I wouldn't be able to evade him all weekend long, especially if we were obligated to "experience" things together.

"Thank you. You do, too," I finally replied, and I meant it. The knit beanie was gone, so his chocolate-colored curls were free to playfully hang over his forehead. The starched collar of a button-down shirt flapped over a V-neck sweater, a solid gray color that looked so soft against his chest, I just wanted to cuddle him. His thick-framed glasses were such the quintessential nerd accessory, but admittedly sexy. Like some kind of off-duty superhero.

"Listen, I'm sorry about—"

"Hey, I just wanted to apolo—"

We started at the same time, and then stopped mid-sentence.

"Ladies first," he said.

My heart sped up. I didn't want to be first. "I...um...I didn't mean to kiss you." His eyebrow sprung up. "I didn't mean to kiss you back?"

Jesus. It came out as a question because I realized just then that I didn't even know what I was apologizing for. He was the one who kissed me out of nowhere. I shouldn't be apologizing for responding to something *he* initiated. Sure, I could have pushed him away. I probably *should* have pushed him away. But I was caught off guard. And then there was the fact that I hadn't been kissed in years. But he didn't know that. And there were the sex noises penetrating through the walls. It made me imagine things and stimulate certain areas of my body and—

"You don't have to apologize," he said, pulling me out of my speeding thoughts before they derailed. "I'm sorry for kissing you. It was completely inappropriate. I've never done something like that to someone I've just met. Honestly, I should be thanking you for not slapping me."

I took another pull of my champagne, internally asking myself why I hadn't. "It's okay. Really. We can totally pretend like it didn't even happen."

He glanced down at his shoes and nodded. "Yeah, no...that makes sense. It won't happen again. It's just..." His eyes drifted back up to mine, and then he leaned in. "Did you feel funny at all? Like maybe something was pushing us together?" he asked, his voice nearly a whisper.

I took a small step back when I noticed that my eyes were following his lips. What did he mean by 'pushing us together?' Because if he was talking about destiny or fate or things like that, I wasn't completely sure I believed in it. The memory of his hand caressing my face flickered through my mind, and I blinked the images away. "I don't know what you mean," I confessed.

His brows came together, and his eyes moved between me and whatever he focused on behind me. "It was like I didn't have control over what I was doing. I heard the sex sounds, and then my mind just switched—"

"Ooh, sex sounds? From where?" Gwen sashayed to where Aidan and I stood, one hand daintily grasping her glass of champagne and the other pinching the calyx of a bright red strawberry. Preston joined her, his fingers wrapped around the stem of a wine glass. He swooshed the maroon liquid around and smelled it before bringing it up to his lips.

Aidan met her expecting stare then looked back at me. "Oh, uh...we were just talking about... McCall and I kind of heard you two. Earlier. In the hallway."

Gwen squinted at us. "In the hallway?"

I had to clarify. "We could hear you two...doing things through the walls in the hallway."

Gwen glanced at Preston, who shrugged. "Doing things like what?"

Really? Was she seriously going to make us say it?

"There were sounds coming from your room," Aidan reiterated.

"But what kind of sounds?"

"Sex sounds!" I blurted, ready for the charade to be over. I scanned the room, worried that someone else might have heard my outburst, then leaned in and spoke in a quieter tone. "Aidan and I heard you and Preston having sex."

Gwen's perfectly arched eyebrows shot up, and a lipstick-stained grin slowly crept up her face. Then she snapped her head toward her husband, her blonde hair dramatically whipping with her movements. They both chuckled. "That wasn't us."

"Look, we weren't talking negatively about you or anything," I said, trying my best to alleviate the obvious embarrassment Gwen felt by her denial of it. Though, she didn't strike me as someone who was bashful about things like this. "We were just saying that we heard you." I left out the part about Aidan and me kissing. Gwen would make a big deal about it, and it was no big deal. Aidan certainly didn't think it was a big deal, anyway.

"No, really. We haven't had sex here. I mean, not yet." Gwen's teeth glided across her bottom lip, and she winked at her senior husband. Preston's wrinkles stretched into a cheeky grin.

As much as I wanted to look away, I couldn't help but admire how into each other they were. It was completely evident that Preston viewed her as his trophy wife. He probably paraded her around his old friends as if she were the hardest prize to win at a carnival, but he won it. What surprised me the most was how Gwen viewed him. She reciprocated those adoring eyes. Even touched him as she spoke. Ran her fingers through his gray hair. It was all kind of sweet.

"Well, if it wasn't you two who were having sex, then who was it?" Aidan asked.

"Tom and Ellen?"

"No. No way," I said, recalling poor little Missy's soggy face when we ran into her and Tom in the hallway after she'd been sick. "How could they when they have two kids sharing a room with them?"

"And it wasn't you two?" Gwen asked, pointing a pink manicured nail between Aidan and me.

"No. No, no, no," we both declared simultaneously.

"Well, it must have been two of the employees then," she said matter-of-factly. Landon mysteriously appearing out of nowhere came to mind. "Now, should we talk about the elephant in the room, please?"

I was careful not to look over at Aidan, but I could feel his eyes on me. Shit. I didn't want anyone else to know about the kiss. It was enough that Tom probably figured it out when he exited the bathroom. The way I not-so-nonchalantly backed off Aidan. What if these people judged me for kissing someone I barely knew? Because I definitely should have been judged. His kiss could have turned into something worse—like the R word—and I didn't stop it. After what I had been through in the past, you would think that I'd report him to Madame Clara and have him removed from the premises for harassment. But the truth was—and I hated that I was admitting this—I hadn't been that close to someone in years, and I kind of liked it. And now I felt kind of guilty for liking it.

Didn't matter, anyway. It was painfully obvious he didn't mean to do it.

Gwen leaned in, and I braced myself. Ready to deny anything she had to say. "What the fuck was all that about at dinner?" she said. I let out a breath and glugged my champagne until it was completely gone. "That was insane, right?"

Preston decided to chime in on this one. "It was rather inappropriate. I didn't condone physically disciplining my own children. And if a stranger did so... I can only imagine what Tom and Ellen are feeling right now."

"And what about me?!" Gwen barked. I flinched, and Aidan recoiled from the unexpected rise in her volume. "That woman attacked me first!"

I barely knew Gwen, but it didn't shock me that she'd make what happened to that little girl about herself. Preston placed a hand on her back and rubbed, which must have been some kind of indication for her to lower her voice. Madame Clara had left us in the parlor alone, but who knew when she'd pop up again and start supervising us from the corner of the room.

"Who the hell is she to tell me I'm dressed inappropriately?" Gwen took a step back in her six-inch heels and gestured at the gilded dress that dazzled in the glow of the fireplace and fit her body like a glove. "This is Alexander McQueen. You do *not* cover up an Alexander McQueen."

"But you covered it up," Aidan said, and I choked back a chuckle. In her defense, what else was she supposed to do? Madame Clara was one scary bitch.

And then it hit me. Madame Clara would make the perfect antagonist in a story. Everything about her screamed *I'm the wicked witch of all four cardinal directions*. Or an evil stepmother. Yes! She could totally pass for an evil stepmother who was dead set on destroying her stepdaughter's life.

No. Wait. That was *Cinderella*. I had no interest in writing a retelling. But whatever story I wrote, the villain was going to be a woman with the same cantankerous attributes as the woman who ran this house. And her character arc would never change or grow, because something told me this was how Madame Clara had always been, and nothing or no one would ever make her evolve.

I missed the reason why Gwen decided to cover herself up after Madame Clara had demanded it. Something about the shawl belonging to another designer whom the first designer respected… I didn't know. I didn't care because that woman—the one with the water pitcher who filled our glasses at dinner—sauntered into the parlor just then and stole my attention. This time, she was carrying a fancy metal tray with another round of cocktails. Her hair was still stick straight and hiding most of her face, which was just as gaunt and sallow as it was earlier. With her focus on the tray and the assortment of liquor, ice cubes clanking with every step she took, the long-haired girl hooked around the button-back chairs and set the tray down on the coffee table, replacing the one with empty glasses on it. I mentally willed her to glance up at us, just for a moment, so that I could examine her eyes. Check the color of her pupils against the lambent light from the fireplace. Maybe they would reflect a completely different color.

She didn't look up. And as quickly as she came, she was gone without anyone else in the group even noticing her. Stealthily. Never making a single sound.

"…and it was really hard for me, you know? Being bullied is like the worst thing that could happen to anyone." Gwen sniffled into Preston's chest, and he coddled her—although there were clearly no mascara-streaked tears running down her cheeks.

A part of me really wanted to believe she wasn't going to be the predictable, privileged, rich girl who only cared about herself and designer clothes. I'd written those kinds of people into my books. They were always the worst. Helpless. Easy to manipulate. Inevitably doomed to die.

There was a moment of silent reflection—at least for me—over how this conversation went from Missy getting manhandled by Madame Clara to Gwen's tortured past before anyone spoke again.

"So, I think I'm going to head upstairs to my room," Aidan announced awkwardly.

Gwen perked up and was back to normal in an instant, like she wasn't just fake-crying on Preston's Royal Oxford shirt. "Wait! No! Let's hang out a little longer. Look, they brought more alcohol."

That poor drink girl. No one even noticed her enough to give her a proper pronoun. Also, I wasn't sure I wanted to stay for more of Gwen's teenage sob stories about how much money she had and how people didn't appreciate that. I came from a wealthy family, but certainly not Gwen's kind of rich. And even if I did, I doubt I'd be anything like her.

It was time to get my laptop open and write some words. I still wasn't completely sure what my next book was going to be about, but I had more than enough mental notes to brainstorm and come up with something. I could probably write a whole novel based on Madame Clara alone.

Gwen gallivanted over to the tray of drinks, picked up a champagne flute, and hurried back to me, shoving the glass in my face. "Come on. We're going to drink and get to know each other."

"I think that's a lovely idea, honey," Preston affirmed before taking a seat on the loveseat. Gwen plopped down next to him then pulled his chin toward her and planted a loud, sloppy kiss on his lips.

I twisted my gaze to Aidan, who seemed to be waiting for me to make a move. Since dinner, the anxiety had calmed down quite a bit. And since finishing this glass of bubbly, it seemed the alcohol was suppressing it. Keeping the edge off. As a matter of fact, having another drink might not be a bad idea.

I drank at home in the comfort of my apartment every now and then. Not sure if I should be bragging about that bit of information because one hundred percent of the time, I was drinking alone. But it was always just a glass of wine with dinner. I never drank to excess. It would be a tragedy if I decided to get drunk on the same night an intruder broke into my apartment. Although, it might be difficult for a robber to gain access into my gated community and get past my personal alarm system. And while I wasn't under the influence the night that hobo attacked me, I swore that I would never allow myself to ever be intoxicated enough to lower my inhibitions and let my guard down.

I eyed my empty glass. I *did* say that I was going to lay off the benzos for the weekend. Sipping on champagne would only loosen me up a bit more. Relax my nerves enough to finally stop thinking about the emergency pill I stuffed inside my bra—the one I had been thinking about every single second since I crammed it in there. And, anyway, I wasn't going to get drunk on just one more glass.

I lifted my eyebrows at Aidan as indication that I was down to have another drink. He shrugged then waved his hand in front of him. "Ladies first," he said and followed behind me to the seats across from Preston and Gwen.

Relax, McCall. You're going to be okay.

Chapter Eleven

My feet were cold. My feet and my legs. And my arms. Icy cool shivers generated goosebumps on my skin, which started at my shins and blossomed up through my body like the efferves-cence of a freshly poured glass of soda. My eyes popped open but were met with a wall of darkness. It didn't register that I was in my bedchamber, in my bed, until I rolled on my back and felt the silk sheets underneath my body. I attempted to move my limbs, but my muscles felt so heavy. As if they were weighed down by a twenty-pound blanket. Except, I didn't even think there was a blanket covering me.

With concentrated determination, I lifted my wrist close to my face to check the time on my smartwatch. It was blurred, but the time said 3:17 a.m. My arm dropped back down to the bed with a heavy thud.

It was completely black and completely silent in my room, but somehow the ceiling I couldn't even see was spinning. I slammed my eyes shut, worried that the whirls would force my stomach to heave everything I had fed it, including all the alcohol. Lots and lots of alcohol. More than I ever had in one sitting.

Glimpses of the girl with long, raven hair flashed through my mind, the way she returned over and over again with trays of cocktails, replacing our empty glasses with sparkling new ones filled with the crisp freshness of champagne for me and Gwen, and zesty old fashioneds for Aidan and Preston. Preston switched to the mixed drink when Aidan talked him into it—jokingly claiming that whiskey was more manly than wine. I had stolen a sip or two to test his theory, and sure enough, I concurred. It was too *manly* for me. Gwen nearly fell out of her chair when I coughed and choked on the astringent burn that coated my throat. I quickly followed it with a huge gulp of my champagne, the cool bubbles alleviating the bite of the bourbon.

I lay still in my bed for a while, eyes closed, reminiscing on just a few hours ago when the four of us were in the parlor. I wasn't drunk enough to have blacked out and forgotten about everything that happened. It was pretty fun, I would have to admit. Once the alcohol began to dull my senses, it also relaxed my nerves, putting the anxiety monster to sleep. The need for the emergency medication stashed inside my bra had completely been wiped away, which was for the best. I was thankful that I hadn't taken it earlier. Mixing benzos and alcohol would render me an inebriated mess. Probably not the best idea while surrounded by a bunch of strangers.

But they weren't really strangers anymore, were they? Getting to know Aidan, Gwen, and Preston was a good time. *They* were a good time. Although Gwen was a brat, there was a reason for it. She was born in Beverly Hills with a silver spoon already shoved in her mouth, having been brought up in a family that had way more money than my well-to-do parents. Her father was an oil tycoon. Her mother was a former model or actress or something. And the rest of her family were all overachievers and earned a wealthy living. It seemed I had misjudged her earlier—she wasn't after Preston for money because she had plenty of her own.

My Preston intuition was absolutely on point, however. He did have children from previous marriages and grown grandchildren. He was a little younger than I thought—by just two years—but it was completely clear after hearing about how their love story began that Gwen and Preston were truly happy together. Maybe even made for each other.

"He hired me to plan a Christmas party for his company," she'd said, placing a hand on Preston's knee. "After meeting him for the first time, I just knew we had a connection."

Gwen immediately went into detail about their first date, their first kiss, and even the first time they slept together, gushing over how Preston was so much more experienced than any other man she'd been with. Preston just sat back and smiled at her as she spoke, his lips nearly reaching the crow's feet of his eyes. He didn't seem to mind that she was giving us TMI, just looked utterly pleased by the mere sound of her voice.

Their courtship was short-lived, lasting only six months before Gwen popped the question one snowy evening on top of the Empire State Building. Could you believe it? The idea of seeing Little Miss Spoiled Brat down on one knee asking a man to take her hand in marriage was hard to grasp. She certainly didn't look like a woman who'd submit to any man. Preston, of course, said yes immediately, also adding, "I already had a ring. She just beat me to the punch."

"It's true! It's true!" Gwen sang and giggled. "He had the box inside his coat the whole time." She lifted her hand, revealing the enormous yellow diamond resting on her left ring finger. The flickering flames from the fireplace reflected light on the many facets of the stone, creating a glittering radiance that physically moved me. I gasped at its brilliance. Literally gasped out loud because I had never seen anything like it before. The thing must have cost Preston a fortune.

The conversation moved to Aidan. Good old kiss-me-out-of-nowhere-in-the-hallway-full-of-dead-people-photographs Aidan.

Aidan was a thirty-year-old born into a modest Cuban American family. As he sort of mentioned when we first got off the bus, he originally lived in Alabama with his parents but moved away with his dad at a young age to New York when they got divorced. He doesn't have the Southern accent I so stupidly assumed he should have when we first met, but I could hear a slight drawl in his words the more and more he spoke.

Aidan goaded us into guessing what he did for a living, and it actually became a rather entertaining game. Preston guessed that he was a bike courier or bike messenger because he lived in the city and had pretty good knowledge of all the places Preston mentioned visiting whenever he flew to New York on business. It was a decent guess, though anyone could be well-educated on landmarks and street names of the place they grew up in.

Gwen guessed that Aidan was... I thought she said a waiter cater? Although I could remember things, the alcohol still fuzzed up my memory a bit, despite sleeping off a few hours of it. But I was almost certain she said waiter cater. Cater waiter? Some kind of person who served food and drinks at parties. Which, in any case, was an honest way to earn a living if you asked me. In Gwen's eyes, however, that title was probably beneath her.

I guessed that Aidan was a professional computer hacker. To this, he smirked and gave me a nod of approval. For a second, I thought I had won the game! I had even shrieked in delight. But after taking a big pull of his drink, Aidan said, "You are *all* wrong."

Preston groaned playfully about not being right. Gwen rolled her eyes and mouthed "whatever." But when Aidan pointed at me and did a little head-wobble thing—evidently, being blitzed brought the sassiness out of him—he said, "*You* were a little right."

"What, you aren't a professional?" I asked, laughing and snorting in between words as if it was the most clever comeback. Gwen joined in with me and we laughed hysterically for several minutes. Though, thinking back on it, it wasn't even that funny.

"No!" he hollered then smiled really wide, showing off a mouth full of straight, gleaming white teeth. "I work with computers. I'm a video game designer."

Cackles came rolling out of me, exploding out of my throat before I could stop it. Between each breath, I said, "I knew it! I knew you were a nerd!" Gwen raised her hand up at me and we high-fived. Only, it wasn't a successful high-five because she slid off the loveseat, champagne sloshing over the sides of the glass flute she was desperately holding on to. This made her convulse with laughter. One of those types of laugh where nothing came out of her mouth, but her shoulders shook uncontrollably.

Aidan's head rolled back, his face suddenly sour. But it only lasted a second before he shrugged and grinned. "I'm a big kid."

Gwen and I cracked up some more, two hens clucking like we'd been friends for decades, until Aidan finally cut us off, "What about you, Miss McCall Harris? What do you do for a living?"

The hazy memory of this part embarrassed me. Although I was in my room alone, lying in my bed with last night's dress on and what I assumed to be a bit of a hangover from all the champagne, I still felt the need to hide my face in humiliation. Despite the difficulty of moving my arms—I felt so sluggish and gross—I covered my face then pulled at my skin as if I could just wipe away what I did. It was stupid really, but for some reason, when Aidan asked what I did for a living, I equated that to him taking a dig at my anxiety issues. Unfortunately, I wasn't so drunk that I could blame all my actions on the alcohol causing me to lose control. I was the kind of drunk where I knew what I was doing but just couldn't stop myself from doing it.

After Aidan asked me the question, I immediately slapped him across the face. Then I stood up and pointed a finger at him as he held his cheek and stared at me in shock. "Fuck you! You don't know me!" I shrilled. My words were slurred, the volume of my voice raised and obnoxious.

I winced at the recollection of Aidan's expression. The way the confusion slowly crept through his face. At the time, however, I was completely offended. When Aidan asked me what I did for a living, those innocent words entered my brain and mutated into some kind of vengeful assault on me. He asked a question that I felt was made to directly point out my flaws.

It was completely ludicrous! Aidan didn't even know me and would have no idea the struggles I dealt with on a daily basis regarding my troubled past and the anxiety and depression that stemmed from it. He wouldn't know a thing about the man attacking me when I was a teenager and the years of therapy I had gone through to make me brave enough to even be standing in front of him in the first place, because I had never told him.

"You have no fucking idea," I had said before storming off and up the stairs back to my room. I slammed the door behind me and dramatically threw myself on the bed, and the last thing I remembered was covering my shaking body with the duvet, trembles caused by either the annoyingly cool and constant draft pricking at my skin or what had just happened downstairs.

Thinking back on it now, with a clearer head, I understood exactly why I did what I did. The years and years of therapy with Dr. Finn had pretty much taught me a thing or two about how to analyze my own behavior at times. The hypersensitivity I had over the subject played an enormous part in my outburst, and when you mixed that with the guilt, indignity, and embarrassment over having major anxiety about something that happened many years ago, it could concoct a convoluted idea of how I thought other people viewed me. Regardless of the fact that no one even knew me all that well. The self-consciousness was constantly working in overdrive. Sometimes it felt like all of my flaws were hanging on the outside of my body for all to see. And the second someone even looked at me, they could automatically tell how fucked up I was. Which was why I hated being put in the spotlight. Add a little alcohol to the equation and there you go. I became a hot mess.

Had I not been super-duper buzzed, I probably would have realized that we were asking questions in a circle and eventually it was going to be my turn. The anxious bubbles in my stomach would have been brewing, and if it became too much, I most certainly would have excused myself to secretly pop the pill hidden inside my bra. But the ease of the night combined with the laughter and the bottomless cocktails lowered my inhibitions. For the first time in a long time, I was actually having *fun*. Forgetting about all those what-ifs and just going along with life for a moment.

Unfortunately, it didn't last very long. I had to apologize to Aidan, and maybe even to Gwen and Preston for my rude and violent behavior. Even thinking about that word— *violent*—and associating it with myself made me shudder with a whole new wave of mortification and guilt. Violence should have no part in my life, for it was what ruined it in the first place.

I reached down in search of the duvet to bury my self-disgust, at least until I absolutely had to get out of bed, but the comforter was nowhere within arm's reach. Frustrated that I would have to finally open my eyes to the darkness and move, I huffed and swore under my breath before lazily lifting myself into an upright position. And right as my eyelids fluttered open, I flinched and gasped, nearly choking on the air I had so vigorously sucked in. There, in the darkened and silent corner of my room, stood a shadowy figure.

Chapter Twelve

I couldn't move. Couldn't breathe. Just kept my eyes trained on the mysterious black silhouette in my room. The curtains on the window above the writing desk were slightly open, only a sliver of moonlight dimly illuminating the top of the monstrous manuscript Landon had given me. It cast shadows on the rest of the room, making every piece of furniture look like something it wasn't. I tore my eyes away from the figure and glanced around, comparing the desk chair to a person sitting down and the bedposts to the side view of four very skinny people. Everything looked like it could have been a person.

Then, after blinking in rapid succession—in a small effort to blink away the champagne-addled mist that was still slightly fogging my brain, which could have been contributing to some kind of weird drunken hallucination—I focused again on the figure and tried to recall seeing a chair in that same spot earlier. The object could have been the silhouette of my coat I had placed on it before I'd left my room for dinner.

But I was wrong. The figure tucked in the corner of my room was human-shaped and tall—around six feet—and there was no mistaking it for a chair. There weren't any identifying features to make out. I couldn't tell if it was a man or woman. Couldn't tell if it had long or short hair. There were no facial expressions visible. I wasn't even sure there was a face to observe. The only description I could give was its height, the entire length of it cloaked inside a big, black blotch only a few steps away from where I sat on my bed. It stood between the window and the door that led to the hallway, and I couldn't help but notice how strategically located it was. Right in between the only exits.

No options. I had no options. No way to take flight. To run away from this thing that was currently violating my space with its unknown motives. With its unwanted presence.

My entire body flushed with cool tingles that traveled from my fingertips to my toes at the same time my heartbeat began to speed up. Nauseating swirls in my stomach initiated involuntary shakes... All signs that an anxiety attack was coming on fast and strong. I was frightened, and all I could think about was the man—or woman—in the alleyway the night of my sixteenth birthday. Flashes of ashen and blistered hands on my wrists came flooding back. Pulling me toward him as he opened his mouth and sank his teeth into the layers of the skin on my neck. And those eyes. Those silvery eyes and the rancid odor emanating from their clothes and hair and pores. I swore I could smell it now in this room with me, and I fought with everything I had not to gag.

Bravely, I decided to speak up. "Hello?" I asked, my voice so strained and hushed, I could barely even hear it myself. My throat was desert dry, and fear constricted my vocal cords. The figure didn't move. Didn't make a sound.

"Wh...what do you want?" I croaked, but there was still no answer. What felt like decades of silence filled the space between us. My body was now trembling from panic, waves of intense jolts coming and going every few seconds.

"Hey!" I managed to yell, half-worried and half-hoping that I would wake someone up. The longer this person stood in the niche of my room, quiet and still, the quicker my fear began turning into irritation. I just wanted the damn thing to get out so this awful anxiety attack would begin to subside.

Frustrated and not sure of what else to do, I picked up one of the pillows from my bed and hurled it across the room, praying I'd thrown it far enough to reach the corner. It did, but as soon as it made contact, the inky, six-foot silhouette morphed into a cloud of black smoke. The vapors dissipated into the air, and the pillow plopped onto the floor right where the figure had been standing.

"What the fu..." I couldn't even finish the sentence. Everything just stopped. My breathing, my movements. And the silence was now deafening. I was left quivering in my bed alone.

I watched the lukewarm water flow out of the faucet and pool into the palms of my trembling hands before splashing it all over my face. It felt amazing. Exactly what I needed to cleanse the residual terror left over from what I'd just experienced. Thankfully, I found enough courage to get out of bed and leave my room, but not before turning on both the Tiffany lamps on my nightstands to make damn sure the strange and scary person made out of smoke was definitely gone. It was. There was only the silky, maroon pillow lying on the floor in its place.

Having to trek down the deserted hallway filled with pictures of dead people added more fear to the fear that was already there, but it was the only way to get to the single bathroom on the second floor. I made sure not to accidentally look at the black-and-white photos, focusing only on making it to my destination in the dreary glow of the candle sconces barely lighting my way.

I wiped my face dry with the hem of my sweater dress because no way was the communal hand towel going anywhere near my skin. Once I got it as dry as I could with the polyester fabric, I opened my eyes expecting to see my reflection in the mirror above the sink. The disheveled counterpart of a woman with smeared mascara all around her eyes, coming down from an awful anxiety attack brought on by some kind of...ghost sighting? Champagne-infused delusion? Who knew?

But there was no mirror. Strange. I had used this bathroom earlier in the night—however, that was after a few glasses of bubbly had muddled my mental awareness and I probably didn't even notice. There wasn't one in my room either, and if my memory served me right, which may or may not have been credible, I hadn't seen one anywhere in the house so far. It was kind of weird, but I wasn't worried about it at the moment. I didn't want to look at myself, anyway. Pretty sure I looked how I felt—sloppy.

I was not happy about having to walk down the eerie hallway again, but I wanted to get back to my bedchamber ASAP. Sleep probably would not be happening for another hour or so. My heart had slowed its thumping, but my nerves were still actively trying to calm themselves. My adrenaline would certainly cause issues with sleep.

Actually, I was in the mood to write. This was supposed to be a writing retreat and I hadn't written one word on my laptop. Just had a notebook with a few scribbles of some ideas and descriptions. I hadn't come all this way, out of my element, far from the isolation I felt so perfectly comfortable with, not to do what I had set out to do.

Granted, this trip had already opened me up to things that had been physically and mentally challenging for many years. I couldn't remember the last time I had dinner with people other than my parents. WITHOUT medication. And sitting around socially drinking and having engaging conversations with a group of strangers in my adult life was certainly a first. I mean, I hadn't laughed so hysterically like that since I was a teenager. And let's not forget about that kiss! A man actually kissed me, and I didn't try to punch him or flee.

To be fair, I ended up slapping him across the face, but that was a total mistake. The first thing I would have to do when I saw Aidan was to apologize.

I poked my head out of the door first before completely exiting the bathroom, just to make sure I wouldn't be running into someone else, or *something* else. I was in no mood for any more creepy run-ins with ghostly silhouettes or tall, mysteriously handsome staff members. All I wanted was to get back to my room. Maybe even take a pill to help me sleep for the rest of the night. Or not. I was brave enough to skip taking it before dinner. And, obviously, that thing in my room was an illusion caused by the lingering inebriation from the alcohol earlier in the night. My brain felt calmer now, and it would totally get back to normal once I was in my room and sitting in front of my computer.

With my arms wrapped tightly around my own body in an effort to keep the apprehension in check, I scurried down the hallway back to my room. I kept my focus forward straight, avoiding any accidental glances at the disturbing pictures on the walls. And when the sound of a creaking door came from behind me, I picked up my speed and held my breath, changing my footfalls to tiptoes.

Get back to the room, McCall. Get back to the room!

"McCall?"

I stopped. The voice that whispered my name behind me was familiar and friendly, so I turned around. Aidan stood in the center of the corridor, wearing plaid pajama pants and a white T-shirt.

"Oh, hey," I said, embarrassed by my appearance. He looked like someone who actually got ready for bed. I looked like someone who couldn't hold her liquor and passed right out.

"What's up? Are you okay?" he asked in a hushed tone, scratching his head as he stepped closer to me.

I wrapped my limbs tighter around my torso, suddenly self-conscious. This guy had seen me almost naked, and now, I was still in last night's clothes and my breath probably smelled like stale grapes. My encounters with Aidan had been nothing short of just plain humiliating. I was surprised he was still even talking to me after I'd slapped him.

"Yeah, I'm fine. Just had to use the bathroom."

He closed the space between us. "Hey, listen, I just wanted to apologize for anything I said that might have offended you."

How awkward. I was sure he was referring to my violent behavior earlier. How ridiculous was it that he was apologizing to *me*? I was the asshole who'd done it without any provocation. All he did was ask me a simple question, and I completely blew it out of context.

"Are you kidding? I'm the one who's sorry. I have never slapped someone in the face like that before. I'm so sorry. I just..." I held my words in, wondering if I should open up to this person about my past and what I dealt with now. The only people who knew about my issues were my parents and Dr. Finn. What would Dr. Finn say if I told her I was considering admitting my mental instability to someone else? She'd probably congratulate me on crossing yet another milestone.

I decided to continue. "When you asked me what I did for a living, it triggered something inside me, which is completely absurd because what you asked had nothing to do with anything."

Aidan squinted at me, wrinkles forming around his eyes. "What did it trigger?"

In a moment of silent consideration, the distant sound of thunder softly resonated in the hallway around us. The storm that Madame Clara had warned us about must have been rolling in.

Aidan's question came back to the forefront of our conversation. I expelled a huff of...defeat? Relief, maybe? I didn't know, but the thought of letting things off my chest exhausted me before I'd even started. I didn't like to talk about my sixteenth birthday unless I was in the presence of a medical professional who was licensed to handle the emotional meltdown that happened when I did.

I backed into the wall of the hallway and slowly slid down the paneling until my ass hit the thick Persian hug. "I have never really talked about this with—"

"Someone you punched in the face?" he asked, grinning on his way down to join me on the floor.

"I didn't punch you!"

"You might as well have. There was some serious power coming from that left hand."

I glared at him, watching his expression carefully to see if he was joking or not. His chocolate-colored eyes were bleary. The faded pillow mark on his cheek was evidence that he was probably sleeping pretty good for a while, but it was clear that he didn't get enough of it. Finally, he smirked at me, that adorable little mole stretching with his lips, and I knew he was just giving me a hard time. I returned a weak smile then switched my gaze down to my legs extended out in front of me because I just couldn't bring myself to look him in the eyes for what I was about to say.

"It happened at my sixteenth birthday party. Some...man," or woman, but it I didn't voice it, "attacked me in an alleyway. Broke my arm in three places and bit my neck." I didn't lift my head but purposely gripped a fistful of my wavy hair and pulled it away from my neck, revealing the proof to Aidan. The cool air collided with the gnarled skin that made up the scar, causing it to ache. "Ever since then, I've had...issues."

Aidan reached out and gently smoothed my hair over my shoulder to inspect the marred tissue. I usually never allowed anyone, especially someone I barely knew, so close to it, but I felt comfortable with him.

When he'd gotten a good enough look, he allowed my hair to fall back into place.

"You have issues. You mean PTSD?" he asked casually, as if it were no big deal. His nonchalance prompted me to look at him. "My brother had debilitating PTSD when he came back from Iraq. Depression, anxiety, anger issues, you name it. He once beat his motorcycle to pieces with his bare hands because it wouldn't start. And this was coming from a guy who never got mad at anything before he was deployed. Who once found his ex-girlfriend in bed with another man, and he just walked out. Any other guy would have probably clocked the dude at least once."

I raised my eyebrows in astonishment and sympathy. While I didn't necessarily have anger management problems, I could empathize. Well, actually, I could have been developing them now. Hitting Aidan had something to do with anger, I was sure. But having any kind of mental disorder could affect a person in so many different ways, which was why it took time to correct it. It wasn't like a cold or a headache. Taking an over-the-counter medication wasn't going to fix things right away. It took lots of time and effort and practice and planning. You had to find the source of the problem, analyze it, break it down, force yourself to dredge up those deep, dark memories of your past, which sometimes required a type of selective serotonin re-uptake inhibitor to even feel comfortable enough to talk about it. It was a long process to endure.

"You said he *had* PTSD?" I asked, wondering how his brother was able to overcome it. I was curious, but the thought of him living a normal life without the nagging ball of dread oscillating in his stomach made me a tad bit jealous.

"He eventually got better." Aidan's glance dropped down to his hands. "But it wasn't until we found him unconscious in his bed one day with an empty bottle of pills next to his body. If we hadn't found him in time, he would have died. But that was his rock bottom."

I remained silent for a moment, unable to find the right words. I couldn't say I was sorry. I'd feel a little like a hypocrite. Obviously, the memory of his brother attempting to commit suicide was a difficult one. It hurt him. It was difficult for me to think about, too, because I had considered doing the very same thing. Committing suicide. Finally ending the years of fear and self-doubt. The years of sadness and constant flashbacks of a man harming me, the scene replaying over and over again in my head on a loop. Wondering what if this happened and what if that happened? After a while, it got old, and I just wanted it to stop.

There was quiet for only a beat longer before Aidan spoke again, clearly wanting to move on from the subject of his brother.

"Why did he attack you?"

I shrugged. It was the same question I asked myself on a daily basis. Why would some random guy attack a teenage girl? I had already deposited the presents into my friend's car, so I didn't have anything of value on me. Not even a purse. No wallet. It was clear to anyone on the street that I wasn't carrying anything. He didn't take a thing from me.

The initial theory from the police was that the man was trying to perform a sex crime, but it didn't feel that way. He didn't touch me in my...private places. It seemed the dirty man was determined to bite me. We wrestled for a while when he'd grabbed me by my wrists, which resulted in my broken arm, but his gray eyes remained fixated on my neck and chest region the entire time. I remembered it clear as day.

The final assumption was that this homeless man was on some kind of drug, bath salts or meth, and there was no specific reason why he chose to assault me. I was just at the wrong place at the wrong time. The man might have attacked anyone else put in his path.

"Did they ever find the asshole?"

I shook my head. My heartbeat suddenly doubled, signifying a possible panic attack coming on. Aidan was unknowingly daring me to go down a path I had never really gone down before—sharing information that only very few people knew about. I could easily shut him down. Tell him I didn't want to talk about it. But someone other than my therapist was interested in my past, so maybe I should take advantage of this moment. After all, this was the weekend of new beginnings, right?

"They never found him," I began, immediately regretting it. "For days after the attack, detectives had me looking at hundreds of mugshots in binders. I was even brought into a lineup."

"No shit. Like, you standing on the other side of a one-way mirror?"

"I know. It was surreal. Like I was in a movie. I mean, there I was, a little teenage girl standing in front of these grown-ass men. Dirty, mean-looking men. Unshaven. Their clothes soiled in God knows what. One of them was even missing a leg. I think they called him Shaky Joe or something like that."

"Well, was it actually a homeless man who attacked you?" Aidan asked.

"I'm not sure. We all assumed he was a hobo by my description. He stunk and he was skinny and pale and just disgusting. But none of those guys had his eyes." I wished I hadn't said that because I knew Aidan would want me to elaborate.

"His eyes?"

I fiddled with a pill of fabric hanging off my dress. "Yes. His eyes were...they were..." The long-haired housemaid's gray eyes flashed in my mind.

Aidan's hand squeezed the ball of my shoulder. "You don't have to. It's okay."

Relief settled over me like a refreshing blast of cool air. He understood how difficult it was for me, and I appreciated it.

"Why don't we get some sleep?" he suggested. "I'm beat, and I would like to wake up in time to have breakfast. I'm pretty sure Madame Clara wouldn't be happy if we missed it." He stood up, extending a hand to help me off the floor. I took it.

"Yeah, I wouldn't want to be grounded for the rest of my stay," I scoffed.

"Need me to walk you to your room?" Aidan grinned, and

I knew he was just being silly because my bedroom door was literally steps away.

"Actually, I think I'll sneak into the kitchen downstairs to get some water," I replied, my mouth suddenly desperate for moisture.

He yawned before saying, "I can walk you there if you want."

I did. I really wanted him to escort me because the rest of the house was just as creepy as this hallway, but I didn't want to keep him from getting the sleep he really wanted. It was obvious how tired he was.

"It's okay. I won't be long. I'll see you in a few hours."

"Okay," he said with another yawn before dragging himself back to his room. Quite frankly, I probably should have dragged my own ass to my room, but I hadn't drunk anything since I woke up and the champagne from earlier had sucked me dry.

I managed to get past the rest of the hallway without accidentally looking over at the death photos. Now all I had to do was make it down the stairs, walk through the dining room and into the kitchen which, according to Madame Clara, was off limits. But the house was quiet. Everyone was asleep, and there was no harm in just getting a glass of water.

I tiptoed down the stairs, my feet landing only on just one or two spots that produced a faint creak. When I made it into the foyer, a strange noise caught my attention. Moaning. Once again, the sound of moaning penetrated the walls. And this time, it was very nearby.

Instead of hooking a left into the dining room, my curiosity followed the sensual noises, which seemed to be coming from the parlor. The parlor door was cracked open, the flickering flames from the fireplace inside casting shadows into the lobby.

Slowly, I approached the opening, careful not to touch anything around it. I wanted to remain unseen and unheard.

Standing away from the entryway, I leaned into the gap between the door and its frame, widening one eye to get a good peek inside. And there was Preston. Sitting on the button-back loveseat, his head pressed against the backside. His hands were gripping the thighs of a woman who was mounted on his waist. She was wearing a thin, silky, red nightgown. Her face was buried deep into his neck and her body was moving. Back arching inward then out. Straddling him as if she were an erotic dancer in a strip club.

I could easily tell it was Preston, his gray hair and wrinkled skin giving it away, but I couldn't see the woman's face. All I knew was that it was NOT Gwen. Her hair was not blonde. It was black. Long and black like a certain Hazelhurst Manor housemaid.

Chapter Thirteen

It hurt. Whatever was making jabs at my brain, straight through my skull and into the gray matter that filled its hollow space, needed to stop. Every couple of minutes, a jolt of pain would shoot across my frontal lobe, behind my eyes, to the occipital bone of my head. It woke me out of sleep and covering myself from top to bottom with a blanket and a pillow did not help.

Surrendering to the headache, I opened my eyes and flung the comforter off me. Now I was cranky. Cranky and hungry and, apparently, suffering from a hangover. I lifted my wrist into the air to check the time. 7:15 in the morning. Not good. I barely got a two-hour nap. It could have been a little more, but things kept swirling around my mind. My brain had held my thoughts hostage, refusing to allow me to put them aside for the sake of sleep. How could I sleep? The whole night was insane. The whole day, even. There hasn't been a dull moment yet, but the last encounter I had was what had kept me awake. Kept me pondering. Agonizing over what I should do about what I'd seen.

There was no doubt in my mind that the man sitting in that velvety, button-back loveseat in the parlor was Preston. He wasn't looking straight at me, but I could see his gray hair, which gave it right away. Preston was the only guest in this house with it. Unless it was Chef Winston, which I highly doubted. He was older than Preston, and smaller.

There was a woman in a scarlet silken negligee on top of him, straddling him, rolling her body in ways I could never. She glided over his lap like water, as if dancing to sensual music only she could hear. Her back was facing me, but I couldn't keep my eyes off her. She was mesmerizing.

It clearly wasn't Preston's wife, Gwen. The woman didn't have platinum-blonde hair. It was long and black. So very black. And while I couldn't get a glimpse of her face, my gut knew exactly who it was. The girl in the third-story window. The woman with the hauntingly familiar eyes pouring our waters at dinner. The pale, hollow-cheeked housemaid in a vintage dress serving our cocktails.

When I'd spotted them canoodling in the parlor through the slightly opened door, I couldn't take myself away at first. I stood dumbfounded and spellbound by the sensuous scene playing out in front of my eyes. But it didn't take long for me to realize that I was witnessing something bad. Seconds later, I hurried back up the stairs to my bedroom and locked the door behind me. I changed into my pajamas and found a nearly empty bottle of room-temperature water at the bottom of my suitcase. It was warm, but it moistened my mouth enough to curb the thirst I had been looking to quench in the first place, which was the whole reason I went downstairs. Just innocently trying to get myself a glass of water.

Now, it was early in the morning. I lay in bed, staring up at the coffered ceiling and the colorful light reflecting from the stained glass of the Tiffany lamps. Everything else that happened earlier in the day had completely faded away, taken over by thoughts of how I was going to break this to Gwen. Because I had to, right? As a...friend, if you could even call us friends. But not only that, as a human being. Because it would be the right thing to do, even though it made no sense whatsoever.

I didn't know Preston and Gwen as far as I could throw them, but I was convinced that they were the real deal. Their public displays of affection looked authentic, despite the fact that it made me queasy to think about being with a man that old. I liked them, I genuinely did. Preston was kind and Gwen was a girl's girl. She would most certainly tell me if my husband was caught cheating behind my back. If not for the purpose of being a woman looking out for a fellow woman—girl power and all that jazz—then, at the very least, for the sheer benefit of having something to gossip about. Gwen did also seem like the kind of girl who could be a shit stirrer, but that was beside the point.

A ferocious clap of thunder roared overhead, its intensity disrupting my thoughts. I glanced at the window above the writing desk, but my view of outside was ninety-eight percent obstructed by the thick, gold drapery. I carefully maneuvered out of bed, trying in vain not to rattle my brain too much. The headache seemed like it was only getting worse. It had to be related to dehydration. I was parched.

After reaching the curtains, I pulled at the tassels and spread the fabric apart, revealing a second-story view of tall, barren trees underneath a gray sky, the heavy sound of rain bearing down. The dense thicket combined with water pouring down in torrents made it near impossible to see anything in the distance. Madame Clara was right. The weather turned out to be pretty bad.

Landon's manuscript caught my attention, the worn, brown leather cover scarred and discolored. I wished I hadn't agreed to read any of his book. There was no way I would have the time now that I wasted last night on getting drunk. That was one full day of my writing retreat lost. I would have to somehow make up for it by finding the time to attend these sit-down meals and nap and figure out what the fuck I was even going to write about! Today would be my only day to fully immerse myself, for tomorrow night I would be traveling back to the airport in that uncomfortable old school bus.

Great. Suddenly, the thought of that bus not returning to pick me up popped into my head. What if the driver didn't come back in time? Would an Uber come way up here to scoop me up in time to make my flight back home? What if there was no way of getting transportation?

I shook my head, fighting the what-ifs off, and focused on Landon's book instead. Gingerly, because it seemed like one semi-strong tug might sever the flimsy fabric, I unwrapped the ribbon binding the manuscript shut and opened it to the first page. The cursive handwriting was very neat, the angle of each letter sloping elegantly to the right. This immediately drew me in. There was something about handwritten words that made me appreciate what I was reading even more. There was personality behind each sentence, creating a kind of intimacy between the reader and its author. I could almost picture the writer sitting down and penning his or her thoughts as I read, like I had a front-row seat to their whole process of writing. If it wasn't such a pain in the ass to transfer handwritten chapters to my computer, I would definitely do most of my writing in a notebook.

I ran my fingertips over the page, grazing the letters indented into the aged, creamy-colored paper. The ink was embedded so deeply into the fibers, like Landon could have been angry while writing. I had to know if his words matched what I was touching, so I read the first few lines.

I awake in a puddle of blood, drenched in the smell of liquid metallic. My eyesight is blurred, but even as they begin to focus, there is no recognition in my surroundings. No perception of how much time has passed. No memory of what has happened to me. I am lying in a bed, still in my nightshirt from the evening before. Where I had rested my head to sleep in the comforts of my own home, in my own bed next to my wife. Now, I am no longer there. I search the room for something familiar, anything to ease the sudden rise of apprehension. This is when I realize that my wrists are tied to the bedposts. I glance down at my feet to find that my legs are spread apart, each ankle tethered in place. I struggle against the restraints; however, they are pulled taut, hindering my movements.

And then I see a silhouette. Tucked into the corner of the room, it appears to be a woman, standing, the shadows of the darkness accentuating her corseted torso and the ruffles of her bustle.

I am alarmed by her presence. Concerned about the subdued state for which my appendages are currently in. However, for reasons I cannot explain, those details do not matter anymore. The scent of the blood—mine or someone else's—suddenly incapacitates me. My mind mainly, for it is evoking a hunger in me that I have never felt before. An emptiness. A hollow pit deep within my bowels.

I am starved, and I must feed.

BOOM!

I flinched and cowered, clutching onto Landon's manuscript as if it could somehow save me from the loud noise. The long clap of thunder rumbled overhead, the sound vibrating the entire house. *Jesus.* Between Landon's words and the jarring thunderbolts detonating in the sky, I nearly yelped out loud. I had never heard a thunderstorm like this one in Miami, and God knew it rained constantly there. Maybe it was because the B&B was high up in the mountains. Closer to the sky? Who knew, but it was scaring the crap out of me. Like *War of the Worlds* going on out there.

I set Landon's massive book down, but not his words. They repeated over and over in my head as I gathered my toiletries, padded down the hallway into the bathroom, took a shower, and brushed my teeth. He said this was a manuscript, but he didn't say what the story was about.

Didn't matter, though. I had only read a few paragraphs and already, I was sucked in. Who was this protagonist and why was he tied up? And the silhouette? Was she his captor? And the hunger?

Immediately, my author brain went straight to the genres I liked to read and write: fantasy and horror and science fiction. Blood and hunger. Vampires. My therapist said it made total sense. After the harrowing event that happened years ago, my psyche had become drawn to stories of similar context. Because I could control it. Close the book if it got to be too much. In my opinion, the years I had spent living as a recluse only made me that much more creative. All I had were my thoughts and lots of time to read books written by great authors, to learn from their style of writing. Apparently, however, Dr. Finn believed this was only feeding into my mental issues. Anyway, that was where my mind went. Chalk it up to my own real-life horror experiences, but my mind automatically went to the worst-case scenarios. Always.

Just those few paragraphs in Landon's book had me eager to sit down and read a whole chapter or two of his story, but after glancing at the time on my watch as I secured it around my wrist, there was no way I could. Breakfast had already begun, and if I wanted to get something in my empty stomach before lunchtime, I had to get downstairs.

As I sat on the edge of the bed and laced my boots over my jeans, I wasn't sure which silent prayer I should send out into the unknown: that Madame Clara hadn't already banned me from breakfast for being tardy or that breakfast wasn't going to be some ridiculously grotesque delicatessen from another century.

I trotted downstairs and entered the dining room to find, as predicted, the other guests already working on their breakfast. I casually scanned the room in search of Madame Clara, but she seemed to be nowhere in sight. This was a relief, but I didn't dare let down my guard. Gwen and Preston were there, and the dread of looking them in the eye was already sinking in. How was I going to face them after what I'd seen last night in the parlor? And why the hell didn't I take a benzo for this? I knew I had vowed for this weekend to be the beginning of new beginnings, but I was starting to feel like I'd picked the wrong time.

Aidan's tired gaze met mine, and he placed a hand behind the antique chair to scoot it out, a clear invitation for me to sit next to him. I gave him a wry grin and tucked my hair behind my ear, a wave of stress hitting me over Aidan drawing attention on me. But as I made my way to the seat next to him, I realized that not everyone was at the table. There only appeared to be Gwen, Preston, Aidan, and myself having breakfast this morning, leaving four empty chairs.

"Where is everyone else?" I whispered to Aidan, pulling my napkin over my lap.

"They left," Gwen said from across the dining room table, which was loaded with morning foods. Dishes filled with croissants, waffles, fruit, bacon, sausage, yogurt... My mouth watered, and I was so, so thankful that this was a buffet-style meal and not one where we were served by the exuberant Chef Winston.

Now all I needed was something to drink. The toothpaste and mouthwash hadn't completely taken away the stale champagne aftertaste, which seemed to be embedded into my taste buds.

I began reaching over the table and transferring food onto my china, finally glancing at Preston and Gwen at the same time. Somehow, despite getting wasted and going to sleep super late last night, Gwen had managed to look like a fucking freshly made goddess at eight o'clock in the morning. She wasn't dressed to the nines. As a matter of fact, I really liked the top half of what she was wearing, which was a very comfortable and soft-looking, light pink hoodie. Her blonde hair was tied up into what was probably supposed to be a messy bun, but it was too perfect to have been spontaneously done. And her makeup. It was natural, but natural in the way that was *made* natural with the expert knowledge of how to apply makeup that way. Gwen did not look the least bit hungover, and I was almost certain she drank way more champagne than I did.

Preston didn't look as crisp as his young wife. There were deep bags under his eyes, the dark, bluish circles showing his age. I wondered if his heavy heart had already been weighing him down from the infidelity. Was this his first act of adultery?

He had drunk just as much as we all did, and it wasn't only dainty glasses of bubbly. He started with wine, but Aidan talked him into something harder later on. He could have been too drunk to even know what he was doing. But then that would mean the woman riding him like a horse had taken advantage of him, and that was definitely not cool.

I studied the married couple without making myself known, watching the way they interacted with each other. Trying to pick up any tension between them. But there wasn't any. Gwen giggled at something Preston whispered to her, and then she wiped a crumb from his bottom lip before kissing him. Still two people very much in love.

And then I saw it. A round, reddened splotch on the left side of his neck, peeking out just above his collared shirt. I watched with my head down and my eyes up as Gwen curled her fingers into Preston's gray hair and kissed his cheek, right before her hand slowly dropped from his hair down to his neck. She caressed his skin, her long, manicured fingernails lightly stroking the spot that without a doubt looked exactly like a hickey.

Preston didn't have that hickey last night. Not while we were all in the parlor together. Not before I caught the dark-haired girl sitting on top of him, burying her head in his neck.

Gwen had to have seen it. There was no way she could have missed it. And if she'd seen it, and they were still being all lovey-dovey in this very moment, then my suspicions were off. It could have very well, and most likely, been his own wife who gave him that love bite.

I cleared my throat when I realized I'd been staring for too long and had better stop before I was caught. When I was able to tear my focus away from scrutinizing their marriage, Gwen's words finally struck me, and I had to ask to better understand what she had said. "What do you mean they left?"

"We don't know," Aidan answered. "Apparently, they left in the middle of the night."

I turned to him. "But we were awake in the middle of the night," I pointed out to him quietly, not necessarily wanting anyone else to know that. "And where did they go?" It was raining and we were high in the mountains. There was no way a cab would come up here so late at night. The only way would be if the bus came back, and I doubted that piece of crap would be chugging its way around steep curves in the dark.

Aidan shrugged. "I have no idea. Madame Clara announced it when we came down for breakfast. She just said they won't be joining us because they left. I'm guessing it had something to do with Clara freaking out at their daughter, though."

To be fair, as a parent, I would have been pissed off, too, if some stranger laid a hand on my kid. Tom did go off on Madame Clara, but even I could tell he was holding back. I completely understood their desire to leave Hazelhurst Manor. But leaving in the middle of the night, in a storm with two young children, didn't sound very smart. Surely they could have waited until the morning to flee.

I decided not to speak on the matter any longer and concentrate on getting food—good food that I actually liked—into my body. The hunger was beginning to make me feel nauseous, and that was grounds enough for a panic attack.

But my appetite was nearly wiped away completely when I heard the door to the kitchen swing open and saw *her* come into the dining room. The woman. The housemaid with the long, stick-straight, blacker-than-black hair. The same woman who had straddled Preston's body. I didn't see her face last night, but I didn't have to. I knew it was her.

She was holding a pitcher of orange juice and walking toward me, a lady on a mission to fill my empty glass. I stopped chewing, held my breath, and fiddled with the napkin on my lap, hoping not to choke once I finally swallowed the morsels of food in my mouth. When she reached me, she leaned over and poured, and my eyes couldn't help but land on her long slender fingers gripping the handle of the carafe. My gaze traveled from her hand, up her arm, to the satin, shiny fabric of her period dress where it covered her bust.

Then I looked up at her, at her beautiful eyes. No longer cold and gray and haunting. She held her head high, chin jutted out at a confident angle. The timid young woman too shy to make eye contact with anyone wasn't there anymore. Her uniquely crimson eyes met mine, and they nearly took my breath away. Iron-straight hair fell over her rosy cheeks, caressing her blemish-free, ivory-tinted skin. No longer pale enough to indicate she might have anemia or some other acute ailment.

The housemaid smiled sweetly at me after pouring my juice, then sauntered back into the kitchen, humming softly something that I knew I'd heard before but couldn't place, as if nothing—NOTHING—was wrong.

I finally swallowed the mush inside my mouth but kept my head down for a beat longer, giving my heart a moment to slow its pace. I couldn't believe she walked in here all normal with Preston and Gwen sitting right there. Stupidly, I didn't observe Preston's reaction to her presence. But in my defense, something else flustered my train of thought. It was her face.

Yesterday, the woman had looked so pale and gaunt. I would have bet money that she was struck with some kind of illness. But today...just now...she was perfect. Not pale. Not gaunt. Perfect with mysterious and beautifully red eyes. Exactly like the portrait in my room.

Chapter Fourteen

Breakfast ended shortly after the girl with the long, raven hair—a.k.a. Preston's mistress—exited the dining room. Her skin and eyes and cheeks had been full of color and light and beauty.

I kept my head low while I stuffed my face, feeding the anxiety monster in hopes of keeping it quiet. Stress-eating wasn't normally my thing—the nausea created by my worrisome thoughts made it impossible to even think about food. But I didn't want to look across the table at Preston and Gwen, the two of them carrying on as if their marriage was okay. I didn't want to watch Preston, the cheating bastard, laughing at Gwen's inappropriate jokes while he rubbed her back, kissed her shoulder. He carried on as if last night hadn't happened. As if he wasn't hiding something. I might not have had a real relationship with a guy in a very long time, but I knew how to act when I was in one. I knew that loyalty and honesty were important in maintaining a healthy bond between two people who wanted to be together.

As a matter of fact, Preston cheating on Gwen made me angry. Didn't he know how lucky he was to even have a girl as gorgeous as Gwen? Especially at his age? I couldn't foresee Gwen and me leaving this weekend and going our separate ways having exchanged numbers and becoming long-distance besties, but that didn't mean she wasn't good people. She was pretty and funny and, while it didn't take a genius to run her business, she still held her own, which required some kind of intellect.

I struggled with the idea of telling Gwen what I saw. The truth was that I hardly knew them. Was I willing to break up a marriage between two people I had only known for one day?

When everyone decided to leave the table, I hung back in the dining room, giving enough space between me and Preston and Gwen for them to forget I was even there. I was positive I wouldn't be able to avoid them for the rest of the trip, but I could certainly minimize the amount of time I spent around them.

As I pretended to be fascinated by the china cabinet filled with beautiful but unbelievably creepy porcelain dolls of all sizes, Aidan came and joined me.

"These things are so freaky," he said.

I bent down to get a better view of the ones on the lower shelf. "They are, but I bet they're worth a fortune. Look at this one with the long spiral curls and the hat," I said, pointing but being careful not to touch the glass. The last thing I wanted to do was touch something that would make Madame Clara go mental.

"Yeah, I'm sure they did cost a lot of money. They probably break out of this thing at night and walk around the house when everyone is asleep, too."

A chill ran down my spine, and I straightened up to meet Aidan's playful grin. "Great. Now I'll be worried about creepy little china cabinet dolls trying to kill me in my sleep. Thanks."

"Just be sure to lock your door. Though, they could probably fit through the crack underneath it."

"Oh my God. I'm leaving," I said, walking away from him before he could spot the smile on my face. He was funny, but the thought of these dolls crawling into my bed with me was terrifying.

Then again, that thought sparked an idea. A book idea.

I had to grab my notebook and my computer.

"Hey, where are you off to in a hurry?" Aidan called after me. I didn't answer and just waved my hand behind me then rushed up the stairs to my room.

I considered sitting in one of the rocking chairs outside on the porch to begin my brainstorming, but from the looks of it through my bedroom window, the rain was still coming down pretty violently. So, I packed my laptop bag and headed to the library. How could being surrounded by world-famous authors not inspire someone?

Thankfully, there was no one else in there when I walked in, and I swiftly made a beeline for the velvety chair in the center of the room. I was in a really good head space—no anxiety, belly full of delicious breakfast food, and tons of ideas ready to spill out of my brain and onto paper. All thoughts of the other people in this house were pushed away, and now it was just me and my laptop in a room filled with the smell of antique books.

There had to be a good idea swimming around my head somewhere. I just had to find it, because I wasn't prepared to quit my dream of writing a book that would set me apart from so many others and land me a book deal with a major publishing company. My other three books were rejected by tons of agents, which was why I decided to publish independently. Every decline featured one line that went something like: "the writing is good" or "great concept" or "relatable characters," but those kind comments were immediately followed by "doesn't strike a chord" or simply "not for us."

Maybe if I'd sent them a story about a well-dressed billionaire lawyer who was an asshole at his firm but seemed to change his douchebag ways the second a mousy brunette entered his office and challenged him, resulting in pages and pages of seduction and romantic trash that just did NOT happen in real life, then someone might be interested in my work. Because these days, it seemed romance authors were the only ones out there making the big bucks.

I was far from a romance author.

But it wasn't that no one liked my novels. The people who did read them gave me praise. It was just that the industry was a bitch to break into, especially when you were doing it all on your own. And especially when you were competing against the thousands of romance authors out there who pumped out book after book, their covers donning a sexy, shirtless man displaying washboard abs and that gross V near their man parts all women in their thirties seemed to drool over.

There was no bad blood for those romance writers, though. Shit, if anything, I admired them. They knew exactly how to feed the masses. Exactly the kind of bullshit those hungry for unrealistic love affairs wanted to eat.

But I didn't want to write for mass consumption. I wanted to be different. Because my stories weren't as simple as a man and woman fall in love, have lots of sex, and the rest of their lives get wrapped into a neat little bow. Oh, no. The characters in my books had issues, just like me.

Okay, here we go:

An old house.

Woman visiting. Woman visiting an old house. House belongs to a family member?

Woman inherits an old house.

House is filled with antiques. The house is left as-is when family member died. Woman must clean out the house in order to sell it. She goes through antiques. She finds dolls. A doll?

She finds one doll.

The doll is a family heirloom. Beautiful porcelain doll. Long curls. ~~Black hair?~~ Red curls. 18 inches tall. Southern Belle outfit.

Woman cleans up doll and decides she will get it appraised. Might sell it on eBay.

The doll doesn't want to leave the house. It's HER house. The doll begins to do things. Creepy things to make the woman leave. To scare her out of the house.

Turn lights on. Move furniture. Steal things. Slam doors...

SLAM!

The library door startled me and I flinched, my haunted-doll concept jumbling inside my head. I tore my eyes away from my computer screen and found Landon standing behind the other velvet chair across from mine, his hands gripping the back. "I didn't mean to startle you," he said, his voice low and steady. Monotone.

"It's okay. I-I was just really concentrating. I didn't expect anyone to come in."

Landon was wearing pretty much the same outfit he had on yesterday—very old-fashioned, eighteen-hundreds kind of clothing. Only this time, his bowtie was replaced with a silk, ruffled cravat. His shoulder-length hair was slicked back, and he moved effortlessly in front of the chair, smoothing the tail of his coat before taking a seat. He was dashing, and suddenly, I felt entirely too underdressed. Images of myself wearing a corseted gown (one of those shiny dresses that smashed and lifted women's breasts all the way up to their chins) while hanging off Landon's arm flashed before my eyes.

I casually closed my laptop and the notebook of story ideas. I wasn't one to share my unfinished work or brainstorming ideas with people. The few times that I did with my parents, they couldn't stop themselves from pitching their own ideas and offering suggestions on what I should change or add to my story. Taking someone else's ideas, even if it was just a minor suggestion, didn't sit well with me. I would feel as if my words weren't my own and publishing a book under my name that way would just feel icky. It had to be ALL me.

But Landon knew exactly what I was doing. "Are you working on your next bestseller?" he asked as he crossed one knee over the other.

"Yeah," I sneered. "None of my books are bestsellers."

"Is that so? I wouldn't understand why. They were all very well-written."

I gawked at him. "You finished my book?" That was surprising. I only gave him a copy of it yesterday.

"I did. I also found your other books online and read those, too."

That couldn't be possible. Granted, my books weren't nearly as long as a George R.R. Martin novel, but they weren't necessarily one-day reads either. Maybe if you absolutely had nothing better to do. Still, finishing all three in just a few hours seemed overkill to even me, the avid reader. "You read all three of my books? Like cover to cover?"

One eyebrow shot up and he grinned. "I'm a fast reader."

"Cool," was the only word I could think of at that moment. It felt very uncomfortable to ask people what they thought of my work, so I never did. If they enjoyed it, I was sure they would just say so, or leave a nice review. So, I usually just thanked them instead. "Thank you for purchasing the eBook copies. I really appreciate your support." Although, I was skeptical that he read all four of my books in just one night. He had to have just skimmed through them.

"Tell me," he said stoically as he leaned forward. "Where does all that fear come from?"

His words left a bitter taste in my mouth, and I shifted in my chair. "Um...what do you mean? My books are about *overcoming* fear."

Landon bowed his head. "Yes. Each story contains a female protagonist who finds herself in a situation that requires strength and conviction to overcome. They acquire these characteristics as the story progresses; however, these women start out frightened. Terrified of life and the things they cannot control. I admire the courage that each one discovers within themselves, but I am more interested in their weaknesses. What makes them so feeble to begin with?"

I didn't know how to answer this. I was well aware of the fact that my books were based on women who resembled me—women who were afraid of what life could do to them. Each of them scared to put their feet down. To speak up. Eventually, they found their voices and conquered their fears, all while saving themselves and others from a particularly harrowing event. This was where there was a disconnect between my characters and me. I have yet to find my courage. I was still floundering in what broke me years ago. There was no telling when or if I would find my way back out of the hole that had swallowed me up, but I enjoyed writing about women who did. I lived vicariously through the people I made up.

I didn't want to reveal this to Landon, though. Besides the fact that I barely knew him, and I was sure I'd already met the limit of sharing personal information with complete strangers, I found it a little bizarre that he'd be more intrigued by a woman's vulnerabilities.

In an attempt to guide the conversation away from me and my books, I brought up his manuscript. "I read a passage from your story."

He leaned back and joined his hands together, steepling his fingers. "You did? And what were your thoughts?"

A pang of guilt forced my eyes away from his. He took time to at least read the important parts of my novels while I only read one paragraph of his. There was no way in hell I could have read that entire thing. But I didn't really want him to know that I was intrigued with what I'd read. That would just be an expectation I'd be planting into his head, inviting myself to make a commitment to read more of his book when I should be focusing all my attention on my own. Instead, I complimented his writing. "Your words felt very real."

It was simple, but that praise was one lots of authors appreciated. We love it when readers found our work *real.*

Landon didn't say anything. His lips curled up, and he stared straight into my eyes, the purplish hue of his irises once again fascinating me. His glare was mesmerizing, and I was suddenly tingling from head to toe, my breathing beginning to quicken. This man was pretty hot, and it seemed I hadn't truly realized how attracted to him I was until now. As we stared at each other wordlessly, the conversation went from semi-strange to full-on weird. But I couldn't stop looking at him.

My body began to pick up on something else. Something electric. Some kind of excitement spurring between my legs.

Although I was wearing a bra, a tank top, and a chunky, knit sweater, my nipples were rock hard. I was afraid that Landon would be able to see the little beacons of arousal showing straight through the layers. And the private part of me, the me that hadn't been touched by a man in a really long time, was awake and alive and ready to be touched again.

We held our stares for what felt like hours. With each passing second, my thoughts became more and more erotic in nature. I began imagining myself with Landon, in this very room, rolling around together on the floor surrounded by first-edition books, making love. Our naked bodies writhing. Our skin hot and slick with sweat. I had never in my life felt the profound need for a man to be between my legs. It was bizarre. It was exciting. It was absolutely necessary.

Landon remained quiet. His posture never changed. He didn't move an inch. His facial expression was completely frozen. But those mystical amethyst eyes... They were speaking to me. Telling me to get up off this chair and sit on his lap. Straddle him. Kiss him deeply until my breath runs out. And just as I was about to obey his silent commands, a familiar voice broke me out of my trance.

"Hey, McCall," Aidan said as he entered the library.

Landon shifted his eyes away from mine, and I blinked several times to remember where I even was. When my vision came back to focus, there was no mistaking the scowl on Landon's face.

"Hey. What's up, Aidan?" I said, playing all of it off as if my lady parts weren't just pulsating with desire. I crossed my arms over my chest, just in case.

Landon stood up. "I'll leave you two to it." He held out his hand, and I hesitated at first but eventually placed mine in his. Then, as if it were the most natural thing to do in the world, he bowed down and kissed my knuckles. "Until next time, Miss Harris."

Blood immediately rushed to my cheeks and ears. I couldn't bring myself to look at Aidan after Landon had gently released my hand then turned to walk toward the door. I didn't want him to see my embarrassment because, holy shit, no one had EVER done that to me before.

Before he could leave, Aidan stopped him. "Are you Landon Hazelhurst?" he asked.

Landon brought his hands together behind his back and stood erect. Confidently. Just like I would imagine a gentleman standing back in the 1800s. So proper-looking.

He dipped his chin at Aidan. "I am."

"And your mother is Madame Clara?"

"Yes, she is."

"Cool. You guys have owned this place a long time, huh?" Aidan asked, and I wondered where he was going with this or if he was just making small talk.

Landon responded without hesitation. It was probably a normal question guests of the bed-and-breakfast had asked many times before. "It has been in our family for centuries, yes."

Aidan nodded pleasingly. "That's pretty awesome. Hey, your mom wasn't in the dining room today. We actually haven't seen her yet this morning. Is everything okay?"

This time Landon didn't answer right away. In fact, he shifted his weight then looked down at his feet before chuckling. "I know my mother can be quite overbearing. She prides herself on being a good hostess to her guests. Unfortunately, she is locked in the study, attending to some business."

Aidan nodded again, sticking his hands into the pockets of his jeans. "She's a hardworking woman."

“Indeed, she is. Well, I must go check on the others. Madame Clara should be done shortly. In the meantime, if you need anything, please do not hesitate to ask.” And with that, Landon exited the Hazelhurst Manor library.

Aidan turned to me with raised eyebrows. I furrowed mine back at him, trying my best to get what he was not telling me. There was a heaviness in the room now. Those questions weren’t just about making small talk. They were asked for a particular reason, and I wanted to find out why.

Chapter Fifteen

Aidan marched over to one of the library bookcases. He stood in front of it and scanned the books before reaching out, pulling one by the spine, quickly reading the cover then pushing it back into place. He moved to another row of books and picked one, pulled it out only halfway, examined the cover, and then pushed it back in.

"What are you doing?" I asked, standing up from the cushy, velvety chair and gathering my things. Obviously, I wasn't going to get any work done in here. I truly didn't want to have to lock myself in my bedroom all day—not with that blinking bitch hanging on my wall—but it seemed to be the only place I would get some peace and quiet to focus on my writing.

"Searching for something," Aidan responded. He finally removed a book completely off the shelf, but it only took him a second to figure out it wasn't what he was looking for after quickly flipping through its pages.

Once I had my laptop bag packed, I met him at the bookcase. “Searching for what?” I watched him. He wasn’t frantic about what he was doing, just determined.

Aidan didn’t look at me. “Do you believe in the supernatural, McCall?”

“The supernatural? Like...ghosts?”

“Sure. Ghosts are supernatural. But the word doesn’t only pertain to the paranormal.” He picked up another book, skimmed through it, then set it back onto the bookshelf.

I crossed my arms over my chest and thought about his question. He was right. The supernatural could mean anything. Ghosts, zombies, witches, monsters, magic. Did I believe in the supernatural? Well, I was an author of fiction who wrote a book about the zombie apocalypse. Did I believe that one day the whole world would be taken over by the brain-eating dead? No. Not even a little bit. I didn’t really believe in ghosts, either. I wrote purely for entertainment. And that was how much I believed in the supernatural—fictional entertainment.

If those things were real, wouldn’t we have seen it by now? Centuries and centuries of life had passed by. I would think that at some point supernatural beings would have been a part of our reality. It was probably why I didn’t completely lose it last night when I thought I’d seen an apparition standing in the corner of my room. Don’t get me wrong, I was freaked out, but I might have been completely petrified if it was an actual person. Now *that* was a different story.

Monsters were real. And they didn’t have to be big, ugly, green creatures that manifested in our nightmares. Sometimes monsters looked just like any other person in the world. And then one of them catches you in an alley, alone and vulnerable, with every intention of harming you. Maybe even killing you. Making you scream for mercy.

That was what I believed in.

"Well?" Aidan said, bringing my focus back on him. He was now facing me, looking through his glasses that had slid down the bridge of his nose.

I exhaled a frustrated puff of breath. I didn't have time for this. Every minute away from my laptop meant that I wasn't working on my new book, and it only solidified the fact that this trip was for nothing. "What's your point?"

Aidan leaned in closer to me. For a moment I thought maybe he was about to kiss me again and I braced myself. I had about half a second to decide if I was going to let it happen or slap him. Thankfully, he stopped moving and whispered, "Vampires."

I stared at him, my mouth agape and my brow furrowed, waiting for him to finish his sentence. But he only returned an expectant look, waiting for me to say something.

"Um...what?" I asked.

"I'm a Chaser."

"But I thought you were a video game designer," I said, confused. Did I remember this wrong? It wouldn't surprise me. I was pretty drunk last night.

"I am. That's my day job. But at night...at night I chase." He was still speaking in a low voice, so I followed his lead and whispered back.

"What are you chasing?"

Aidan lifted his head up to the ceiling and spun around in a circle. He seemed to be searching for something. When he was done being weird, he took me by the elbow and guided me closer to the corner of the room, away from the door.

"Okay," he started, maintaining a low volume. "I'm a member of a group called the Chasers. We search for supernatural beings across the globe."

"Like ghosts," I stated plainly.

Aidan didn't appreciate my condescending tone. Either that, or he was frustrated with the mention of ghosts again. He shook his head vehemently. "Yes, ghosts. And witches and vampires and demons."

"Demons?"

He ignored me. "I'm part of a big community of Believers. People who believe in the existence of entities other than humanoid beings. Any manifestation of the occult, really. Supernatural beings with magical abilities like telekinesis, shape-shifting, immortality... Things like that. Basically, any force that defies the laws of nature as *we* know it. Chasers travel the world in search of those entities."

It took everything I had not to laugh out loud. Aidan couldn't be serious. I knew he was a nerd, but this was next level. Ghosts weren't real! And neither was magic or supernatural beings. If it were, the entire world would know about it, and there wouldn't be any so-called Chasers chasing them around to prove they were real. There were worse things to be worried about. *Real* things. Like murderers and rapists. *That* was real.

I decided to play along, even though I didn't have time for Aidan's wackadoodle theories. Jeez, and I actually kissed him yesterday? "So, what happens when you find them?"

"Nothing. We just document what we've seen by taking pictures and recording videos. We aren't trying to disturb the S.O.U.Ps."

Late nights at home, lounging on my couch snacking on peanut butter M&Ms and watching those ridiculous ghost hunter shows came into mind. The shaky cameras and creepy voices that were most definitely added post-production. It was all so fake. Then my brain registered what Aidan had just said. "Did you just spell the word *soup*?"

Aidan rolled his eyes. "I did, but we don't like to say that." There was a little bit of sass in his tone, and I got the feeling that he got asked that a lot. "People get it confused with SUPEs, which is short for superheroes," he said, moving his hands in circles as he spoke.

"There are superheroes, too?" Seriously, what had I missed over the past few years living as a recluse?

"No!" he shrieked, then chuckled. "It's a comic book thing. Anyway, S.O.U.P. is an acronym for Supernatural, Otherworldly, and Unearthly Phenomena. We don't want to harass them or anything. We just want proof. There are some other groups who try to capture them. Find out more about who they are and where they come from. But I'm not trying to be an asshole. Besides, it really helps out with my video game designs to just observe them."

Aidan had a good point. Sometimes creativity could be best expressed by using what we knew and have experienced. I'd only written one book about a "supernatural" being—my other books featured a cult and a serial killer, which did absolutely exist—but I'd certainly thought about telling a story about ghosts or vampires. If he was right and S.O.U.P.s did exist, it'd be pretty badass to see it for myself then articulate it down on paper.

Too bad S.O.U.P.s weren't real.

I adjusted the strap of my laptop bag, readying myself to walk away from Aidan, the Chaser. "Okay, well...I've gotta get to my room to do some work. I'll see you later." I turned on my heel, but before I could take a step toward the door, Aidan hastily grabbed my wrist.

"I have proof."

I glared down at the hand wrapping about my arm then at him. He let go immediately, a compunctious glint in his eyes.

"What?" I asked.

"I have proof that S.O.U.P.s exist. I can't show you video or pictures because I don't bring that stuff with me when I travel. I keep it safe at home. But I can show you something that might help you become a believer."

As much as I found that statement hard to *believe*, curiosity prevailed. But anxiety tickled the back of my throat. Fleeting what-ifs began to cross my mind. What if Aidan wanted to show me something that could harm me? What if whatever he had was illegal, and now that I'd seen it, the cops would find me guilty of aiding a criminal? What if what he showed me scared me or heightened my anxiety?

I fidgeted and cleared my throat, cursing myself in my head again for not taking my damn pill this morning. Seriously the stupidest idea ever to choose this weekend to start being brave.

"Well?" I asked Aidan hastily. I didn't mean for it to come out that way, but waiting was only making my nerves worse.

Once again, Aidan searched the library, as if someone had entered and we wouldn't have seen them come in. When I assumed he felt safe enough, he pulled the collar of his hooded sweatshirt away from his chest then reached inside. A quick little ping of panic shot across my stomach. The fear of the unknown.

Out came his hand, along with a necklace that dangled from his fingers. Some kind of small glass vial hung off the silver chain and I squinted at it, trying to figure out what was inside. It swayed as he held it up in front of his face, and all I could tell was that the vial was corked and whatever was inside shimmered white with every swing.

"What is that?"

Aidan smirked. "This is the feather of an angel."

"Ha!" My hand shot up to my mouth, trying to somehow stop the obnoxious yelp that had already escaped. Aidan frowned. "I'm so sorry. I didn't mean that."

It was apparent that Aidan truly believed in the supernatural and that this thing hanging off his neck was an *angel's* feather. I wasn't in the business of making people feel bad or judging them. Who was I to do so? I could only imagine what people thought of me and my mental issues. My parent's friends. People at my job. Even my landlord. The last thing I wanted to do was insult someone who clearly had his own mental issues, because let's face it, you had to be a little cuckoo if you believed in S.O.U.Ps.

Thankfully, Aidan accepted my sincerity. "It's okay. I guess I can't blame you." He buried the vial into his fist. "We got a tip about an undercover angel. I went to check it out. Found out where he lived and broke into his apartment, and sure enough, I found this."

"So, because you found a white, glittery feather, that means this person is an angel?"

Aidan pulled his sweater away from his neck again, dropping the necklace back inside. "Well, there were other things, too. Look, I won't be the least bit upset if you don't care about or believe in this stuff. I don't expect you to. I just figured since you seem really cool and you're a writer, you'd be interested in maybe helping me out."

I shrugged and contemplated his words. He was right. I didn't care about this stuff. What I cared about was doing what I had set out to do, and what this weekend was supposed to be all about. Writing. But the honest-to-God truth was that I still didn't even know what I was writing about! I had come up with an idea about a creepy doll that came to life and haunted a house. But, come on. Seriously? A doll! I should probably name the story *Chucky* or *Anabelle* then call it a day. Who was I kidding? That idea was garbage.

Maybe joining Aidan on his hunt for...whatever he was even looking for, would benefit me and spark another story idea. A better story idea. Besides, we'd still be in the bed-and-breakfast. The evidence Aidan needed had to be in this house, which gave me options. If I got too anxious, I could always simply run to my bedroom and take a benzo. No need to worry. I had options.

I stood tall. "I'm in."

"Really?" he asked, a dubious expression falling over him.

"Really. Let's do this. Let's go find a S.O.U.P."

Aidan clapped his hands and did a little jig, once and for all confirming that he was a legitimate nerd. A cute one, though. I couldn't help smiling at his excitement.

"I've never had a partner in crime before. Especially someone so pretty."

Blood rushed to my cheeks, and I averted my eyes away from his. I hadn't been called pretty in a very long time. If he didn't shut up right now, a whole new set of worries was going to pop up. Stuff I didn't normally care about, like whether or not my hair was done right. Or if my outfit was acceptable for hanging out with someone I liked.

I quickly changed the subject. "So, what's our mission? What are we chasing at Hazelhurst Manor?"

Aidan's lips widened and parted, revealing a shit-eating grin. "I already told you. Vampires."

Chapter Sixteen

Unfortunately, most people these days equated vampires to that infamous story about a bunch of sparkling bloodsuckers who each had different superpowers. Also, unfortunately, I was one of the many tweens who jumped on the whole picking-teams bandwagon (team Edward all the way). As a writer, I appreciated that the author of that series put herself out there and wrote a book for the masses, creating an unforgettable story that people continued to talk about years later. It could very much be on its way to becoming a cult classic. But as someone who was currently trying to be persuaded into believing that supernatural beings were real, there was absolutely no way in hell anyone could convince me that a vampire would willingly step into the sun to show off his twinkling bare body.

So, when Aidan had turned me around and put his hand on the small of my back then guided me to sit in the oversized velvety chair before he took a seat next to me, I couldn't help asking him to clarify his meaning of the word *vampire*. "Are you talking about vampires who only come out at night and sleep in coffins, or vampires who gallivant around high schools during the day like they don't have anything better to do?"

Aidan lifted a finger to his lips. "We should be careful. We don't know who could be lurking around."

I fidgeted in my seat and glanced over my shoulder, suddenly feeling as though someone was watching us. The painting of the woman in my room came to mind, and I briefly wondered if Hazelhurst Manor could be a breeding ground for *all* things supernatural.

"These vampires are definitely not drama queens," he started. "They are the real deal. Coffins, hypnotism, metamorphosis...the whole shebang."

"Metamorphosis? You mean changing into something else?"

"We can't say for sure that they can morph or shapeshift into anything."

"Like into a bat?"

I meant that as a joke, but Aidan nodded. "Maybe. We do know that they are capable of taking form of a cloud of smoke, which is probably only an extension of their ability to teleport. I'm not sure if the smoke is what's left behind when they vanish into thin air, or if they actually turn into it. It could very well be that their superhuman speed leaves behind a bit of exhaust." He furrowed his brow and looked off into the distance, as if really getting lost in his thoughts.

I got lost in my own head, remembering last night when I woke up to the dark silhouette hanging out in the corner of my room. Could that have been a... *Jesus!* I couldn't even bring myself to say it in the privacy of my own mind. I convinced myself that what I was seeing had to be an effect from drinking so much champagne. But what if it wasn't? That would mean that I really did see that figure. It was real. It was real and in my room. But if that really was a vampire, then I might as well just say goodbye to the last shred of sanity I was barely holding on to. There was no way my anxiety would be able to remain controlled without help for the remainder of the weekend.

Aidan didn't notice my momentary zone-out. "Then again," he continued, "They're only capable of vanishing and reappearing a short distance away. I'd say about fifty feet."

"How do you know this stuff?"

His eyes met mine. "It's what other Chasers have documented about their own encounters. I've spent a lot of time researching myself. And I'm not going into detail about the history of vampirism. I'm sure you're aware that vampire lore dates back centuries, and we would be here all night talking about it."

Understandable. But suddenly, I was struck with a bout of the giggles when I pieced together what he was really saying. "Wait a second," I said, holding back a full-on laughing fit. "You're here because you think Madame Clara is a vampire? And Landon and that waitress? And Chef Winston? And that they can turn into bats?"

Aidan didn't return a laugh or so much as smile to my somewhat serious and slightly silly questions—because when else would I ever ask if someone was a vampire? His expression remained solemn. His eyes were steady and laser-focused on mine. And the next words that came out of his mouth were so low and deliberate and honest that they almost made me become a believer right then and there. "Yes. I think at least one of them is, but it's probably safe to say they all are. Vampires normally nest together, and I believe that we are guests at a vampire dwelling."

I squinted at him, focusing on his mouth and hoping to spot his lip quivering against his urge to grin like he was about to reach the punchline of his joke. But Aidan didn't falter. He was dead serious.

My mind reeled, quickly recollecting the physical features of Madame Clara and the rest of the people who ran this B&B. The chef, the waitress, the mysteriously handsome man who lurked around the library. They all seemed pretty human to me, despite the rare genetic eye color condition that they all collectively inherited. Even Madame Clara herself. Aside from their antique style of clothing, which could easily be justified by working at a historical landmark, and their pasty skin, which could be a consequence of living in the middle of the woods where the sun may not shine too often, they appeared normal. The long-haired waitress might have looked a little dead yesterday, but she was much more put together at breakfast this morning. Glowing even. No one had fangs. No high-collared cloaks. No blood mustaches.

"Okay, well, what makes you so certain that there are vampires at Hazelhurst Manor?"

Aidan glanced back at the door leading out into the hallway, and then to me. "Before the quarantine, a member of the Chasers stumbled upon this place when he was looking for a little getaway. When he found out how old it was, he started investigating."

"Oh, come on," I chided. "Just because this place looks haunted, doesn't mean it is." Certainly, Aidan didn't believe every historical Victorian home was riddled with S.O.U.Ps.

"Chasers are optimists. We have to be. We're always open to the possibility, no matter where it is. Or what it is. Since most S.O.U.P.s are immortal and have lived for so long, places like this are usually our number one location to investigate. And as much as the world has evolved over time, many S.O.U.P.s tend to prefer to live as they did long ago. Witches and vampires mostly. With this place in particular, it was more than just aesthetics. It's the location. Sitting high in the mountains surrounded by nothing and no one. It's the stories of the townspeople."

"The story about the man killing and eating his whole family?" I asked, recalling the spooky tale Gwen said she'd heard.

Aidan shrugged. "If vampires live here, then I'm assuming that story is probably true."

"But wouldn't people know if they did? I mean, how could vampires survive in seclusion? Don't they need blood to stay... alive or whatever? How do they get blood without getting caught at some point?" I had so many questions.

Aidan placed his hand on my knee. "That's why I'm here. To find out as much as I can."

"And then what? What do you do with the information?" I asked, my voice slightly raised. I brought my hand up to my mouth then mumbled, "I'm sorry."

I was getting frantic and maybe a little bit annoyed. I couldn't quite understand how Aidan, someone who seemed like a smart guy, would get himself wrapped up in something like this. Something so absurd. I wasn't the kind of person who was completely closed off to the possibility of things happening out of our realm of understanding. I had faith in God and heaven and miracles. Things that couldn't quite be explained by science. Many people didn't believe in what they couldn't see. Did that mean it wasn't real?

I'd assume that if supernatural beings were walking around on Earth, at some point they'd be found out. There'd be tangible, up-to-date evidence, not some ancient drawings of vampires and werewolves and witchcraft. We would just *know*!

"We don't do anything with the information," Aidan answered. "We just know that it's there. That it's real. We leave the S.O.U.P.s alone, unless they are actively hurting someone."

I shook my head. “But how do you know that they aren’t?”

Aidan chuckled. “Honestly, there wouldn’t be much we could do. S.O.U.P.s are much more powerful than regular humans. Maybe in only one way, but most of the time in multiple ways. The last thing I would want to do is piss them off and find myself in a really fucked-up situation. With that said, there have been very little findings suggesting S.O.U.P.s harm humans in this day and age. If they are, they do it very quietly.”

We were both quiet for a beat—I assumed we were thinking the exact same thing, which was what a S.O.U.P was capable of. If they were anything like what we saw in the movies, they could possess an endless amount of superhuman abilities.

I shook the mental picture of a large-nosed witch with long, black fingernails casting spells. “Well, now what?”

“I have a plan to get inside that attic, and then the cellar. There has to be some evidence in there. I need to find their dwelling. Where they keep their coffins or blood reserves. But first I want to check the grounds outside. See if there’s anything worth finding out there.”

“Didn’t Madame Clara say she wasn’t letting anyone hike because of the weather?” I asked, suddenly worried that I’d slip in the wet mud and fall down the side of the mountain. I wasn’t a hiker, that was for sure. The closest thing to a mountain Florida had were man-made sand dunes.

Aidan stood up and offered his hand. I took it, standing up with him. “She can’t stop us.”

“Oh, no? How about the weather then?” Right on cue, thunder rumbled above our heads. I pointed up, giving Aidan a told-you-so smirk.

“We’ll be fine. Let’s go change into some warmer clothes and head down for lunch. It’ll be starting soon, and then we can sneak out afterward.”

Now I was concerned about lunch. Breakfast was delicious, but I had a feeling lunch might be another weird-ass meal from the olden days. Just another reason to be anxious: going against the owner's rules to explore the dangerous land surrounding a possible vampire den with a belly full of something gross.

"McCall!"

I stopped in the middle of the hallway, allowing Gwen to catch up with me. She was just stepping out of her bedchamber.

"Where are you going?" she asked.

"I'm just going to my room to change before lunch." We walked to my door.

"Oh, cool. I'll join you," she said, turning the brass knob and entering my room. Not like I had invited her in or anything. Which I definitely wouldn't have. I was still contemplating whether or not I was going to tell her about Preston and the waitress.

Gwen glanced at each four walls. "I'm glad to see we all pretty much have the same size room. I was worried that Preston and I might have gotten hosed or something. The bedrooms here are definitely not what we're used to. They don't even have closets!"

I set my laptop bag down. "I don't think there really were closets in the old days."

She pulled a face. "That's tragic." She reached for Landon's manuscript on the desk, and I attempted to stop her, extending a hand out to intercept.

"Oh, that's not—"

She picked it up and flipped through the pages. "What's this?"

"It's..." Should I tell her it was Landon's? Did he want other people to know about it? "It's just something that was here already. I guess maybe it belongs to Madame Clara."

Gwen tossed it back on the desk, uninterested. I wondered if she'd be interested in anything that belonged to Madame Clara. "It looks old. Just like everything else in this place." She sighed before plopping down on the edge of my bed.

I took a moment to admire her outfit today—a glittery turtleneck top with jeans and fur-lined boots that rode up to her knees. I was thankful that she dressed modestly this time. Besides the fact that it was always chilly in this house, there was less of a chance of Madame Clara chastising her outfit.

I proceeded to get my warmer clothes ready for the excursion Aidan and I had planned for later. I hadn't anticipated going outside all weekend because of Madame Clara's warning and my declaration to stay inside to write, but I was glad that I had packed wool socks and thermals. The temperature outside might have been the norm for people from around here. Especially considering it was only fall. But for someone like me, who lived in a place that was usually seventy degrees on Christmas day, it might as well have been Alaska.

Gwen lay back in the bed, her blonde hair fanning out around her head. "If it wasn't for the stupid pandemic, I'd be on a beach right now sipping on a frozen margarita."

"You might be able to have one here. I'm sure Chef Winston could blend up a cocktail for you," I joked, refusing to mention the waitress.

"Yeah right. That old man probably doesn't even know what a margarita is." She giggled. "Oh, but I bet that little server girl with the long, black hair does." Crap. "I think she was the one mixing our drinks last night."

I began rummaging through my suitcase as the anxiety started to bubble in my stomach. The plan to stay medication-free for the rest of the trip was still in place, but I just had to look at my bottle of pills. Remind myself that they were there if I needed them. The conversation we were having made me nervous. It had been years since I'd been in a predicament like this—the last one being in high school with my high school friends. I didn't have friends anymore. There was no drama in my life. Drama made me uneasy. It was unpredictable. Just like people were.

I had to tell Gwen about the raven-haired waitress. This woman wasn't my friend. I barely knew her. But from one female to another, it would be the considerate thing to do. God knew I wouldn't want to be the reason to break up a marriage, but Gwen had a right to know that her husband cheated on her.

On the other hand, I could just let her find out on her own. If he was indeed a cheater, this certainly would not have been his first, or last, rodeo. They'd eventually go back to California and she'd find out, without me meddling in their business.

I shuffled my clothes around in the bag.

"So, what's up with you and Aidan?" Gwen asked in that gossipy, high-pitched voice girls do when there's something juicy to talk about.

"Nothing," I said, my eyes focused, anticipating the sight of my orange bottle of pills. But I still couldn't find it. The beats of my heart sped up, my hands beginning to tremble. "Shit." I dug through, pulling articles of clothing that I'd just folded that morning and throwing them into a messy pile on the bed.

"What's wrong?"

"I can't find my medication," I answered wildly, suddenly agitated that Gwen was even in the room and asking me questions.

Gwen didn't even care about my frenzied state. She didn't move. "What do you take?"

Normally, I was very taciturn when it came to my mental health. If it wasn't my therapist or my parents, you would never catch me discussing my issues with anyone else. This most definitely included treatment. But in the moment, I didn't care who was near me. My main concern was finding my pills. My only option to escape the madness of my own mind.

I switched my search to my laptop bag, pulling out my computer and notebook and pens and tossing them aside. "It's just medication for my anxiety..." I mumbled, trailing off to concentrate less on words and more on what I was looking for.

"Oh, shoot. I've got Xanax, Ativan, Valium..." She rattled off the name of the benzos like it was a shopping list. "They're all lying around my bathroom counter back home. If I'd brought them, I totally would have given you a few. Actually, I kind of wish I had them last night. Those babies are yummy with alcohol. But everyone is fucked up in the head somehow, right? Maybe Aidan or even Madame Bitch Face might have some to spare. God knows she needs them."

It was starting to get harder to control the shaking in my hands. Right after I flung my bag across the room to search someplace else, I spotted the pill bottle buried inside the clothes I'd just emptied from the suitcase. I grabbed it, shook it once to hear the sound of the pills, and let out a sigh of relief.

"Sounds like you found them." Gwen turned on her side to face me, her luscious hair flying over her shoulder and cascading down the side of her head as she rested her cheek in the palm of her hand. "Anyway, what do you mean nothing's going on with you and Aidan? You two are adorable together. I mean, you did slap him last night, but that was like a love tap. I've done that a ton of times. He might have actually liked it." She winked and grinned deviously at me.

I closed my eyes and concentrated on my breathing. Lowering my heart rate. Steadying my hands.

I have my pills. I have options. I have my pills. I have options. I have my pills.

"McCall?"

Finding the pills immediately abated the panic, but the mantra helped, too. I knew Gwen was wondering what the hell I was doing, but I didn't feel comfortable explaining. I finally acknowledged her. "Well, I already apologized to him."

"You two should totally hook up. Make it a one-time thing. You're on vacation! And you don't live near each other. It could be a one-and-done, and then you go your separate ways."

"Aw, that's such a sweet love story! I can't wait to tell my children one day," I teased, feeling much more at ease once I began refolding all the clothes I pulled out of my luggage.

Gwen was completely oblivious to my brief panic attack. "You're right. It's hard to find the perfect love story." She fell onto her back again, smiling from ear to ear and exhaling a long, pleasing moan. "I was lucky to have found mine."

Shit! Why did she have to mention Preston?

"I know people don't get our relationship. Everyone always comments on how much older he is. And they constantly want to know what the sex is like. The truth is, the sex is awesome! Are we doing wild handstand sex positions? No."

Please. Please stop talking about Preston.

"But he's really good in bed. He knows how to please a woman, that's for sure. And he doesn't even care if he doesn't get off. You know how most guys, like, freak out if they don't finish? Preston is okay with it. He says as long as *I* cum, it doesn't matter. And—"

"Preston cheated on you!" It came out before I could stop it. Like vomit. Word vomit. Because if she didn't stop talking about doing sex handstands with Preston, I might have actually vomited.

She stopped rambling then sat up, turned, and squinted at me. "What did you say?"

I walked around the bed and leaned up against it, right next to her dangling legs. I almost rested a hand on her knee to comfort her but decided against it. Gwen was not my friend. "I...I saw Preston with the server girl last night. The woman with the long, black hair."

"You saw them what?"

I couldn't look her in the eye. "I saw them kissing in the parlor."

Gwen's eyes slowly drifted from me to her hands on her laps. She stayed that way for what seemed like forever, and I considered pulling her in for a hug. Her heart seemed to be breaking right before my eyes, and although Gwen was *not* my friend, she most certainly needed someone to act like one at the moment.

But before I'd made my final decision and leaned in toward her, she abruptly gripped me by the elbow and stood up. "You're lying."

She stood tall, the heels of her boots adding at least four inches on me. I glanced up at her and shook my head. "I'm not lying. I went downstairs to get a drink and I saw them. In the parlor. The girl was sitting on top of Preston. Straddling him. And if you didn't give him that hickey, then I think she might have."

Gwen's eyes widened before they narrowed at me, burning a hole right through my forehead. Maybe I shouldn't have said that last part. "He told me he cut himself shaving, and I believe my husband."

I retracted my statement immediately. "Then maybe I'm completely wrong." Of course I was wrong. Why did I even suggest something like that to a woman about her husband? The man had to be telling his wife the truth about the shaving mishap.

The raven-haired girl might not have given him that hickey, but I sure as shit knew what I saw. And I saw a woman seductively draped over Preston's private area, and she was not Gwen.

"I'm so sorry to be the one to tell you this," I said sincerely. "But I saw that waitress with Preston last night and they were embracing and—"

"He would never do that to me," she seethed, stepping closer to me. "You're just fucking jealous, you bitch!" And before I could move out of the way, she pushed my shoulders back with forceful exertion, shoving me into the thick, wooden bedpost. My spine collided with the solid wood, and I groaned loudly from the spasm it caused that radiated from my back to my lungs. Gwen stormed out of my room, slamming the door behind her. I fell into a heap on the ground, grabbing for my back and wincing at the ache.

That didn't go over so well. I hadn't expected Gwen to get hostile. She was incredibly sweet, even for being a ritzy, spoiled young woman. That whole exchange went from 0 to 60, and I didn't even know what just happened.

Well, that was certainly the last time I would try to open my mouth and do the right thing. I naively thought that Gwen would appreciate my honesty. Then she'd cry on my shoulder, and I would awkwardly try to console her. On the flip side, she didn't even know me, and I should have also anticipated that kind of reaction. Just...not a violent one.

Another perfect example of how people were so unpredictable.

Chapter Seventeen

I shut the bedroom door behind me, feeling the back pocket of my jeans as I stepped out into the shadowy hallway. The key to the safe formed an outline in the denim fabric, and a sense of security washed over me. After a round of what-ifs, I had decided the best place for my pills to go was the safe. For about a half an hour, my brain fought back and forth with itself, arguing about whether or not I should continue with making this weekend THE weekend to work on my fears and anxieties. In the end, my heart prevailed.

My options were still limited. I didn't have a ton of escape plans set in place. I couldn't leave the property if I wanted to or call Dr. Finn to get verbal encouragement. I couldn't even really call my room a safe place because weird black clouds of smoke visited me at night and the portrait hanging on my wall was watching me. But I had my benzos. And if I needed to, I could pop one and in fifteen minutes be in a state of total serenity. None of that stuff would matter.

In the beginning, I had no qualms about taking my medication. I was willing to try anything to help with the daily discomforts of life itself. The decision to kick the habit of using them wasn't influenced by my therapist or my parents. If anything, Dr. Finn encouraged me to take them if I felt that was what I needed. And taking them over the years have, without a doubt, saved my life. So why was I so fixated on breaking the habit?

Well, it was for the exact reason I started taking them: to have control. For the past nine years, I have allowed what happened to me define every aspect of who I was. The stinky, ashen-colored homeless man with silver eyes took a bite out of my neck and left a hole in my life, altering my personality, forcing me to alienate myself from people who might be able to show me what it was like to love and be loved, and completely distorted my view of the world. Because of the asshole, I have become a recluse and I'd missed out on so many opportunities and experiences that a woman my age should be having.

Dr. Finn and I had many discussions about weaning me off medication, should I decide against taking them. I'd managed to go about two weeks without it once but ended up having a nervous breakdown one day at work when I thought I had spotted the bastard who attacked me near my apartment building. After that, I hadn't been able to curve the dependency. I guess it could be worse. I could be an addict who relied on harder drugs to give me the courage I needed to make it through life. Cocaine was a known recreation for a lot of the well-to-dos who attended my parents' country club, and they seemed to have no trouble getting through life. In fact, those ones I knew for sure who used it were usually the most successful and the life of the party.

Benzos were just my drug of choice.

I reached the second-story landing, glancing up at the darkened stairway that led to the attic. I was conflicted. A part of me was dying to know what was on the other side of that door, now that I knew there could be something belonging to a S.O.U.P. (if S.O.U.P.s were real), but another part of me didn't think it was such a good idea to be snooping around in places we were specifically told not to. If, hypothetically, there were really vampires around here, I wasn't too sure I wanted to be the one to discover them.

A chuckle escaped my throat as I descended down the steps. The idea of the supernatural actually being real titillated the part of my brain responsible for my imagination. It would be so crazy cool to learn that the characters in horror and science fiction novels were actually based on something real. Then again, it could also be the stuff of nightmares. What if this bed-and-breakfast was, in fact, run by vampires? How much danger could I be in at this very moment?

I passed through the foyer and entered the dining room where Aidan, Gwen, and Preston were already seated at the table. Madame Clara was standing close by, all prim and proper like a giant stick had been placed perfectly snug right inside her rectum.

"So glad you could finally join us, Miss Harris," she deadpanned.

I flicked my wrist to trigger the light sensor on my watch. The time illuminated in a lime green hue. 12:05 p.m. Five minutes late.

Shaking off the nervousness beginning to form in my stomach from Madame Clara calling me out, I took my seat next to Aidan. He graciously picked up the carafe of water and poured some into my glass as I unfolded a napkin and placed it over my lap. "Thank you," I whispered. My eyes drifted to the empty spots around the elongated table, leaving me wondering how Tom, Ellen, and their kids were doing. I hoped that they got to the airport okay.

I stole a quick glance at Gwen and Preston, who both didn't even acknowledge that I had joined them for lunch. Preston was now wearing some kind of ascot or scarf covering his neck and the shaving wound. He sat back in his chair, eyes down to his empty plate and fingers fidgeting with the utensils next to it. Gwen's hands were under the table and she was staring down at them, and I knew that she was secretly on her phone. She had to be pretending to be using it to deliberately avoid eye contact with me because our phones didn't work. Madame Clara was clearly not fond of electronic devices, so she'd probably lose her shit if she saw Gwen with one at the dining room table.

I wished Gwen wasn't upset with me. The whole pushing-me-into-the-bedpost incident might have been out of line, and physically hurt, but my back was feeling better and I didn't want to part ways tomorrow evening knowing that I have gained an enemy who lived across the country. It shouldn't bother me at all. Chances were that I wasn't going to see Preston or Gwen ever again, but it would make me feel a whole lot better to know that I didn't ruin someone's marriage.

"My apologies for missing breakfast this morning. I had some important business to attend to," Madame Clara said, her frigid stare switching back and forth between all of us. "I hope that whatever needs you might have had were met in a timely and satisfactory manner by the other staff members who were available."

Gwen raised her hand as if she were in a classroom, but she didn't wait for Madame Clara to call on her. "Actually, no. I asked the tall butler guy for the girl with the long, black hair to come to my room. You know that housemaid lady?"

Madame Clara narrowed her eyes, her lips pursing. "Her name is Pandora."

Gwen huffed, smiling sardonically. "Well, PAN-dora didn't show up."

"Was there something Landon couldn't help you with?"

"I didn't want his help," Gwen responded through gritted teeth. "I wanted her."

Shit. Shit. Shit. My heartbeat quickened. Did Gwen want to confront Pandora about making out with her husband? The good thing about this was that Gwen somehow came to her senses and decided to believe what I said. There might have been a conversation between her and Preston, and Preston probably admitted to it. He looked like the kind of guy who would, anyway. Like, he would own up to any wrongdoings because why not? The man was ancient and old people didn't lie, did they? And he just seemed so in love with his wife. At the moment, he was rubbing her back as she spoke to Madame Clara, supporting her even though he was in the wrong. It could have been a total mistake. We were all drinking pretty heavily last night, after all.

The bad thing was that if Gwen confronted Pandora, she would reveal that I was the one who told her—there weren't many other people around here to accuse—and Pandora might want to seek revenge on the tattler. If she lived by the "snitches got stitches" rule, then I'd better prepare myself. Especially if she was a vampire.

Oh God. My palms were beginning to sweat. This was too much drama to handle for one weekend. I should have known that Gwen would confront the mistress. She was rich and blonde and sweet, but there was a little firecracker underneath all that makeup and expensive clothing.

Madame Clara straightened herself, a signal I was beginning to pick up that meant she was about to end the conversation once and for all and her word was going to be the last. “Pandora will not be serving as your concierge for the remaining duration of your stay. If you need anything, Landon or I will fulfill your requests.”

Gwen pulled a face. “Did she leave?”

“Mrs. Prescott!” We all flinched at Madame Clara’s sudden stiff-lipped outburst. “The whereabouts of my staff when they are not on the clock isn’t and-slash-or should not be the concern of our guests. Quite frankly, it is rather rude to inquire about anything pertaining to their personal lives. The only interest you should have is whether or not your needs are being met.”

Gwen’s large breasts rose and fell with every accelerated breath she took. She was fuming. I was surprised we couldn’t visibly see steam blasting out of her ears.

“In the meantime,” Madame Clara finished, “Landon and I will do everything in our power to ensure that your experience at Hazelhurst Manor is...pleasurable.”

The two of them stared daggers at each other and we all sat still, waiting for something to happen. There was a mental duel going on, a fight the rest of us couldn’t see. Gwen had to be cursing Madame Clara with every bad word she could think of. And Madame Clara was probably doing the same, only in a very passive-aggressive, condescending kind of way, which I thought was worse than the *f* word.

Finally, Gwen opened her mouth to speak, but Madame Clara beat her to the punch. “Now,” she addressed the rest of the table, her voice elevated and regaining control of the room. Gwen leaned back in her chair, her full, glossy lips pressed in a hard line. I felt sorry for her. All Madame Clara had done since we’d been here was berate her. Part of me wanted to stick up for

Gwen, but the other part—the cowardly part—didn't want to get scolded by either of them. "Chef Winston has prepared a very special lunch."

Right on cue, Chef Winston and his cart rolled in, the overwhelming aroma of meat following him. He wheeled it to the head of the table then smiled at us, the biggest lopsided grin I'd ever seen. Teeth tarnished with years of staining.

The dinner cart contained three items: one large oval plate and two smaller ones, all covered by shiny, metal domes. Exactly the kind of thing I would see at the country club my parents had been members of since before I was born, where we'd eat every Sunday for brunch since I could remember. And by the way the old man was beaming with enthusiasm, it was apparent how eager he was to show us all what was underneath the lids.

Chef Winston's fingertips pinched the knob of the largest dome and at exactly the same time he lifted it off the plate, Madame Clara announced what our eyes were seeing. "Boiled calf's head."

A head. An entire head of a baby cow on a plate.

She continued, "This beautiful cut of meat was raised by Chef Winston himself, and prepared in a creamy, buttery sauce with capers and fresh parsley."

My stomach rolled with a heavy onslaught of nausea in its wake. The baby cow's head lay motionless. Dead. Its eyes hollowed out and its mouth partially opened.

Chef Winston moved to reveal what was under the other smaller domes. Madame Clara said, "The head is accompanied by caramelized calf's brain and braised calf's tongue."

It took everything in me not to retch all over the table.

"Did it come from that...calf?" Aidan asked, and I shot him a dirty look before elbowing his ribcage. He shrugged innocently, insinuating that he was simply curious.

"Yes, the tongue and brains belonged to this particular calf." Madame Clara nodded at Chef Winston. "You may carve and serve now."

Chef Winston commenced the carving of the calf's head by first slicing through its cheek. The room fell quiet, and there was only the sound of the long, serrated knife sawing through the meat and into the bone. I cringed but couldn't bring myself to look away. The precision Chef Winston displayed while cutting up this poor baby cow could have been an art form. It was such a barbaric thing to do, but he was extremely delicate with each piece of meat he methodically incised and removed, placing equal amounts onto each plate.

Once he was done, our meal was served. The plate sat in front of me, three different portions of the baby cow's head soaking in a buttery, brown sauce with parsley and capers. As if the splash of green would somehow liven up the revolting dish. Okay, if I was being honest, it didn't look half bad. But my eyes couldn't help drifting over to the skeletal remains of what used to be an adorable little farm animal.

"Don't look at it," Aidan whispered to me, a fork full of meat in his left hand. "We've got to get some food in us if we're going for a hike. Just eat a little bit." He bravely shoved the fork into his mouth and chewed, followed by a hard swallow. Then he forced a smile.

I had no misgivings about eating meat. I was a carnivore through and through, but only if I didn't have to actually *see* where my meat was coming from. As much as I wanted to push my plate of food away and declare the basket of rye bread sitting in the middle of the table as my lunch, Aidan was right. If we were going to spend a few hours outside hiking through the woods, I should make sure I had the energy to keep up. I was pretty hungry and having hunger pains didn't do my anxiety any good.

I picked up my fork and poked at the various layers, trying to decide which piece would be the best to start with. When I finally felt ready, I pushed a small morsel past my lips and chewed.

Chapter Eighteen

I tried. I really did. But my stomach was not happy with what I had fed it.

My head hovered over the toilet bowl, one hand gripping the edge and the other holding back my own hair. I didn't have time to pull it into a bun. As soon as lunch was done and we stood up from the dining room table—after I'd forced myself to eat at least half of what was on my plate—the calf's tongue and brains and whatever else was part of its head lurched straight back up from my stomach to my mouth. It wasn't the taste that had made me sick. I couldn't believe I would admit this, but the meal itself wasn't the most terrible thing I had ever eaten. However, knowing exactly where it had come from screwed with my head the entire time I sat at the table. That, coupled with Madame Clara watching us and knowing Gwen was upset with me, and the anticipation of Aidan and me venturing out into the hard rain and dense woods just didn't mix well with the food.

Right as I finished splashing water on my face, there was a soft knock on the door. "McCall? Are you okay?"

It was Aidan. I opened the door to a concerned look on his face.

"Yeah, I'm okay. That food was just a little too...authentic for me."

"You're not kidding." He rubbed his belly, and I felt his empathy. "Hey, if you don't feel up to going on that hike, it's totally cool."

I wiped away the cold sweat from the back of my neck. "No, it's okay. I'm still in. Just let me run up to my room for a minute." I pulled the sleeves of my sweater over my hands and squeezed the fabric into my tight fist, trying to hide the shakes from Aidan. Sickness made me super anxious. It made me feel like I didn't have control of my body, and that was unacceptable.

Aidan nodded and stepped away from the bathroom door. "I'll be waiting for you in the parlor."

"Okay," I said over my shoulder as I concentrated on getting to my bedchamber. I just needed a moment to myself. A moment to do a breathing exercise or two to regain control and ground myself.

Once I made it inside, I silently closed the door and locked it, leaning back against the wood and slamming my eyes shut. *One more day, McCall. Just one more day and you will have finally survived a weekend away from home all alone.* After all these years of fighting my own mind, of living in fear. After living in the shadows of what happened to me, I would finally be able to feel like I was actually healing. It would be an enormous milestone. One that would certainly restore at least a little bit of the person I used to be before the vicious attack that upended my life.

I opened my eyes and they drifted to the safe underneath the writing desk. My escape was locked away in there. If at any time I needed refuge from reality, all I had to do was take one of my pills.

My cellphone sat on the desk next to Landon's manuscript. Part of me wished that there was reception to touch base with Dr. Finn. Just to let her know that I was doing okay. But the other part of me, the bravery buried deep down inside somewhere that was fighting its way to the surface, was happy that I couldn't. This was a test like no other, and I was determined to pass it.

After taking a few minutes to compose myself, I stepped out of my bedroom and closed the door. Down the Hallway of Death I went, to the staircase and into the foyer. I walked with a confident stride, proud of myself that I had not even stuffed an emergency pill into the cup of my bra.

Okay, I was proud, but that didn't mean that I wasn't worried. I might have felt a little stupid, too. Was it a good idea for a person prone to panic attacks—because of the unknown—to venture out into the *unknown*? I put my money on no. What if I began to hyperventilate? And the lack of air made me pass out? What if I fell and hurt my ankle, and Aidan wasn't strong enough to carry me back, so he would have to leave me alone? In the wilderness. With no water. What if I choked because I had nothing to drink? What if he couldn't find me when he came back, and I was left out there all alone on the forest floor? Then I'd starve. What if the crows picked out my eyeballs and tore at the tendons in my arms and legs?

"Over here, McCall," Aidan called to me from the doorway of the parlor, knocking me out of the irrational rambling that I knew wasn't good for me. No more what-ifs from here on out. If I kept it up, I might as well not even leave the house.

I peeked into the parlor room. Aidan took a long gulp of what was left in his cocktail glass, and Preston and Gwen sat in the loveseat near the fireplace having a drink of their own. Preston's arm hung over Gwen's shoulder, and her head was nestled into the nape of his neck. She didn't even look up at me. They both just sat there, watching the fire and cuddling as a married couple would do on a romantic getaway. A clear indication to me that either she truly didn't believe me when I told her I saw her husband making out with the housemaid, or they had quickly gotten over it and moved on. Somehow, I didn't see Gwen accepting that her man cheated on her. I didn't know her well enough to make that assumption, but why would she? She wasn't with him for the money. She had her own. And she had to know that she was young and gorgeous and could probably have any man she wanted, especially one her own age.

"You ready?" Aidan whispered near my ear, his warm breath tingling my skin and sending goosebumps down my back.

"Yup." I glanced behind me. "Are you sure they aren't going to catch us?"

Aidan shrugged. "Who cares? She warned us about going outside after the storm, but she didn't make us sign a contract about it. I don't remember anything like that in the application. Do you?"

I shook my head.

"Besides, what's she going to do? Kick us out? We leave tomorrow, anyway. We paid through the weekend."

He headed toward the front door, reaching up to silence the bell before it alerted everyone in the house of our secret departure. I turned to follow him, sneaking a glance over my shoulder one last time at Gwen. To my surprise, I caught her watching us, and I immediately twisted back around. I was embarrassed that she caught me looking, but happy that she was at least a little bit curious about what we were doing. When we got back, I would have to pull her aside and have a heart-to-heart. Whether or not she chose to believe her husband was cheating was her choice, but she had to know I would never lie about something like that.

It took a beat for my eyes to adjust to being outside. The inside of Hazelhurst Manor was so dim that even the clouds that hid the sun stung. It didn't take long to get used to it, though. It wasn't raining anymore, but the overcast sky covered the house and the surrounding forest with a blanket of silvery haze.

As we plodded down the short stairwell onto the moss-covered walkway that led to the forest, I felt like I could have been experiencing some kind of environmental shock. It was gloomy when we had arrived, but what I was seeing now was a different kind of bleak. Everything was a muted shade of gray. The vintage house, the stone path leading to the trail, the leafless trees, even the mud. There was gray in the air, a kind of vaporous mist that consumed everything. Where I came from, there was still color when it rained. Miami was known for its art deco and teal-colored ocean. Some of the wettest days occurred while the sun was shining high up in the sky, and a rainbow could always be found somewhere over the horizon.

Now, as Aidan and I commenced our search for...I didn't even know what...the feeling of being so far away from home hit me like a ton of bricks. It was cold and damp and dreary out here, and I wasn't a fan.

A few yards away, the stony pathway ended just past an opening into the wooded area, changing into a brown sludge. My boot sunk, generating a suction sound with each step. We approached a weathered wooden sign that read *Blood Bond Trail* and a small map underneath, an illustrated pathway that zigzagged through the trees and formed a circle back to the manor.

"Charming trail name," I commented as we walked past it to begin our hike.

"S.O.U.P.s can be blatantly transparent, and humans are oblivious. Most live among us and we have no idea who they could be."

I glanced back at the house once more. We weren't far yet. This was my chance to back out. Tell Aidan I didn't feel good or something. I did get sick earlier, so it wouldn't be hard to use that as an excuse.

Aidan must have sensed my hesitation because he said, "Don't even think about it. You look like you want to go back, and you're not going back."

I pulled a face. "What?" I placed a hand on my chest, hoping to convince him that I was surprised by his accusation. "I don't wanna go back."

The narrow walkway of the trail opened up, and we began our trek through the crowd of tall, skinny trees with bare branches.

"Listen, you don't have to hide it from me. I get it," he said. "I could tell something was a little off with you the moment I saw you."

"No you didn't," I scoffed. I was offended. Aidan didn't know me very well, and I refused to believe that someone could just look at me and know that I had issues. I didn't give off that crazy vibe, did I?

"I could tell in your face," he explained. "The way you watched everyone around you when we got on the bus at the airport. Even when you looked at me. You were skeptical. And when we got off and stood in front of the house, you looked back at the bus leaving like you almost wanted to chase it down and jump back on."

The brisk October air suddenly felt cooler against my skin. I shivered and closed my jacket tighter around my body, dipping my chin a little lower into my scarf. The thought of someone being able to just look at me and know that I was scared was disconcerting, making me feel exposed. It was apparent to me that the people I spent time with on a daily basis knew, at the very least, that something was strange about me. At work, I kept to myself. Didn't talk much to my co-workers. Didn't join them for lunch or attend weekend gatherings with them. I spoke to my neighbors on very rare occasions, but they saw me come and go. There was no doubt that they were familiar with my schedule, which consisted mostly of coming home and staying there for most of the day.

One of the struggles I had was worrying about what I looked like to the rest of the world. And hearing it right now, coming from someone I might actually like, made me ashamed of myself. It made me want to change more than ever.

We both stepped over a large log covered in bright green moss, halfway buried into the muck. Aidan reached out and gingerly grasped my elbow to keep me steady. "It's nothing to be embarrassed about, McCall. You went through something very traumatic. PTSD is real. I saw some of the same things in my brother."

I couldn't look at him. "Yeah, well...it's just annoying, you know? It's like, I want to get better. I want to get over what happened to me. It's not fun always having to look over my shoulder or worry about who might attack me next. The anxiety just takes over and sometimes it's too hard to overcome. It wins every time." I bit my bottom lip, stopping myself from saying any more. This was the most I'd spoken about my feelings outside of my therapist's office.

"Then don't let it!" Aidan countered. "You have the ability to control—"

"Don't go there," I interrupted sharply, moving away from a long, brittle-looking branch projecting out of a tree. "We don't have the ability to control anything. Life happens, and we don't know who, what, when, or where it's going to happen most of the time."

Aidan sucked his teeth at my statement. "That's bullshit. You might not be able to have control over what happens to you, but you have control over how you react to it."

I grew silent, allowing the words I had been hearing for years to percolate in my mind. I heard him, just like I'd heard Dr. Finn say the exact same thing over and over to me. And their wisdom was spot on. Gaining control over how I reacted to things happening around me, or things that *could* happen, would basically be the end-all to my crippling anxiety disorder.

But it just wasn't as easy as saying *this happened, so this is how I'm going to feel about it*. It took a lot more psychological fortitude for a person like me, who doubted herself and everyone around her constantly, to control my response to situations. Everything that happened in life, however big or small, warranted some kind of reaction. I could not imagine myself being one of those people who just let things slide off their shoulders. Like some kind of hippy-dippy girl or something. There had to be questions. There had to be answers. There had to be a plan for what might happen next.

Aidan must have mistaken my moment of quiet, inner dialogue as offended silence. "I don't mean to put any pressure on you or tell you how to live. I know it's easier said than done."

"It's okay." A gust of damp wind weaved through the trees and between Aidan and me. My hands dove into the pockets of my jacket. "This is kind of the reason why I don't usually tell random people about my issues. They always think they can fix me just by saying a few encouraging words."

"Yeah, but what I'm saying comes from experience. I watched my brother hit rock bottom, burn, and then come out of the ashes. I know what helped him get through it."

He was right. His words actually had weight behind them. But he still couldn't fix nine years' worth of damage by simply saying he understood.

"Also, I hope you don't consider me a random person anymore. We've kissed, I've seen you half naked, and you slapped me across the face, all in a matter of twenty-four hours. Doesn't that count for something?" he asked, his tone light and playful.

I turned to him and smiled. But before I could respond to his adorable wit, my boot slid out in from of me. Aidan reached out for my arms to stop me from falling, but it was too late. My right leg shot straight out, and my left knee collided with the muddy ground, leaving me in an awkward half split that stretched the muscles in my groin. I winced. Maybe I could do splits when I was younger, but definitely not anymore.

Aidan curled his arms under my armpits and pulled me up as I struggled to find my footing in the muck. I held onto his biceps while he practically lifted me clear off the ground and gently planted me upright. His muscles flexed underneath the layers of clothes, and I was pleasantly surprised by his strength.

"Are you okay?"

Aidan was taller than me by nearly a foot, and when I glanced up at him, I forced a smile to try to hide my embarrassment. "I'm fine. Stupid mud."

He held me close and gazed down at me, his brown eyes never leaving mine. The corner of his lips curled up, and my heartbeat quickened inside my chest. Aidan was kind of dreamy, with his wavy, chocolate-colored hair and thick eyebrows to match, his olive complexion, and stubbly bristles that ran along his squared jawline, encasing his mouth. And that mole above his lip only added more charm.

In the gloom and fog, surrounded by barren trees and only the occasional sound of birds cawing in the distance, there was almost a romantic quality to the setting we were currently in. Enchanting, even. My writer brain kicked into gear, immediately imagining myself writing this exact scene into one of my stories. Only, a gentle rain would begin to fall as the two main characters leaned in for a kiss.

My eyes drifted from Aidan's lips up to the sky, willing the clouds to—

"What the hell?" I asked, my attention taken from Aidan and the moment that might have ended in a kiss by what I was seeing in the sky.

"What?"

I pulled away from Aidan's steady, gentle grip and pointed up. He followed my finger. "The clouds."

We both watched as a large ring of gray clouds hovered above Hazelhurst Manor and some of the surrounding forest, swirling in constant motion.

"I knew it," Aidan said, grinning.

Chapter Nineteen

Standing within the depths of a graveyard forest, a thin layer of mist rolling at our feet, Aidan and I glanced up at the sky together. The view of the sprawling Victorian mansion was now obscured by hundreds of tall trees surrounding us in all directions, their many branches naked but still blocking the curves and points of the house's turret and arched windows in the distance. And despite the leafless timbers soaring high above our heads, reaching into the sky, we could still spot the blanket of gray and black hovering directly over the manor.

If I remembered it correctly from science class back in grade school, the lumpy, angry-looking clouds were called cumulonimbus clouds, which were usually associated with thunderstorms and torrential downpours. It made total sense considering the cracks of thunder exploding over us all night long and what sounded like a monsoon falling on the wooden roof. Currently, the dense sheet of heather-gray puff wasn't generating thunder or rain, just narrow bolts of neon blue and purple shooting across its width every minute or so.

"What do you mean you knew it?" I asked dubiously. I couldn't figure out what weather patterns had to do with our current vampire mission.

"They're controlling it," he said as he dug into his coat pocket. He retrieved his phone and held it up to the sky to snap pictures, rotating it vertically and horizontally like some kind of professional photographer.

"What are they controlling?"

Aidan tapped the screen on his cellphone a few more times before sliding it back into his pocket and stepping over to me. "The weather. Some vampires are able to control the weather. It's a type of safeguard. To protect them from the sun."

Even though I was still on the fence about whether or not Aidan was full of shit, it was nice to hear we'd been hunting your run-of-the-mill vampires and not the ones who twinkled in the sunlight.

"Well, that's convenient," I remarked.

"From what we understand by the investigations we've done so far, only the very old vampires have the ability to do this."

I thought about Madame Clara. Despite having a face that could pass for a thirty-something-year-old woman, my gut told me she'd be the old vampire of the nest. She had that whole seniority, what-I-say-goes-because-I'm-in-charge-and-everyone-else-is-garbage-compared-to-me kind of vibe. Although, Chef Winston might come in as close second, simply because he looked ancient. "What about the ones who aren't old enough? Do they just burn to death?"

Aidan started down the soggy trail again and I followed.

"They end up living underground and only come up at night."

I wasn't sure if it was because part of me might have started to believe Aidan's vampire theory or that the temperature had dropped a couple of degrees within a matter of seconds, but a chill found its way through my layers of clothes and into my bones. I shivered.

"Makes sense," I said, my teeth clattering. I wished I had brought my notebook. Writing a book about vampires wasn't set in stone yet, but whatever he said could give me ideas to create a supernatural of my own. It didn't matter, though. None of what was happening this weekend was normal, so chances were, I'd remember every single thing he said.

Aidan started to unzip his jacket. "Here. I have another layer underneath," he offered.

It was a sweet gesture, but I wouldn't allow it. "No, don't. I'm just not used to this weather." I stopped to zip him back up, and then we started walking again. I snuggled deeper into my coat. "So, tell me a little bit about these vampires without having to explain their history."

"Well, you gotta know that vampires have been around for centuries," Aidan explained. "Back in the old days, they pretty much did what they pleased. Wreaked havoc on villages and turned people left and right."

"'Turned' as in, made them vampires too? How does that even work?" I asked.

"We don't exactly know the whole procedure for turning humans into vampires, but we know that it takes more than just a bite," Aidan said. "They continued to make new ones, but not quick enough. Over the years, the world grew in population and began to evolve. And technology evolved, too, so it became harder for them to hunt and get around without going unnoticed. They'd get found out and get killed or jailed."

Instantly, my brain went straight to the many hours of watching late-night TV alone in my tiny apartment, catching a special or two on witches back in the 1600s. Over two hundred men and women were accused of witchcraft, a lot of them executed and burned at the stake. "Like the Salem Witch Trials," I muttered quietly, but Aidan caught it.

"Exactly," he confirmed. "Things like that went on all over the world for different kinds of S.O.U.Ps without being formally documented. A lot of times with local citizens acting as judge and jury. Anyway, because vampires were having to hide out, this meant they weren't getting the proper nutrition to stay *alive.*" Aidan used air quotes for that last word. "They started to die off, and their population got smaller and smaller. There's still a decent-sized community of vampires whose members live in different parts of the world, but not nearly enough to overrun the human populace.

"As a matter of fact, it's like that for most S.O.U.Ps. They were much more prevalent back in the day, when life was simple and there weren't cameras and futuristic weapons and complex science. Most S.O.U.P.s are afraid of getting caught in fear of getting locked up and tested on like some kind of lab rat. So, they just keep to themselves. Stay out of people's way or try to blend in."

Aidan tore a twig off a low-hanging branch and began to crack it, first in half then little by little, and dropping pieces to the ground as we walked. He seemed so comfortable with the conversation, explaining the history of supernatural beings to me as if we were talking about...well, anything other than supernatural beings. I, on the other hand, glanced down at my Doc Martens and watched as the clear soles sunk into wet silt with each step, a smidge unsettled by the idea of S.O.U.P.s having to live in fear. Afraid of showing who they really were. Having to hide their truth and themselves from the world.

The way I hid myself from the world.

The way I *feared* the world.

But we were chasing vampires, and vampires killed people. Sucked them dry and left them for dead. Or worse. Transformed them into monsters against their will. How could I carry even an ounce of empathy for supernatural beings who caused harm and may or may not be fictitious?

Aidan didn't think they were, though. He continued with his theories. "Each vampire has different abilities, depending on their age and practice. It's hard to tell exactly what the ones at Hazelhurst Manor can do. Madame Clara does a good job of looking normal. And since she runs the place, she's probably got a tight leash on the others. But vampires are capable of all kinds of things. They're easily the creme de la creme of the S.O.U.P.s. Metamorphosis, weather control, super strength, super speed, hypnotism..."

"They could hypnotize people?" I asked, surprised but I didn't know why. Movies and books portrayed vampires as hypnotists. Could stare you right in the eyes and make you do whatever they commanded. Which had me thinking... Could it be possible that these fictional shows and books were actually based on real life? I mean, they had to get their ideas from somewhere.

"They could, yeah. Vampires could also manipulate emotion."

"How so?

Aidan hesitated, and we walked in silence for a few feet. I started to think he hadn't heard my question until he finally spoke up. "I think it could be the reason why you and I have been so...up and down."

Keeping in line with his stride, I glanced over at him, my brow furrowed in confusion. "What do you mean 'up and down?'"

He kept his gaze down, and I got the sneaking suspicion he was too embarrassed to look at me. "Haven't you noticed that our emotions have been all mixed up? One minute we're kissing and the next minute you're slapping me in the face."

"First of all, you're the one who kissed me. And second, I was pretty drunk last night." Those were legitimate explanations for why I did what I did.

"First of all," he mocked, "I have never in my life tried to maul a woman I'd just met. And second, you weren't *that* drunk, McCall."

A twinge of hurt deflated any thought of Aidan actually liking me. "So you're saying you wouldn't have kissed me if vampires weren't forcing you to?" I tried to keep the tremor of emotion out of my voice, but my words wavered.

He detected it and stopped, gently gripping the back of my jacket to stop me, too. "Hey, I didn't mean it like that. You're beautiful, McCall, and someone I would most definitely kiss. I just wouldn't have done it so soon. I like to get to know a girl a little before I'm shoving my tongue down her throat."

I bit my bottom lip and focused on the trees behind him, too abashed to look him in the eye.

"All I was saying was vampires have the ability to mess with people's feelings. It's like they're playing a game, and we're their pawns."

His hand slid down my arm and found mine, squeezing my fingers before letting go. I nodded, and we turned to continue our walk down the trail. I felt like I was being so high maintenance and conniving—pouting and convincing a guy into telling me I was beautiful. Forcing him to express feelings he might not even have for the sake of keeping me from getting my feelings hurt. It felt icky, but no guy has shown any interest in me, compelled by outside forces or not, in a very long time. It was important that Aidan's attraction to me was real. Knowing this would boost my confidence and self-esteem. Not in a vain way, but in a therapeutic one.

Gwen. While the news that her husband might possibly be cheating on her could have most certainly provoked a hostile reaction, something inside me wondered if her emotions were being manipulated, too.

"Mirrors," I blurted, attempting to break the awkward silence that now lingered between us as we trudged down the path. "Why aren't there any mirrors in the house? No reflection?"

"Quite the contrary. There's a reflection, just one they prefer not to see. The mirror shows their true age."

"Whoa. I wouldn't wanna know what a three-hundred-year-old human really looks like," I said.

"It's not a good sight, that's for sure," Aidan concurred.

Peeking over at Aidan, I spotted the corner of his mouth turned up into a smirk. His knowledge and sanguinity of the supernatural was endearing.

"Vampires are my favorite S.O.U.P.s. They have so many abilities. So many tricks of the trade."

"Aren't you afraid of them?" I asked. I found Aidan's fondness of the supernatural to be enchanting, but there had to be some part of him that was a little bit scared of what they were capable of. He could put himself in very serious danger, considering their abilities and strengths.

Aidan shrugged. "Sure. It's only logical that I be scared when I'm dealing with mysterious entities, but that's why I became a Chaser. People fear the unknown, but I chase it."

People fear the unknown, but I chase it. The words turned over and over inside my head, the connotation so closely related to what Dr. Finn had been telling me for years and what even Aidan had said about controlling my reaction to things. After so many years, I had never considered flipping the switch that way. The possible outcome of having this mentality had me wondering... Could chasing my fears really help me?

"And besides that," he continued, "it's fun as hell to travel to all these different places."

He had a good point.

"The vampires. Do we know for sure that they drink blood?" I asked, immediately feeling like an idiot. Of course they did.

Aidan snickered, but not in a condescending way. More like he was delighted about my interest. "Yes. Lots and lots of blood."

"But if they need so much blood to survive, and they stay in hiding, then how do they get it?" Hypnotizing people, sucking their blood, and then sending them on their way was one way to do it. But not if they didn't have that particular ability.

"Vampires are smart. Especially the older ones. They've had years and years of practice, using trial and error to determine what works best for them. They're a part of a community, globally, but they make sure to keep a very low profile. Breaking off into smaller nests spanning across continents. There might only be one family of them living in one country. And they figure it out. Adapt. Whether it's living on humans or animals, they figure out how to get that blood to stay alive. Although, it's been long believed that vampires live longer on human blood. If they feed exclusively on animals, eventually they could wither away and die. Not the appropriate nutrients or something like that."

Somehow, that made complete sense to me. But I couldn't tell Aidan that. Not because I was ashamed or embarrassed. It was because what lay ahead of us had stolen all the words right out of my mouth.

With all that has happened on this trip so far—Tom leaving with his family, the disgustingly authentic food, the phantom presence in my room, the cheating husband, the lack of calming medication metabolizing through my body—I'd completely forgotten where Hazelhurst Manor was located geographically. Which was why my jaw dropped when we emerged from the dead forest onto the edge of a cliff, high up on a mountain overlooking miles and miles of gloriously lush woodland and the blue, cloudless sky above it. I'd never seen anything like it. A sea of overgrown trees thriving, their green and orange and yellow-colored leaves brilliant against the rays of sunshine shooting down upon them. The juxtaposition of what was in front of me and what was behind me left me speechless as Aidan and I slowly advanced closer to the precipice.

"Wow," Aidan breathed. "This is beautiful."

"It's like a postcard," I said, finally finding my voice.

The view in front of me was vivid and picturesque. It evoked a feeling of joy from someplace deep within my stomach. Suddenly, I was overcome by how much I'd miss the beauty of this place once it was time to go back home. But there was something else entirely different behind me. I could feel it on my back, watching me and breathing down my neck. It was dark and haunting. A sensation that induced a chilling shudder down my spine and forced me to turn around and gaze up at the sky.

Clouds and thunderstorms weren't foreign to someone who lived in Florida, where tropical weather often went hand-in-hand with rain. What had me a little perturbed was how the shelf of clouds only hung over the house. While I couldn't see the house from where we stood, I had a roundabout approximation of where it was. The edge of the cloud was quite visible and clearly only covering Hazelhurst Manor. As if perfectly stamped by using a circular cookie cutter.

What was more, as I spun in a circle and scanned the rest of the sky, it was unmistakable—there was an evident contrast between what hung over the barren forest and the land below this mountain. Just like on the bus ride over, when everything suddenly changed from bloom to gloom.

Aidan glanced up with me. "That cloud isn't just there to mask the sun," he said, his voice deepening and scaring me a bit. "It's there to keep us inside, too."

"You think Madame Clara actually *made* it rain this weekend?"

"Possibly. Kept us all locked up in a house so she could get what she wanted," Aidan said.

I gave Aidan an incredulous glare. Two and two were starting to piece together. "Hold on. You think they're running a bed-and-breakfast to suck the blood of their guests?"

Aidan faced me and shrugged. "Dogs might not eat where they sleep, but vampires do."

"I'm pretty sure it's 'eat where they shit.'"

His lips slowly widened across his face, his adorable smile forcing heat into my cheeks and ears. "I know, but vampires don't shit."

"But how do they get the blood? And when? I think I'd know if I had been bitten, even if they managed to hypnotize me. There'd be a bite mark." The scar on my neck tingled, and I fought the urge to soothe it.

"Not if they have the ability to heal. And vampires are resourceful. They wouldn't necessarily have to bite someone. This bed-and-breakfast is a front for Madame Clara and her family to lure people here. I can't tell you for sure how they're doing it, but I promise you that they're feeding," Aidan said. "Know how we can tell? Pandora, the housemaid. Friday night she looked awful. Like complete shit. Super pale skin, sunken face, gray eyes. And Saturday, she was perfect.

"So somewhere between serving us parlor drinks and pouring juice at breakfast the next morning, she drank blood. Human blood. Because animal blood wouldn't be that strong enough to completely change her appearance like that. She would not have had those red eyes."

The eyes. I shook my head, knitting my brows together and wondering how Aidan could be right. There could be a number of reasons why Pandora went from looking sickly to fine in a matter of hours. It could have been a 24-hour bug. Or a mental thing. God knew there were times my anxiety was so bad, I couldn't bring myself to even get out of bed and brush my teeth or my hair. I wouldn't dare glance in the mirror on those days, but if I did, the reflection of a very grotty, pasty-faced shell of a woman would be staring back at me. There were times when it came in waves, and the next day I would feel much, much better. Enough to at least shower away the grimy film that the anxiety and depression left behind.

That could have been Pandora's situation. As for the eyes, it was probably just a weird eye condition, like Madame Clara said. It had to be.

"Apparently, you don't believe the whole story Madame Clara gave us about the rare genetic eye color condition," I stated.

Aidan shook his head. "Not a chance."

Then, suddenly, there it was. It popped right into my head, an epiphany of epic proportions. I literally gasped out loud and shot Aidan a look of disbelief because...I believed him. It didn't make sense, except it completely did. There could be no other explanation except this one. And it wouldn't have been so easy for me to finally teeter off the edge of doubting him if it hadn't been for what I saw last night with my own two eyes.

I reached out for Aidan's arm and whispered, "Preston. I saw Preston last night in the parlor with Pandora. She was sitting on top of him and... I thought they were kissing or something. I thought Preston was cheating on Gwen." But he wasn't, and I could see that now.

I felt remorseful. I shouldn't have suggested that Gwen's husband was cheating on her. That poor woman had to question her marriage and the love her husband had for her because of me. "I didn't see any blood or anything, though. From the angle that I'd seen them, I couldn't tell."

"The mark he had on his neck this morning, and the way she changed from yesterday to today. It all makes sense," Aidan said. "She must not have the ability to completely heal someone. She does come off as somewhat of a newbie to me. I wish I would have seen them, too. It'd be nice to have a picture of a vampire in action."

"She hypnotized him," I attested, defending the old man. He loved Gwen. He had to have been forced to allow a young woman to sit on his genitals while she stole his blood.

"Maybe, but I'm willing to bet Madame Clara prefers to do things nice and clean, without the possibility of being found out. Pandora leaving that mark on Preston's neck was a sloppy move. She probably needed his blood badly. She probably couldn't help herself."

We both took a moment of silent reflection. I didn't know what Aidan was thinking about, but I was wondering how the hell I would explain this to Gwen. If she didn't believe that her husband would cheat on her and took such offense to it as to hurt me, then I wouldn't expect her to believe that a vampire stole his blood.

Aidan stepped forward until we were inches apart. He reached out, gently swinging a bundle of my long hair over my shoulder, then pulling down my scarf. The nippy air kissed the part of my neck that had been warmed by the layers. The part of my neck permanently marked by the gray-eyed man in the alleyway. Aidan made contact, zapping me with a surge of coolness from his fingertips. I flinched, but he only lightly grazed the scar before his hand cradled my face. Everything stopped, including my breathing, as he gazed into my eyes. I braced myself for a kiss, but instead he said, "I think this is a vampire bite."

It rolled off his tongue so nonchalantly that I had to ask him what he said.

"I think you were bitten by a very hungry vampire when you were a teenager. It explains his appearance. Especially his gray eyes and the smell. He was literally rotting away and needed to drink blood."

I pulled away from his hands. My stomach rippled, pushing a wave of nausea up my throat. My hands started to tremble, and I knew for sure that it wasn't the cold causing it. I pinched the thin skin between my thumb and my forefinger as hard as I could, enough to cause pain and an indent from my fingernail, hoping that it would take my mind off the panic attack that was quickly coming on. It was a technique I had used in the past to quell the panic. The pain would temporarily divert my focus away to something else.

But it wasn't working, and my vision began to blur. I could feel the blood draining from my face, and the back of my neck began to sweat, my heart thumping in rapid succession. My breathing became labored, and suddenly, the clothes on my body felt constricting. They needed to come off. I tore off my scarf then my jacket as I struggled to catch a breath and slip out of my boots.

Aidan's mouth fell open as he watched me descend into manic mode right before his eyes, but only for a moment before he realized what was happening. He quickly came to my aid, urging me to leave my clothes on because we were outside in the cold. But he didn't understand that the cold was what I needed.

"McCall, it's okay," he tried to convince me as he struggled to wrangle my wrists, stopping me from pulling the rest of my clothes off. I put up a fight at first but gave in soon after, the exhaustion of all my emotions coming down on me like an anvil. I fell into him, allowing myself to melt into his chest as his arms wrapped around my body and squeezed.

It was true. A vampire. A fucking vampire had bitten me.

Chapter Twenty

There were goosebumps on my skin. It was cold. I knew I still had my clothes on, minus my big coat. Aidan was kind enough to pull it off when he practically carried me back to my room from the trail. I vaguely remembered trudging back, barely hanging on to him in a catatonic state. Sometime during my anxiety attack, after he shared his theory about a vampire biting me when I was sixteen years old and when I realized that he was right, I went into total shock. It was kind of like an out-of-body experience. I was present, but I wasn't. I was aware of what was happening, but my body just stopped working. My limbs were operating at half capacity, and my brain had checked out. I couldn't wrap my mind around the fact that a vampire even existed, let alone having attacked me all those years ago.

Aidan thought it would be best to take me back to my bedchamber so I could nap the shock away. I was pretty sure I dozed off because now that my eyes had fluttered open, it was completely dark, the shadows of the gloomy sky no longer casting a light gray filter into the room. I was too languid to move and check my watch, but my internal clock told me it was probably close to dinner time.

I trembled then pulled the blanket Aidan had gently tucked me under higher up to my neck and shut my eyes, releasing the tension in my back and settling deeper into the unforgiving mattress. Maybe if I just lay still and breathed steady, reminding myself that the weekend was almost over and that I'd be home soon, it would all get better. So what if I didn't get any writing done? It wasn't like I couldn't go home and do it. I didn't need to travel to an entirely different state and stay at a remote, haunted mansion to find myself again. To find my bravery again. To feel inspired to write. I didn't need help because I was a writer, and creativity ran in my blood. Imagination fueled my stories, just like it fueled my anxiety. I produced my own fears.

In a perfect world, I would jump out of this bed and forget about my past. No, not forget it. *Embrace* it. Use it as a motivational tool. An unfortunate event that empowered me. Hell, in that make-believe world, I'd be a fucking motivational speaker who traveled from place to place, retelling the courageous story about how I managed to escape a...vampire?

I shut my eyes tighter, squeezing my eyelids together as hard as I could. Was it possible that an actual *vampire* attacked me and bit my neck? I shook my head. No. There was no way. It couldn't be possible because vampires didn't exist. And neither did ghosts or witches or angels or S.O.U.P.s.

My eyes popped open.

Why did the part of my brain that was supposed to rationalize things never work? It had to be broken. Dr. Finn thought drugs and therapy would help fix the chemical imbalance, but I wasn't so sure anymore. There had to be some kind of mechanical error. A chunk of brain matter lodged someplace it shouldn't be, because as I was lying in my uncomfortable bed inside the secluded bed-and-breakfast high up in the mountains of Maine, I was utterly convinced that it was run by vampires. Nineteenth-century, weather-manipulating, blood-sucking supernatural beings who slept in coffins (I was guessing).

The idea that maybe I'd finally crossed over to the clinically insane side did cross my mind. Except, I just couldn't get over the dark-haired housemaid, Pandora. The way she changed so drastically. The way her eyes went from gray to crimson. Who the hell had red eyes, anyway? Genetic condition, my ass!

But what now? What was I supposed to do now that I believed I might be spending the weekend with a bunch of vampires? I could kick my ass into gear, pack my things, and run out of the house screaming like a banshee for help—though, I doubted anyone would hear me up here. Still, I had to assume that the people in this establishment posing as regular old humans were dangerous. After all, one of them might have been responsible for breaking my arm and biting my neck all those years ago.

Wait.

Could that have been possible? Aidan said there were vampires all over the world. But could one of the Hazelhursts been the one to attack me in Florida?

I chuckled. A vampire living in Miami? I could just picture a man with milky white skin sporting a banana hammock and sunglasses, lying in the sand with a tanning reflector while sipping from a tall glass of blood through a straw, a tiny umbrella hanging off the side. A man...or a woman.

My gut might be telling me that the person who assaulted me was a vampire, but I still wasn't sure if it was a male or female. He or she put up one hell of a fight, that was for sure. A female vampire could have just as much strength as a male,

I would guess. I managed to escape, but the cops and everyone else concluded that it was a drunken and starving hobo who didn't have it in him to overpower me completely. Could I have overpowered a *vampire*, male or female? If it was a starving vampire, low on blood and desperate to quench his or her thirst...then that didn't sound too farfetched. And I shouldn't forget the evidence that glared back at me whenever I looked in the mirror: the scar on my neck. What maniac would bite someone on the neck? Someone hopped up on drugs, maybe?

There was still a tiny portion of my brain that questioned this entire situation. The smidgen of rationale that poked its little head out every now and then. The thought of Madame Clara and Chef Winston and Pandora and Landon being vampires still didn't compute in that part of my brain. Sure, they were a family of weird and intense, pasty-skinned people, but that didn't make them supernatural. There was the blinking portrait and the black smoke in my room, and let's not forget the gray/purple/red eyes. It could be the lack of solid proof that was keeping me from hiking down the steep mountain in search of rescue. After all, there was no absolute certainty that Pandora was drinking Preston's blood last night.

The fear of the unknown loomed over me like the angry, gray cloud hanging above Hazelhurst Manor. There were tendrils of dread swirling around my stomach, anticipating that something terrible was about to happen and yet, morbid curiosity was keeping me from taking my chances on climbing down the mountain in search of safety. Or could it be that I had already achieved what I set out to do this weekend? Find that backbone the rat bastard from my past took from me when I was barely old enough to even know who I was yet?

I sucked in a breath of cool air then dramatically exhaled. This weekend was supposed to be about finding my bravery *and* starting my next novel. Not just any novel. THE novel. The one that would jumpstart my writing career. I had ideas, especially now that I was introduced to the possibility of S.O.U.P.s existing. But those ideas didn't mean shit if I didn't get them down on paper.

A new wave of fatigue washed over me. That was the thing about mental issues—it was exhausting. The anxiety created constant worrying, which left me foggy and unable to focus. The depression made me lethargic and feeble. Normally, after a really bad panic attack, I could sleep for an entire day, completely neglecting everything around me.

It was safe to say that this writing retreat was a bust. The day was nearly over, and the bus was scheduled to pick us up and transport us to the airport tomorrow afternoon. Aidan might be wondering how I was doing, but the uncomfortable bed felt too comfortable at the moment. I needed just a couple more hours of rest to recuperate from that psychotic breakdown earlier.

Madame Clara won't be too happy when she realizes that I won't be coming down for dinner. Oh well. I guess Chef Winston will only be serving his disgusting food to Aidan, Gwen, and Preston. I pondered over what Chef Winston would try to pass as food tonight.

Ugh...Gwen.

There was no rule saying that I even had to speak with her. Especially now since her husband might have fallen prey to the vampire chick. How would I even go about telling her such a thing?

"Hi, Gwen. Listen, I was mistaken. Your husband wasn't making out with the housemaid. She was just sucking his blood. She probably even hypnotized him so...good news! He didn't really cheat on you!"

I could just ignore her and Preston altogether. As a matter of fact, that was just what I would do.

Okay, the Gwen-and-Preston issue was squashed. I had to keep telling myself that it was none of my business, regardless of the fact that he might have been forced to do what he did. Hmm... Did that qualify as a form of rape, though? What if he was really hurt? What if I didn't tell the man that he was taken advantage of, but then later it would cause a variety of physiological issues for him? As someone who suffered from mental disorders, I wouldn't want to wish that upon anyone else.

Okay, maybe I'd wish it upon the asshole who attacked me. I hoped he or she suffered from a lifetime of guilt and regret and...impotence, if it was a man.

I shook my head vehemently. No matter. It was none of my business. Gwen and Preston were not my issue anymore because in just one more day, I would never have to see either one of them again. That was one problem solved.

The next dilemma had to do with my book. I shrugged. No dilemma there. As soon as I got home, I would hunker down in my studio apartment and produce a quality bestseller that'd get me noticed by the big boys. Once I got out of bed, I'd be sure to scribble every single thing about this place and what Aidan told me about S.O.U.P.s in my notebook of story ideas all the way back to Miami.

Which led me back to Aidan, the Chaser. What was I going to do about adorable, sweet Aidan and his charming little mole? We kissed, he saw me half-naked, I slapped him... He carried me through the mud all the way back to my bed and tucked me in. How could I ignore that?

I smiled and shimmied under the duvet at the thought of kissing him again. The truth was that he actually understood me and my fucked-up head. He got it. He didn't ask why. He didn't even offer his advice, which my parents seemed to think was the only topic of conversation to have with me whenever we were together. Advising me on ways to forget the past and move on. Offering their guidance on how to get over my anxiety and depression. I couldn't help but feel like they were judging their youngest daughter, the only one of their children who wasn't married with kids.

This was the closest I'd gotten to a guy in a long time, and I was interested in getting to know him better, despite the fact that he called himself a Chaser and wholeheartedly believed that supernatural beings lived among us. Because now I might be a believer, too. Well, only if I found solid proof. And that meant I'd have to go searching for it.

Satisfied with the decision to officially, truly, join Aidan on his vampire hunt, if he'd have me, I turned on my side and pulled the blanket up to my chin, nestling deeply into the bed. I still needed a short nap to restore my energy fully.

Right as sleep pulled me into its lulling embrace, an odd sensation interrupted. The feeling like someone's hand was slowly sliding down the side of my body, starting at my shoulder, down my torso, and to my hip. My eyes shot open, and I attempted to yank the duvet over my head—a stupid knee-jerk reaction to fear that little kids did, like it was supposed to save them from the bogeyman.

But my blanket wasn't accessible. In fact, it was the thing that was causing the odd sensation. I could feel it now sliding down the rest of my body, as if someone was standing at the foot of my bed and tugging. I immediately sat up and glared down, spotting two glowing red eyes glaring at me from above the edge of the bed. I gasped and swallowed a scream then quickly stretched across the bed to switch on the Tiffany lamp. When the stained glass illuminated, I turned back to the eyes, but they were no longer there. Instead, there was only the bunched comforter at my feet.

Chapter Twenty-One

"McCall! Are you okay?" Aidan exclaimed, standing in front of the writing desk in my room.

His voice startled me, as I wasn't expecting anyone else to be in my bedchamber with me. "Aidan! What are you doing here?"

"I was just reading," he said, holding up Landon's gigantic manuscript.

"In the dark?"

"I didn't want to wake you up. I was using the flashlight from my phone." He held up his other hand, the fluorescent dot on the back of his phone shining so brightly it stung my retinas. Aidan quickly shut it off when he noticed me squint. "I heard you making noises and breathing loudly, but I didn't realize you were awake. I thought you were just dreaming."

Clamoring over the bed and onto the floor toward him, I reached out to grab hold of Landon's book. "What are you doing with that?"

There was a slight annoyance that Aidan was reading it. It had less to do with Landon's trust in me to keep his work out of someone else' hands and more to do with Aidan thinking it was perfectly okay to just come into my room and pick up anything he pleased.

Aidan snapped his arm back before I could take the book from him. "Why didn't you tell me you had this?" he questioned with suspicion in his tone.

I chuckled. "I didn't even think about it."

"You didn't think about having the autobiography of a vampire?"

"What?" I asked, genuinely confused. "What are you talking about? Landon gave me his manuscript when he found out that I was an author. He said he wanted my opinion on his story."

Aidan stared down at me for a beat, and I watched the black frame of his glasses slide down the bridge of his nose. I widened my eyes and shook my head at him mockingly. A second later, his shoulders slumped and he tilted his head. "This isn't a manuscript. I don't know why, but he gave you his autobiography. This is the story of his life."

I snatched the hefty book out of his hands and flipped through its aged pages, skimming through paragraphs and words, catching phrases like "*...that evening, the hunger bested me...*" and "*...the salty taste of the barkeep's blood is nothing like sweet Adeline's...*," and "*Mother insists that we begin to satiate our thirst by feeding from bags.*"

"Why would he give me the story of his life?"

"I have no idea," Aidan said. "Maybe he's just trying to mess with you or something. I snapped some pictures of a few pages. The Chaser society appreciates any kind of original literature we could find. A few of the members like to turn it into fan fiction."

"Then you should probably know that there's a vampire bible downstairs in the library," I informed him. "But it's sealed up inside a glass case. I doubt you would be able to get inside it without them knowing."

"How do you know about that?" he asked, his voice once again carrying slight wariness.

I squinted at him. "Do you think I'm keeping this stuff from you on purpose?" If so, it might have actually hurt a little. Aidan and I hadn't known each other long enough for me to be expected to divulge my deepest, darkest secrets to him, but why in the hell would I intentionally withhold information about S.O.U.P.s? I wasn't the Chaser here.

"Well, it certainly wouldn't surprise me. Some Chasers like to make it a competition."

I punched him in the arm. "I'm on your team, dumbass. You think I want to compete when there are blood-sucking vampires in the midst? I just want to get the hell out of here as soon as we can."

Aidan rubbed his arm, which I knew was just for show because I didn't even hit him that hard, and a cheeky grin crawled up his face. "Ow! Okay, you should really stop hitting me. Also, we can't leave until we get some more evidence. You agreed to help me, remember? I'm not letting you back out now."

He was right. I'd made a commitment. In reality, I didn't owe Aidan my word, but I did owe myself a chance at finding that courage buried within myself.

The thought of Aidan dragging my dead weight through the forest while I suffered one of the worst panic attacks I'd ever had flashed through my mind. It was possible that I *did* owe Aidan my word, because he certainly was not obligated to care for me.

I nodded in agreement. "Hey, thank you, by the way. For helping me out earlier."

He smiled sweetly. "Don't worry about it. I wasn't going to leave you out in the cold, alone. Besides, I got another little peek at your bra when you tried to rip off your clothes."

I swatted at his arm again, but this time he giggled and blocked my open palm. "Okay, I'm going to the library to see if I can take a few pictures of that book."

"It's in the corner, underneath a velvety sheath and a vase," I informed him.

"Got it. You get ready for dinner. We'll choke down whatever crap Chef Winston has cooked up, and then we'll meet in the parlor to discuss our next move. Come up with some plan to get into that attic and the cellar."

In my opinion, the idea of trying to gain entrance into the attic or the basement had disaster written all over it. Most specifically, the basement. Didn't vampires sleep underground, inside coffins? But Aidan was the Chaser here. He had to know what he was doing.

"Don't you think it would be too dangerous to try the cellar?" I asked.

He stepped toward the door to the hallway. "Maybe. Who knows?"

"Um...*you* would know, right? Aren't you the Chaser?"

"Never been inside a vampire lair," he said nonchalantly, shrugging as if it were absolutely no big deal. "I'll see you at dinner." He opened and quietly shut the door behind him.

Excuse me? Aidan had never been inside a vampire lair? What did that mean? Was I following the lead of a Chaser who didn't have experience chasing vampires?

After edging myself back onto the bed, I sat up against the headboard and pulled my knees up to my chest, wrapping my arms around them and hugging them tight. The memory of those red, glowing eyes glaring back at me from the foot of the bed came tumbling back. It had to be a reflection from the forest outside.

It had to be.

It had to be.

It had to be.

After several minutes passed of convincing myself of it, what-ifs began to swirl around inside my head, slowly summoning my deepest fears from the pits of my stomach. The terror began to claw at my insides as I simulated every scenario possible, all trajectories leading toward my impending death.

Before I knew it, I was standing in front of the safe under the writing desk, trembling, stomach lurching, trying to decide if I should just give up on my mission to become bold and fearless and pop a benzo. My heart was telling me to deal with the rest of this weekend medication-free and clear-headed. How rewarding would it be if I'd left this place knowing that I conquered my fears and dealt with the anxiety head-on, without any help? That was...*if* I was able to escape.

I wrung out my hands, kneading the tiny bones in my fingers almost violently.

Be strong, McCall.

Be strong, McCall.

Be strong, McCall.

With a few deep, quavering breaths and a single pinch of the skin between my thumb and my index finger, my un-painted nails forcing blood to the surface, I turned on my heels and swung open the door to my bedroom, stepped out into the hallway, and shut the door behind me without looking back. I could do this. I was scared out of my mind about the unknown, but I just had to do this.

The Hallway of Death photography was empty and just as dim and shadowy as it had been since we arrived. The candles flickered inside their glass sconces, throwing dusky light directly to the grim-filled pictures inside their gold frames. I took inventory, scanning the corridor from left to right. No other bedroom door was open. Even the library door was shut, which somehow made me feel like I was doomed. It felt so inviting before, the smell of antique books finding its way into my nose, tugging on my admiration for the written word all the way down from my room. But there was no smell now, and I couldn't help but feel utterly alone.

Dr. Finn's tranquil voice echoed inside my ears. *Practice your breathing exercises, McCall.*

A sudden sense of yearning for Aidan tugged at my heart. Somewhere along the way of this insane weekend, I had designated Aidan as the unofficial white knight. My safe haven. Regardless of whether or not this was his first vampire rodeo, he somehow had the ability to make me feel like I might just be able to control my panic and that he could save me from myself.

A very potent odor of cooked meat snaked its way into my nostrils and I squinched. The memory of the calf's head at lunch threatened to make me gag—of it going down and coming back up. I wished Aidan would have wanted to skip dinner, but I assumed that'd only raise questions from Madame Clara. Still, I'd rather starve myself until I got home than ingest whatever it was Chef Winston had butchered and cooked up.

As I ambled down the long hallway, the thought of downing a tall glass of sparkling champagne made my mouth water. If I wasn't able to take an anxiety pill, liquor would definitely calm my nerves. Although, switching my dependency from pills to alcohol didn't exactly sound like the smartest idea.

So what? I was pretty sure I had a good enough excuse for getting drunk if I wanted to. Three words: family of vampires.

With my mind set on downing some bubbly, eager for that numbing flush to surge through my body, I finally just scurried down the rest of the darkened corridor to the second-story landing. But before I could get down onto the first step, something halted me. A noise.

It was quick and hushed. Probably wouldn't have been heard over chatter or the din of forks and plates downstairs. Maybe not even from the inside of my bedroom. But I heard it.

Glancing over my shoulder and up the unlit stairwell that led to the attic, my pulse quickening with every shallow breath, I considered minding my own business and ignoring it. Except, it happened again. This time I could make an educated guess because the noise was a bit louder. Not by much, though. Someone with very good hearing would only be able to confirm that there was a sound at all, and I'd never had any issues with my hearing.

It was muffled, similar to those sexual noises Aidan and I had heard through the walls of the hallway. But those were distinct echoes of pleasure. This, coming from the attic, was different.

I turned toward the inclined staircase and placed a hand on the railing. These steps were different than the ones that led downstairs to the first floor. They were shorter. Steeper. And the stairwell was narrower, climbing up to what I presumed to be the locked door that Madame Clara had informed us about when we first arrived. Only, it was so completely dark, it could have been a black hole that led to another dimension for all I knew. Wouldn't surprise me at this point.

Mm...aargh...ow...

Moans and groans of pain. The whimpers registered in my brain as a person in need. A person who was suffering. The sound immediately replaced the fear I had of the unknown with a strong impulse to provide assistance. Not that I would know what to do. There was no telling what was behind that door. But I was the only one I knew who'd ever been attacked or harmed by someone. No one was there to help me fight off the bastard, but I would like to think that if anyone saw, they would have rendered me some aid. This could be my chance to pay it forward...in a hypothetical way.

My feet automatically shuffled up a few steps but then stopped when I realized that there might not be a some*one* up there, but a some*thing*.

Chapter Twenty-Two

It played out in my mind as if it were yesterday. A week before my sixteenth birthday party, my five best girlfriends decided to surprise me with a trip to Wet Willy's, the coolest water park around that wasn't three hours away in Disney World. Wet Willy's was a forty-five-minute drive to Fort Lauderdale, but we were still able to make a day of it, piling up into Morgan's car—the only one of us who had her license, which was probably for the best. Not only was Morgan one year older than us, but she was also the only one who'd obey the traffic laws.

We were sure to stuff our totes with all the water park essentials—sunglasses, tanning lotion, junk food, energy drinks, and itty-bitty bikinis that barely covered our teenaged assets. We actually wore those underneath our tank tops and ripped booty-hugging shorts. The beach and water parks were the only places we knew were okay to dress like a slut. We all came from conservative families who were alumni of our private school, the one that required we wear uniforms consisting of crisp, starched oxford shirts and skirts that were never allowed higher than two inches above the knee. Wet Willy's was a breeding ground for practically naked high school girls who couldn't wait to break free from conformity. It was also a hotbed for sexually charged teenaged boys. Hell, every teen who walked through Wet Willy's gates was fueled by hormones.

Besides the twisty water slides and relatively large wave pool, a small portion of the park catered to those who didn't want to get wet. Fairgrounds with a Ferris wheel, a carousel, a couple of wooden roller coasters, and a few other carnival rides.

The girls and I had no real plan that day. We arrived with the intention of having fun and celebrating my birthday, all while strutting our swim wear and flirting with the boys from other schools. We'd grown tired of the ones at ours—the ones we would see every day and had already even dated.

It was pretty much customary to start the day out on the water slides, then once the sun started setting, moving over to the fairgrounds. We waited in all the lines together, plummeted down each water slide one after another a few times over, then rode the waves in the wave pool and basked in the sun on the tanning ledge before finally toweling off and heading to the "dry" side. By this time, we were all starved and eager for that amusement park food—hotdogs drenched in chili and giant cups of soda and oil-soaked funnel cakes.

The day had been a success, which was normally rated by the number of rides we rode and slides we slid down. Without even a second thought, without a single what-if, I had climbed onto every adrenaline-inducing contraption with only one thing in mind: happiness. Everything at that point in my life made total and complete sense. With friends and family and good grades at school, a bright future of possibilities ahead of me, there was absolutely nothing to worry about. I lived every day looking forward to the next, praying that the universe would give me more opportunities to stretch my wings and fly. Which was exactly why when my girlfriend, Emily, shrieked enthusiastically at the sight of a new amusement park attraction, I was first in line to test it out.

"Holy shit! Look how high it is," Mary, the one who was usually the bravest in our group, exclaimed. But there was doubt in her tone. Mary once tore her clothes off on the shore of South Beach and ran completely naked into the lukewarm, teal-colored water on a dare. It might not have been so bad if it was just us girls, but it wasn't. We were in the middle of a birthday bash—a celebration for one of the more popular fellas a grade above us who invited pretty much the entire junior and senior class. Mary wasn't drunk or high, either. Completely sober, as a matter of fact. Someone had dared her to, and without hesitation, she'd done it.

After she had splashed and twirled and giggled in the ocean for a few minutes, Morgan—the more reserved and protective of our little crew—was right at the foreshore waiting to wrap Mary's bare body in a towel. The dare was a piece of cake for Mary because she was gutsy. Adventurous. Spontaneous. I recalled coveting her boldness that day.

So when she watched someone jump into a free fall from about seven or eight stories high, mouthing gaping and head shaking no, I was truly surprised.

"They have bungee jumping now?" Morgan groaned. I knew she was annoyed because one of us was going to be flying off that thing and that meant she was going to worry. As we walked closer, she plopped down on a wooden bench facing the attraction, right where she could keep an eye on her crazy best friends.

"It's bungee jumping, but not really," Emily announced. "The harness is wrapped around your waist, not your ankles." It was now nightfall, and her eyes sparkled with the reflection of twinkling colors from the amusement park rides.

"You gonna try it?" I asked Emily. She blinked hard at me then claimed her seat next to Morgan.

"No. Maybe next time."

Emily was tired, I could tell. Her shoulders slumped and her eyelids hung low, which was totally understandable. We'd spent the day swimming with the sun beaming down on us. Hours under those Florida hot rays would be enough to drain us of energy.

I slid my gaze over to Mary, our eyes meeting simultaneously. My raised eyebrows were a declaration. *It's just you and me*, I thought. I didn't have to say it because she knew exactly what I was thinking.

But surprisingly, she started to shake her head before squeezing between Emily and Morgan on the bench. "Not this time, Mickey." McCall wasn't really the sort of name people usually shortened, but Mary did.

I was stunned. "Really?"

"I'm sorry," she whined. "I'm just...kind of scared of heights."

Scared of heights? "Since when?" I asked suspiciously, challenging her to tell me exactly when she'd become afraid of heights.

"Since always. I'll happily swim with the sharks or roller-skate without a shirt on, but jumping off things high up in the sky is not my thing." She retrieved a cigarette out of her backpack and lit it. None of us smoked—not even Mary, really—but she enjoyed using her fake ID whenever she had the chance.

"It's not high up in the sky," I argued, turning to take a second look at the tower. It definitely wasn't taller than the Ferris wheel standing right next to it, but it wasn't exactly short, either. A quick calculation added up to eight...or maybe nine flights of stairs to get to the top. I couldn't be sure exactly, but it had to be more than fifty feet.

"Looks like you're on your own, Mickey."

"Or you can just not go on it," Morgan suggested. She pouted and looked up at me with puppy-dog eyes. She was so sweet and innocent that most of time she could guilt me into doing whatever she was asking of me. But not this time. This time I was determined.

"You guys suck!" I blurted with a smirk, waving my finger across their faces. Then I twisted on my heel and stormed off into the direction of the bungee.

The entire stubborn walk over, I debated whether or not I should turn back around to join the girls on the bench. If Mary was too scared to jump a few stories down, then how the hell was I supposed to do it? But maybe this was my chance to show her up. Not that I was out to do that. That was the great thing about my best friends—we never competed with each other.

Really, more than anything, I wanted to prove to myself that I was brave enough to do it. Honestly, what was the worst that could happen? If the bungee broke, I'd just land on the cushy blowup platform situated directly underneath.

As I approached the staircase, another thrill-seeker had just jumped the plank. It was a girl with long blonde hair that rose off her shoulders as she fell, something between and a shrill and a giggle escaping her throat the whole way down until she bounced onto the big square inflatable pillow. Once, twice, then a third time before she sprawled out completely, staring up at the sky with a satisfied grin on her face. She was fine. Everything was fine. I would be fine.

I was winded by the time I'd gotten to the top. Thankfully, there was practically no line at all, and I was equally as grateful that one person was ahead of me. I had to catch my breath before jumping; otherwise, I might completely run out mid fall from the adrenaline. I had decided I was going to do this, but that didn't mean I wasn't terrified. The dude in front of me had just gotten strapped up by the bungee operator—a guy with a long, scruffy red beard wearing a backwards cap.

"You wanna count down?" the man asked the younger boy, whose face I couldn't see. I could only see the back of his tall, lanky body.

"No, I've done this before," the boy said. And in the blink of an eye, he ran off the platform. I gasped and nearly yelled after him as I watched him go off headfirst, afraid that he might have tripped and fallen off or something. But when the boy bellowed out a long "HEEEEEELLLL YEEEEEEAH" on his way down, followed by laughter, I realized that his jump was intentional.

The bungee man leaned over the edge and glanced down for a few minutes then waved a hand at me. "Your turn."

My heart began pounding. The butterflies in my stomach fluttered nervously, but not enough for me to back out. I was here. I was ready.

The bearded operator helped me into the harness, tightening the belt around my thighs and my waist. My body jounced with every tug until he seemed pleased with how secure it was on my body. Then, he glanced down one more time, probably to make sure the kid made it off the pillow. A beat later, he was ready for me to go.

"You need me to count down?"

"Um..." That was a difficult question at the moment. If he counted down, it meant that the anticipation would just build and build and build and it'd be the longest few seconds of my life. But if I just jumped...

I closed my eyes, took a deep breath, and went for it. As soon as my feet left the metal plank, my body was weightless. Floating in the air. A euphoric rush filled my head and everything around me just disappeared. There were no sounds, just the roar of the wind as I plummeted through the air. So much different than a water slide or a roller coaster. There was nothing to grab on to. Nothing to lean on. Just me falling through the ether.

I wasn't entirely sure if I'd screamed or not, but there was a thud when my body landed on the pillow.

"McCall! Are you okay?" It was Morgan's shaky voice. I lifted my head and spotted Mary, Emily, and Morgan all watching me intently, their expressions both eager and horrified.

I smiled wide and chuckled. "Haha! Yes! Yes, I'm fine! I'm fine!"

And I was. While there was some apprehension once I'd gotten to the top, it was something the average person would experience when faced with the unknown. There was no long list of what-ifs to follow up on. No subconscious talking me out of doing it. No crippling anxiety attack that would have forced me to leave the park and my friends behind altogether in search of my safe house. I just did it, and it had felt *amazing*.

As I stood in front of the attic door, listening to the muffled sounds of someone quietly moaning in pain, I tried to reach deep down inside myself to find that courage again. For the same tenacity that wrapped around me in layers and which guided me to the ledge that night at Wet Willy's. It was there, I could feel it. All I had to do was trust it. All I had to do was let go of the fear of the unknown...

I gripped the brass doorknob. Aidan said he was going to figure out how to unlock the attic door. But what if it wasn't actually locked?

I twisted the knob and pushed. The hinges creaked.

It opened.

Chapter Twenty-Three

Almost instantly, the moaning stopped. Evaporated into the air. I considered that I might have been hearing things outside of the door, but judging by the other noises I'd been hearing all weekend, it was unlikely.

As soon as I stepped another foot into the candlelit room, I was met with a very potent smell. A coppery odor that reminded me of something raw and bloody. Quietly, and against my better judgment, I shut the door behind me. I didn't particularly want to be alone with whatever was inside this attic, but I also didn't want anyone else in the house to know I was in here.

With my breathing slowed and my body still, I waited for my eyes to adjust to the dull lighting. There were votive candles inside of standing sconces scattered around, casting dancing shadows all over the enormous room. That was what it was—one large room with a sloped ceiling. A quick glance around revealed nothing strange. It looked much like an ordinary attic with exposed beams, random pieces of furniture piled on top of each other, boxes, and antique-looking storage trunks lying around.

Hazelhurst Manor had been around for centuries, and for such an old house, Madame Clara and her family did a fantastic job at keeping it clean and tidy. But I couldn't say the same for the attic space. Globs of cobwebs hung from every possible object it could stick to, and my boots crunched and slid along the dust-covered floor. I cautiously advanced deeper into the attic, vigilant and preparing myself for anything—a ghost slipping up through the slats of the wooden floor or a giant flesh-eating rat crawling out from a hole in the wall. There was really no telling what I might find up here.

My heart started to pound. This wasn't an anxiety thing. Anyone's heart would begin thudding uncontrollably if they happened to be inside a vampire lair getting ready to discover God only knew what. In an attempt to curb the possibility of having a seriously intense anxiety attack, I began to utilize one of Dr. Finn's many coping exercises. Find a focal point. Anything. It could be a clock on the wall or a speck on the ceiling. Anything at all. Give all my attention to this one thing and breathe. Put all my energy into concentrating on that one object I have chosen in the room. Allow the trepidation to pass without giving it life by rolling it around in my head over and over again until I finally just break.

The octagon-shaped attic window with colorful stained glass grabbed my focus and held it there. It was several feet away from me, but it became my point of destination. There was no light shining through because it was night outside, but the flickering flames of the candles were enough to illuminate the bright hues of each pane. It was where I would walk to, then turn around and get out.

I had to investigate. I had to find out what that moan was.

Passing an enormous pile of photo albums on my left and a hoard of stacked books to my right, which took everything in me to ignore what must have been a treasure trove of first editions, I reached what resembled a wall of boxes on both sides of the space. This should have been the point where I stopped walking. But that relentless curiosity fiend clawed at my insides, and I just had to know what was on the other side.

The multicolored attic window remained in my peripheral vision, but I continued to search around me, bracing myself for something horrible hidden after the boxes and at the end of the room.

Mmm...ooowww

Murmurs of a wounded person echoed louder around me, causing my pace to quicken, in search of the source. But when I moved past the rows of cardboard blocking my view, there was nothing. And no one.

Pleeeease...

A mere whisper, but I could hear the pleading.

Let me gooo...

I twirled in all directions, no longer afraid of what the empty attic might reveal but determined to discover what it might be hiding. But there truly was nothing. I stood alone in the shadows of abandoned furniture and books whose authors were long gone and dead. Could it have been that I was hearing things? Not a single drop of alcohol had touched my tongue in over twelve hours, so it couldn't be a champagne-addled auditory hallucination.

Stop it, McCall. Hazelhurst Manor was sketchy as shit, vampire lair or not. I had to stop blaming myself when strange things happened around me.

No longer feeling the weight of a potential panic attack knowing that there wasn't anything up here with me, I turned away from the stained-glass window and headed back to exit the attic.

Whhhyy...

I froze. There it was again! A single, hushed word, but it was there. I knew it.

The inquisitiveness wore off almost immediately, replaced by a wave of frustration. It was beginning to feel like the person in need was mocking me. Playing some kind of crude joke. A vampire joke? If I were to believe anything Aidan told me about vampires and what they did, it most definitely wouldn't be implausible to think that one of the vampires in this house was throwing their voice somehow. Playing games. Or even worse, luring me. Controlling me as if I were a pawn.

The thought of being lured into this attic twisted my stomach into knots. Suddenly, I found myself wildly scanning every corner of the room, twirling in circles to catch sight of a vampire lying in wait behind some boxes or piece of furniture or even up on the ceiling—

Mmm...uuggh

The dancing flame of the candles cast a wobbling light on a brass vent high up on the wall, just like in my room. I edged closer to it, willing another pained whisper to float out of its register.

It wasn't until I stood directly underneath it, glaring upward, that I heard the familiar, grief-stricken words flowed out.

Help me...

I backed away. It was Gwen. The voice sounded like Gwen's. And she was hurt.

With a rapidly beating heart and newfound conviction to help my semi-friend, I rushed out of the door to the attic, silently thanking God that it hadn't been locked by some evil force wishing to lock me away forever. Skipping down the steps to the second-story landing, I scrambled down the Hallway of Death, opening the door to each bedchamber, the bathroom, and then the library to see if maybe Gwen's voice had carried up through the vent from one of these rooms. But every place was empty. There was no one around.

I hurried back through the long corridor and skipped down another flight into the foyer, hoping to smash into Aidan, or even Preston, along the way. But every racing thought slowed down with the quiet that surrounded me. Standing in the middle of the lobby, with the parlor, the dining room, and the hallway that led to the music room and the study all easily accessible, not a single noise could be heard. Only the ticking of the old grandfather clock. No clanking of silverware against china from the dining room. No crackling of wood coming from the fireplace in the parlor.

It was as if I were all alone inside Hazelhurst Manor. No humans. No vampires. No S.O.U.P.s in sight.

Taking a deep breath in and reluctantly silencing the alarm bells blaring between my ears, I poked my head into the parlor then stepped into the dining room, pushing past the empty chairs and into the kitchen where not even Chef Winston could be found barbarically slicing through some sort of exotic meat. I exited into the hallway and flung open the doors to the music room and the study, finding not a single one of the people who were here earlier in the day. Where had everyone gone?

A wandering and brief—and maybe a little bit crazy—thought entered my mind and I stared down at my shaking hands. Could any of this be real? What if it was all a dream? What if this dream never ended? What if I was in a car accident and was now in a coma, hooked up to machines while my mind teetered on the ledge between dying and living, the unconsciousness causing nightmarish fantasies to run amok through my sleeping brain? What if I didn't wake up from the coma and I was stuck in this horrifying world, an alternate reality where things like vampires and ghost and fucking demons existed? What if I was already dead, and Hazelhurst Manor was my hell?

Stop it, McCall!

Stop it!

Stop it!

My hands shot up to my head and I slapped myself in the temple a few times, desperately trying to deactivate the anxiety switch before it could go off. Because I had to. Because if I didn't, I would have a mental breakdown right here, right now, all alone. And what if I did? What if I had the worst panic attack of all time and began to hyperventilate? What if I couldn't catch my breath and I passed out? What if I needed CPR and no one was around to administer it?

Within seconds, the what-ifs took over, along with every possible symptom of a panic attack. Nausea, trembling, palpitations, sweating, chest pain... My vision began to blur, and I stumbled past the music room and study room, back into the foyer. All the walls began to close in around me, warbling in and out as if to be breathing down my neck. I leaned into a wooden accent table, missing my footing and knocking into it with the boorishness of a drunk.

To my absolute horror, the sound of something skidding across the surface before dropping to the carpeted floor pulled me out of the feverish delirium long enough to see that a vase, the same one Madame Clara scolded little Missy for nearly touching, had smashed into a million porcelain pieces despite landing on the Persian rug. Shit! A whole new round of what-ifs began.

What if Madame Clara walked in right now to find that I had broken an antique heirloom? What if she completely lost it, bashing my head into the wallpapered wall before throwing me into the fireplace? What if she really *was* a vampire and she bit me? Bit me just like that asshole years ago bit me?

The scar on my neck tingled as the memories of that horrifying night of my sixteenth birthday came barreling back, and it was the final push, forcing me to hurl myself at the front door of the manor, desperately unlocking it and swinging it wide open. This was the moment I had decided to run away from this haunted vampire house, away from the fears and anxieties that I was sure to eventually kill me.

But to my dismay, as I ran down the porch's steps and my boots made contact with the mossy walkway, a thunderous roar above my head halted me. I glanced up at the sky, at the big mass of clouds churning angrily in puffs of dark gray like it was getting ready to blow. The sky growled at me again, sending down a single droplet of rain that landed directly onto my eye. I flinched and reflexively wiped away the water with my finger before looking down at my hand. But there was something wrong. My finger was red. As I examined it, moving my hand over and back and watching the fat, wet drop leave traces of red on my skin as it slid around with the movement, I wondered if my eye was bleeding. With my other hand, I wiped at my eye again and pulled away—there was a smear of red left behind.

A flash of bright light and then a loud crack forced me to cower. My eyes darted to the left where a lone, leafless tree was now on fire, the flames wildly twisting off the branches into the air. A lightning bolt must have struck it.

The sky commanded my attention again, sounding off the most forceful and earsplitting crash of thunder I'd ever heard.

Its power sent vibrations throughout my entire body, and I couldn't help but gaze into the whirling gray clouds above my head. As soon as I made contact, a barrage of raindrops fell on top of me. All around me. The whoosh of a heavy downpour so loud that I could barely hear myself breathe. Except, it wasn't rain...because it wasn't water falling from the sky.

I glanced down at my body, my clothes, my skin, my hair, all dripping red. The moss-covered walkway was now a red puddle around my boots. It was blood.

It was all *blood.*

Twisting to face Hazelhurst Manor again, I attempted to skip back up the steps of the porch but slipped on the first blood-soaked step. My hands weren't quick enough to break my fall, and my face collided with the unforgiving splintered edge of a higher step. Immediately, the pain of my lip splitting extracted a howl from somewhere deep in my throat. It felt like I had lost all my teeth!

Frantically, I searched the area around me, hoping not to find pieces of my teeth mixed in with the red rain. There was no way to tell if it was my own blood pouring from my face or the blood from the sky.

CRACK!

Another ferocious clap of thunder hit the trees behind me, and I crawled up the rest of the stairs, onto the porch, and back through the front door of Hazelhurst Manor. The welcome bell chimed cheerfully with the swing of the door before I slammed it shut behind me, leaning into the wood and rapidly pulling in deep breaths, trying to calm myself down. Every ounce of my body trembled uncontrollably, including the teeth that I now knew for sure were still there.

It's raining blood.

It's raining blood outside!

But how? How could blood be falling from the sky?

Madame Clara. She controlled the weather. This had to be her doing. What if she knew? What if she knew that I was trying to leave and so she did it on purpose? What if she tried to scare me back into Hazelhurst Manor, tried to stop me from leaving with blood rain and lightning strikes?

Frozen flat against the door, all of my muscles cycling between tensing and shaking, I listened for sounds. But there were none. Not even from outside. The rain and thunder had stopped. The dead, quiet air around me seeped deeper into my bones, forcing all the fear and apprehension and self-doubt to finally boil over. It was too much to handle. I couldn't take it anymore, and if I didn't take a pill right now, I might throw myself into the fireplace.

I launched toward the stairs, taking two steps at a time as I climbed, choosing to ignore the way my blurred vision disoriented everything around me, warping the solid ground as I staggered to my bedchamber.

Pushing into my room, I tripped on the corner of the door and fell to my knees, crawling the rest of the way to the safe underneath the writing desk. My trembling, blood-soaked hands reached for the key from my back pocket then unlocked the safe, aching to get that fast-acting benzo down my throat. It would take close to thirty minutes before feeling the full effects, but just knowing it was working through my body, inhibiting the neurons in my brain and slowing down my nervous system, eased me.

And when the key turned and I swung the thick, little metal door open, my stomach dropped.

The orange bottle of pills was gone. The safe was completely empty.

Chapter Twenty-Four

W*HERE ARE THEY?*

Where are they?

Where are my damn pills?!

Could this be another hallucination? I reached inside the safe, praying that my entire arm would disappear into a secret compartment that I hadn't known about, someplace my pills could have dropped into. But there wasn't one. The safe was only deep enough to fit the width of my laptop, which now I realized wasn't there either. The cache where I had stored two of the most important items I had brought on this trip was completely empty.

I stretched up and grabbed my cellphone off the desk. Then, through a torrent of fresh tears falling from my eyes, I leaned back into the bed frame and began searching for Dr. Finn's contact. The seven digits of her phone number were forever etched into my brain—I had called it enough times over the years—but my fingers were too shaky to dial. My phone only had twenty-one percent battery life left, seeing as I hadn't plugged it in to charge for an entire day because there was no point. No reception. No Internet access. However, I couldn't resist. The habitual tendencies that I'd practiced all these years, to seek solace in one of the people whom I had assigned to be my psychological sponsor, was going to be really hard to shake if I was on a mission to live a life of mental independence again. But there was an exception: having a nervous breakdown alone, miles away from home, stranded on a remote mountain where it rained blood, and imprisoned inside a creepy old house that may or may not be full of vampires.

My blood-stained index finger swiped through the phone and found my therapist's number then smashed on the green call button. With my entire body quaking, I held the cellphone to my ear, trying my best not to drop it.

Nothing happened.

Chest heaving in search of a decent breath, I threw my phone at the door with a force that seemed to be reserved for this exact moment. It bounced off and landed at my feet, face up and glass screen cracked. This turned my crying into full-on sobbing and left me feeling defeated and hopeless, which only made everything worse.

One of the worst parts about having anxiety and depression is *knowing* that I had anxiety and depression. And knowing this made me feel like a complete loser. I was perfectly aware and of sound mind during the times where I slept all day and had mood swings and breakdowns and temper tantrums. I was completely aware that it wasn't normal. I totally agreed with the diagnosis. And now that I was alone, with no one to save me from myself, I just wished that I could ball up into a fetal position and die.

I brought my knees up and buried my head between them, the undeniable feeling of loneliness chaining me down to the spot I sat in, on the floor of my bedchamber. All I needed was just one phone call to Dr. Finn or my parents, and they would send help. Just one call—

Then it hit me. The landline!

Madame Clara said there was a landline in case of emergencies. A phone with a physical connection to the outside world. Or at least, to the nearest town. I could call for help. I could call the police. Or an ambulance—they would probably come quicker. Would they speed up a steep mountain to rescue someone who was only having a really bad anxiety attack? Because there was no way in hell I could say that I needed saving from a haunted vampire house. But an anxiety attack alone probably wouldn't get them to come either.

I could lie. I could say I fell and hurt myself. That I was bleeding profusely, losing copious amounts by the second. After all, if I didn't get out of this house soon, that lie might actually come to fruition.

Without moving too fast—careful not to spur the contents of my queasy stomach—I scrambled to my feet and exited my room. The fact that the house was ominously dark and creepy with those freaky post-mortem photographs lining the walls of the hallway didn't bother me at the moment. There was only one thing on my mind now, and that was to find the telephone.

Believe it or not, the fact that I was placed in the Millennial demographic didn't mean that I was completely clueless about earlier technology. Despite what all those know-it-all-Gen-Xers have said, some people my age actually *did* know a thing or two about what was now considered *retro* or *nostalgic* from the 90s, like beepers and Blockbuster Video and Whitney Houston. My parents owned a telephone. Several of them throughout the house, and I vividly remembered using the cordless. A young

McCall chatting with her middle school gal pals about nothing and everything important.

As my shaky legs carried me down the stairs to the first floor of Hazelhurst Manor, I pondered on where the telephone might be. My parents had one hooked up in the kitchen, another in the office, and one more in the living room. I imagined the Hazelhurst landline probably resembled one of those old-fashioned rotary phones. Those ones where the receiver rested on a gold, elevated cradle. Something someone might pay a lot of money to own nowadays so it could sit in their house as a relic.

The smooth, ligneous railing supported most of my weight as I leaned into it, carefully climbing down each step. Focusing on where I'd be able to find the landline actually eased a bit of the anxiety, and the tension in my chest weakened.

Now that the attack my mind was waging on my body felt like it was finally subsiding, I could concentrate all my efforts on finding the telephone and getting the hell out of here. As soon as my boot hit the Persian rug in the foyer, the search was on.

Starting with the parlor first, I checked every flat surface—the coffee table, the mantel, the end tables near the button-back chairs and velvet settee—and then the walls because I remembered the one mounted in the kitchen of our family home near the refrigerator. Once I was done, I moved into the dining room and searched the china cabinet with the creepy porcelain dolls and the sideboard where a pitcher of water sat on a silver tray. Without a second thought, I snatched the full pitcher from its tray and brought it to my lips, turning it up and swallowing so much water I thought I might choke. I didn't realize how thirsty I was until that very moment.

More than half of the water missed my mouth completely and drenched the front of my body, which actually felt good. It felt cleansing. Rinsing me of the blood rain that had soaked into my hair and clothes and skin. After pulling the glass away from my mouth, I lifted the pitcher over my head and pour the remaining water over me, using my other hand to rub myself and wash off as much of the blood as I could from my face.

When there was no more water left, I set the empty pitcher down and resumed my hunt for the telephone. There was nothing but cooking tools and accessories in the kitchen. Pans hanging from the ceiling pot rack. Stacks of plates drying near the sink. A knife rack affixed to the wall with an array of knives stuck to a magnetic strip. Steak knives, bread knife, paring knife, carving knife, a cleaver...

I eyed the cleaver, its wide steel blade catching the glowing reflection of a candle on the wall. And what if there were vampires in this house? Was I just supposed to lie back and allow them to take my blood, or was I going to at least try to fight back? From everything I'd ever read about vampires or seen in movies, wielding a knife at one wasn't going to kill it, unless the blade was made out of real silver. Unfortunately, Aidan's vampire lesson didn't include the part about how to kill them. Quite honestly, I was more fascinated by Aidan's complete belief in them and S.O.U.P.s in general to ask the hard-hitting, super important questions.

No matter. I plucked the cleaver from the wall and held the wooden hilt tightly, ready to swing with all the force I had. If it wasn't going to kill them, the least it could do was buy me time to run away.

Once the kitchen was thoroughly checked, I moved into the hallway, past the downstairs bathroom and locked cellar door, to the music room and the study. The music room didn't turn up anything, just a piano and a few marble busts of what I assumed to be famous, historical musicians. Nimbly, I moved to the study, careful not to make too much noise. Then, after searching the large, solid wood desk and the walls and the ornate mantel of a smaller version of the fireplace from the parlor, I finally spotted the telephone sitting on top of an accent table next to a brown, leather chair. Without hesitation, I launched myself at the table, tripping and landing directly in the seat as my hand picked up the receiver. Almost as if I had choreographed the entire thing.

A large lump of hope blossomed in my chest. The telephone was nearly exactly as I imagined it. Shiny gold with a rotary dial pad. I brought the receiver to my ear and turned the metal wheel, starting with number nine, then one and one. But there was no sound. No ringing. No dial tone. I picked up the entire phone, only to learn that there weren't even any wires connected running from it to the wall.

That lump of hope quickly wilted, and I threw the vintage phone into the fireplace.

Leaving the study to stand in the hallway, knife cocked and ready to attack if need be, I was once again overwhelmed by the feeling of defeat and immense loneliness. There was no one in this house with me. No way to reach the outside world. No pills to help me escape my own madness. There was only complete silence. Not even the sound of the grandfather clock ticking. Not even the blood rain or fire-starting lightning.

No rain? If it had stopped, should I try to escape into the woods now? In the dark? Alone?

I took a step back toward the foyer and the front door, preparing myself for the amount of willpower and fortitude it was going to take to hike down a steep mountain by only the light of the moon. If I even had the moon to guide me. Who knew if Madame Clara's big cloud of blood rain would follow me?

But I had to try. I had to fight to live.

And then I stopped walking and reversed my steps, turning to face the one door I hadn't opened yet. The forbidden one.

The cellar door.

Chapter Twenty-Five

I had never lived in a house with a cellar or a basement. Never even been inside of one. It wasn't necessarily practical in most of Florida—the water table sat too close to the ground surface. But I was aware that they were ideal in most northern states. On the Home and Garden network, homeowners usually transformed the extra square footage below their house in a multitude of ways, converting their basements into gyms, offices, movie rooms, wine cellars, and even apartments that could be rented out for extra income.

But a real strong instinct was telling me that there was no gym or office or movie room here as I stood in front of the wooden door that led to the cellar of Hazelhurst Manor. All that kept running through my head were flashes of horror movies, where the basement door would lead to a set of creaking stairs, descending into a pitch-black, damp open space that housed evil shadows and ghosts ready to terrorize. There would be a furnace, its iron grill resembling an angry monster waiting to spit flames. And four mysteriously dark corners where anything could crawl out and attack.

Madame Clara claimed that this door was locked. But she laid the same claim for the attic door, and one twist of the knob proved that she was wrong. My assumption was that maybe someone had accidentally left it unlocked, for Madame Clara's stern, unamusing voice echoed in my memories, her words short and to the point: *We ask that guests do not enter*. It was clear that she was not asking, but rather enforcing.

But the attic was easily accessible, and I wondered how easily the cellar would be to access.

Of course, there was the most obvious question blinking obnoxiously behind my eyes—one that I was trying my hardest to not ask myself and it started with two very familiar words. *What if* these doors were purposely left unlocked and a kind of psychological game had begun right at the moment I'd heard the pleading whimper of someone in need? After all, everything I'd learned about vampires from reading books and watching movies was that they could be quite devious. Calculated. Always were two steps ahead of their prey.

Then again, this thought was followed by yet another hypothetical: What if there really was someone in need of help, and I was their salvation? Like Gwen? Or Aidan? Or even Preston?

Before I could reach out to test the knob of the wooden door with metal hinges that led to the cellar, into the unknown, an overwhelming longing for my missing anti-anxiety pills stopped me from moving. I stood in front of it, staring deeply into the grain of the wood, imagining how much easier this would have been if I were able to take just one pill.

Naturally, I hadn't a clue how to explain how the medication worked by using scientific lingo or medical jargon. However, with my eyes closed, I pictured swallowing the tablet. It would travel into my stomach, where it'd then be digested and passed into my bloodstream and carried right to the part of my brain that was constantly working in overdrive. My nerves would begin to relax, my muscles would become less rigid, and my heart would slow its pace. There would, without a doubt, still be some uneasiness about not knowing what I was to uncover in the cellar, don't get me wrong. The medicine was by no means a magic potion that could eliminate *all* worries. But it could make everything much more manageable. A kind of calming lull that embraced me. A transparent shield, where I could still see the anxiety and fears just below it, but it couldn't reach me at its maximum potential.

Thinking about that tiny tablet melting away in my body did create a little placebo effect. Finally, I took one deep breath in and held it as I twisted the knob with one hand while the other gripped the cleaver tight. There was the sound of brass sliding on brass, and when I leaned into the wood, it took a bit of force before the door parted from its swollen frame.

It had opened...

Ugggghhh

And there was the groan of a woman in pain, clear as crystal.

Chapter Twenty-Six

As soon as both my feet met on the top landing of the cellar stairs, just past the door, the music began. A low, slightly static instrumental found its way into my ears, the overused heavy piano chords ricocheting off the concrete walls. I was instantly hit with the odor of copper mixed with alcohol wipes mixed with mildew. Out of those three scents, the acrid, wet smell of mildew was what surprised me the most. Hazelhurst Manor, for being centuries old, was strangely one of the cleanest places I'd ever been to. Madame Clara did a great job of keeping the house shipshape, whether she did it herself or ordered Landon or Pandora to do it. It would make sense if she wanted to keep guests coming back to stay at her bed-and-breakfast. I didn't see it when I'd been looking for information about the B&B, but there had to be reviews somewhere on Yelp or Tripadvisor. If it were true and Madame Clara had been around for a long time, I was sure she had learned a thing or two about how to run a business.

The mildewed odor sat heavy in my lungs when I inhaled, testing my gag reflexes. From then on, I would have to do most of my breathing through my mouth.

Carefully, because I hadn't a clue how sturdy the railing could be, I peered down the staircase, trying to follow the flickering lights of what I assumed were candles casting shadows off the walls deeper into the cellar. I stopped breathing altogether for a moment, stretching the radius of my hearing as far as I could, trying to ignore the weird, macabre classical song that was clearly being played on a record. If I was being completely honest, it was so totally vampiresque I could have laughed out loud right where I stood. It wasn't quite the *Dracula* theme, but something very similar, very synonymous to the soundtrack for *Interview with a Vampire.*

The moans and groans of pain that came through the vents in the wall upstairs and through the thick door of the cellar could no longer be heard, unless they were seamlessly blending in with the orchestral composition filling up the space, and my mind. There was only one way to find out if Aidan or Gwen or Preston were down here, and I had to do it fast before anyone was hurt. Or hurt worse.

If I couldn't leave to get help or call someone to get help, then I would have to figure it out on my own. So, with a bit of newfound conviction to save my kinda sorta friends, I moved down the steps. Naturally, each stair creaked but I wasn't worried, thanks to the classical background music that I was sure to be masking the sound.

As the stairwell turned around a corner, I had no idea what I was going to find. A million what-ifs circled my brain, too many to even pick one to obsessively dwell on. The base instruments of the string selection echoed deeper into my body the closer I got, and before I knew it, I was standing in front of four vampires and their coffins. All of their red eyes on me.

"Miss Harris. We've been waiting for you," Madame Clara huffed, as if to be very irritated by my late arrival. She stood in front of the others, her hands crossed over her groin, her posture perfectly stiff and prim. Landon leaned his back against the wall made of concrete blocks, his top hat tipped over his brow and his hands in his pockets. Pandora stood to Madame Clara's right, swaying gently from side to side, the bustle of her ruffled dress swooshing against the concrete floor. I was reminded of a little girl, the way she moved playfully to the music. But her appearance certainly gave off an older, more mature vibe. Still sporting that freshly fed look, she was a vixen with ruby red lipstick and a corset so tight that her pale breasts were brimming over the fabric. Her hands were gloved, and her sateen fingers twirled a chunk of long, obsidian hair. Chef Winston leaned over a matte black coffin on a metal stand that seemed to have seen better days—the wood splintering and tarnished. He was grinning at me and nodding his head, the layers of wrinkles on his white face jiggling with his movements.

It was only an observation with no written proof—his name wasn't embossed in Old English letters across the casket or anything—but I assumed that Chef Winston was hunched over his own coffin, while the others stood in front of or next to theirs. They were all on trolleys with tiny wheels that boosted them waist-high, but each one appeared to specifically belong to their owners in a way that matched their personalities and characteristics.

While I couldn't quite make out small details, there was enough warm, ambient light from the candles in the cellar for me to make out that Landon's coffin was so shiny and black, a smaller version of himself reflected off it. Madame Clara's coffin was wrapped in silver, with a white, doily-like skirt hanging off the edge and hiding the stand underneath. And Pandora's coffin was velvet, the color matching her maroon outfit so well that if it wasn't for the different textures, her body would have been camouflaged.

"Wh-why—" I had to clear the fear out of my throat before I could finish. "Why were you waiting for me? Where's Aidan?"

From my point of view, there only seemed to be us and the caskets in the room. But way in the corner, behind all the vampires staring at little old me, I spotted a door.

Madame Clara ignored my questions and stepped forward, her face showing indifference. My feet became rooted to the ground as I watched her descend upon me, bracing myself for a fight after I swung the cleaver at her face. But within a matter of nanoseconds, she flashed toward me the rest of the way and managed to somehow snatch the cleaver out of my hands and return to the exact same spot she was in before I could even figure out what happened. Then she dropped it and kicked it at Chef Winston, who picked it up and stuffed the knife into his chef coat pocket.

Well, there goes my only weapon. I released a sigh of resignation.

"Now," she started. "It took an enormous amount of effort and time for me to find a suitable, efficient way to ensure this nest—" she extended a stiff arm, gesturing to the three vampires behind her, "—remains properly fed. And by time, I mean centuries."

My eyes broke contact with hers and I shifted my weight, suddenly feeling very self-conscious and awkward that she was talking directly to me and only me about this. I didn't think I was supposed to even know they were vampires. But she continued, "There have only been a handful of times in the past where we struggled to procure enough sustenance to remain healthy, such as in times of war or economic crisis on a national level."

My mind reeled, recalling history classes in high school and college where I learned about decades and decades of important events and milestones that happened in the country. It was crazy to know that the four people...er...vampires standing before me were around for the invention of the telephone.

"Although we weren't completely immune to the effects of those events, even having lost a beloved member of our clan—" For one brief moment—and I mean so brief, a blink would have missed it—Madame Clara's tight face seemed to have softened, but it was a matter of a millisecond before she straightened herself, lifting her chin up to the air in a kind of defiant gesture. "—but we forged through it. And the recent global pandemic is no exception."

The global pandemic? How would that have affected vampires, or even S.O.U.Ps for that matter? Were they capable of catching the virus and becoming ill? I would assume not. It would be a tragedy to be a supernatural being with magical powers, only to be knocked off your ass by the glorified flu.

The instinct to ask Madame Clara questions remained lodged inside my chest. While there was definitely a fair amount of fascination over the fact that I was really and truly standing in front of—no shit!—*vampires,* I needed to know where Aidan was and if she had killed everyone. But there was no way in hell I was going to interrupt her. Especially not when she was surrounded by people she could easily command to do anything she wanted. So I just listened.

"While we have learned from our past misjudgments, this year had been especially challenging. Unfortunately, due to a small setback—"

Landon chuckled and sneered. "You mean to say, 'due to Pandora.'"

Madame Clara ignored him. "Due to a small setback," she repeated, ignoring her son, "our backup supply ran dangerously low, and we were forced to endure a few months of malnourishment. You and the other patrons were our first guests in over a year. But you must know and understand that an incident like this hasn't occurred in many decades."

It didn't take a genius to know that when a vampire talked about backup supply, they meant blood.

Landon chuckled again with abject mockery. "Yeah, now thanks to Pandora, we have the wonderfully laborious task of covering up not one or two, but *eight* bodies."

Bodies? What bodies?!

My heart began to thump behind my chest wall as I mentally counted the *bodies* he mentioned. Not one or two, but eight. Eight bodies. One, two, three... Wait, how many of us checked in yesterday? Eight sounded like too many. And Tom and Ellen and their kids left last night, right? Oh my God. What if they didn't leave?

Pandora twirled her attention toward Landon and gasped theatrically. "It's not my fault! I only wanted a simple taste. It had been so long," she said, pouting with her fingertip between her teeth as she started to sway childishly again. "Besides, Winston fucked up, too, with those two little dumb kids."

Oh my God. Missy and Max. What did Chef Winston do to Missy and Max?

"Right, and now yours and Winston's ignorance have set us back," Landon spat back. "Your lack of control and Winston's child fetish will be the end of us. And the manor won't be deemed fit for lodging until we rid the bodies from the property and tie up loose ends. We'll have to cancel the next group of guests. Do you understand how damaging that is at this time? Our supply is still critically low."

Pandora stomped her foot. "Don't you think I know that, asshole? It was a mistake!"

Hearing her curse at Landon didn't sound right. Didn't fit with the whole tone of Hazelhurst Manor. Not with the decor or the food or with what they were wearing. And using foul language definitely didn't have a place in Madame Clara's nest. Madame Clara would never stoop so low. Condescension and patronizing undertones were her way of swearing, and it was very effective. Just ask Gwen. That was, if Gwen was even still alive.

"Both of you stop it!" Madame Clara barked. She turned to the tall, handsome man who continued to lean coolly against the wall. "Landon, you know Pandora is still considered a fledgling. Mistakes are to be expected from her." Then she turned to Pandora and Chef Winston. "And you must learn to once and for all control your thirst. Hazelhurst Manor has a reputation to uphold, which determines whether or not we will starve. And Winston, you are no exception either. From now on, children will no longer be allowed to stay. Not for a long while."

Chef Winston's weird smirk fell, and his gaze met his feet. "My apologies, Madame." I didn't expect his British accent, seeing as how I hadn't heard him utter one word since we checked in. His voice was just as ghoulish as his leering eye.

He lifted his head with a renewed creepy smile. "Madame, there is still a fair amount of space in the icebox. It would be my pleasure to prepare the dead for storage. Future guests would be quite pleased with the plentiful provisions Hazelhurst Manor has to offer."

Bile rose from my stomach as I realized what he was saying. *God, please don't tell me Chef Winston served human meat to us at one of those "authentic" meals.*

"That won't be necessary, Winston," Madame Clara said. "We will take care of the dead as we've done in the past."

Again, morbid curiosity threatened to open my big mouth to ask all the questions that weren't important at the moment. About what they had done to dead bodies in the past. But hearing myself asking the question in my head only solidified the realization that this was all really happening. I was really standing in front of vampires, talking about supposedly dead bodies, and although I didn't know who exactly was deceased and who wasn't yet, someone definitely was.

"Where is everyone else?" I asked, my voice shaking with fear. I didn't want to know where they were, but I did. I had to know, because there was a formidable glare in each of the vampire's bright red eyes, and somehow it was a foreshadowing of my own fate, of my blood coursing through their bodies. Because their eyes weren't gray like they had been starving. They weren't uniquely purple like they were earlier in the weekend, an indication I learned meant that their blood tank was just full enough to hold them over.

No. Landon and Pandora and Madame Clara and Chef Winston all had the same glowing, crimson eyes. They had recently drunk blood. And whatever happened to the other guests was going to happen to me next.

Chapter Twenty-Seven

While standing in front of four vampires, I had come to the realization that I sealed my fate the moment I stepped into this house the day before, when I walked into the supernatural unknown. Hell, it probably happened sooner than that—when I'd searched for a vacation destination. A cheap place for me to find the girl I used to be before I got attacked by a random asshole who stole my dignity and courage. To add to the ridiculous notion that a weekend away would magically change the sad excuse for a woman that I had become, I naively believed that I could produce the outline to a future bestselling novel when I hadn't a single idea for a new story in my emotionally disordered brain.

Strangely enough, as I watched Madame Clara, Landon, Pandora, and Chef Winston watch me, apparently patiently waiting for me to answer a question I hadn't entirely paid attention to, my nerves felt calmer than before. There was only a thin sheet of dread hanging over me now, and my stomach wasn't tied in its usual knots. Somehow, my impending doom had created a sense of peace over me. Was I finally learning that there was truth behind Dr. Finn's words: *we fear the unknown*? Now that I actually knew what was going to happen to me, there was less to fear.

"McCall Harris!" Madame Clara snapped. "I would like to advise that you pay attention, as our next conversation will be the difference between life and death."

If life was an option, she had my full attention.

"Under any other circumstance, we wouldn't be giving you this choice. But we aren't the monsters the world has claimed us to be. Not all vampires are out to murder in cold blood. Our nest has only ever wanted to live a quiet life of leisure amongst the trees, on the land that we've inhabited for centuries. And for many, many years, we have done so without incident. Guests are invited to stay in our home for a one-of-a-kind experience, and while they may be unaware of the essential gift they leave with us, we ensure that those people depart with memories of a pleasant vacation."

I didn't ask, but I knew exactly what Madame Clara referred to. Hypnotism. Someone, or maybe all of them, in this nest had the ability to compel people, erase their memories and possibly replace them with different ones. Now the question was, how did they go about stealing their blood? Yes, stealing, because technically these vampires were considered thieves. There was no way anyone would willingly give their DNA to a bunch of monsters.

Madame Clara pressed her lips into a hard line before she said, "Unfortunately, the recent global pandemic has brought the worst out in us. And seeing as how your group were the first guests we've had in a year, some of us were unable to control ourselves." Her eyes flickered to Pandora and Chef Winston, and then back to me. Obviously, they were the fuckups she was referring to in this room. "Because of the misdeeds of my fellow nest members, we were unable to grant The Prescotts, the Humphreys, and Mister Moreno a pleasant departure."

It was true. Aidan was dead. Everyone was dead. My chest caved with grief.

"Your fellow guest mates have provided us with plenty to ration before we are able to book the next group of visitors, which is why we are offering you a choice."

The need to know what choice Madame Clara was giving me clawed at my insides, but for some reason, only one question came out of my mouth before I could stop it.

"What did you do with my pills?" I asked, and I could hear how small and pathetic my own voice sounded. Of all the screwed-up things that were happening at this very moment, I had to ask about my stupid anxiety pills. Not that I necessarily needed them. I was already coming to terms with the fact that I was probably about to die, which was just another sign of how messed up my head was. Just when I thought I couldn't get any crazier...

Madame Clara answered without blinking. "Landon prefers his blood clean."

I peeked over at Landon and met his ruby red eyes, the corner of his mouth slowly turning up. If there was any silver lining, at least the man who would be sucking me dry was a handsome fella—in an 1800s emo kind of way.

There was no more procrastinating. "What is my choice then?" I asked.

For the first time since I had come down the stairs to the cellar, Madame Clara moved. She took two stiff steps toward me. All the muscles in my legs tensed, but my feet remained rooted to the ground.

"In the past, we have found that individuals who are afflicted with some forms of mental instability have benefited from the transformation. Embracing the many attributes our kind has to offer can *revamp* a person. Give them a newfound strength that they've never seen before in themselves. These fledglings end up becoming a force to be reckoned with."

Did she just crack a joke? Did Madame Clara, the meanest and most severe woman I had ever met, just seriously make a pun? Her expression remained stony, but Chef Winston released a phlegmy cackle behind her. She continued, "We have observed you over the course of the weekend and we've come to the conclusion that you are one of the forty million humans in the world who have anxious tendencies."

Heat rushed to my cheeks and my gaze fell to my feet. How embarrassing that a couple of vampires who hadn't been humans for centuries could sense my flaws and fear of life.

"With the transformation comes incredible power, some of it immediately transferred from the maker and some of it taught through immortal years of practice. And with this power comes self-assuredness, courage, and a renewed conviction for what you have become. For the new life and family you will have adopted. You are reborn."

A bone-chilling surge of cool air from someplace in the dank cellar found its way underneath my clothes and into my skin when I began putting her words together. *Embracing the attributes of our kind* and *the transformation.* "Are you saying..." My mouth became dry mid-sentence, and I struggled to find enough saliva to swallow. "Are you saying that you want to turn me into a vampire?"

Madame Clara's expression remained still, her eyes boring into mine. The next couple of sentences out of her mouth were so resolute, each word ricocheted off the walls of my stomach.

"I'm saying that I am giving you a choice, Miss Harris. It's either death or immortal life."

Death or immortal life? Meaning, did I want to die or become a vampire? Well, I guess I was lucky to have had more choices than everyone else did.

"Um, excuse me," Pandora shrieked.

Madame Clara rolled her eyes before turning back to the vampire clan. "Yes, Pandora."

Pandora's lips shifted from a sensual smirk to a pouty pucker. "You said that you didn't want more than four nest members. You said that more than four was too conspicuous," she screeched at Madame Clara, pointing a gloved finger at her.

"And I stand by my word," Madame Clara replied calmly.

Pandora pointed to me. "If she chooses an immortal life, that will make five of us."

"I'm surprised you can count that high," Landon chimed in.

On the inside, I chuckled, but I knew how I looked on the outside. My mouth was agape and I was pie-eyed, staring blankly at Pandora who was sulking immaturely about who knew what while I contemplated whether or not I wanted to die...or die. Because vampires were dead, right?

Pandora ignored Landon's dig and continued whining to Madame Clara. "You killed William because of your rule. The love of my life. You said there was no room for him in this nest," she accused.

But Madame Clara raised her voice over Pandora's. "And you were given an option to go with him, were you not? The two of you were given a choice. William wanted you to have the immortal life. He sacrificed himself so that you could continue living."

"Oh, but now you are allowing a fifth member? That's bullshit!" Pandora's squealing made my ears ring.

Then, from the corner of my eye, there was movement, and a gust of wind simultaneously whooshed through my hair, blowing it up and around my face. A blurry flash of something crossed in front of me, and my body jolted at the unexpected splatter of warm liquid hitting my face. I blinked my eyes one, two, three, four, five times in rapid succession before my vision could focus on what was in front of me again.

Landon was standing next to Pandora's body that had crumpled on the cellar floor, holding a heart dripping blood.

Chapter Twenty-Eight

When I had first started at the veterinary clinic as a receptionist, I only ever expected to worry about paperwork and answering phone calls. Scheduling appointments for rabies shots and grooming. The idea of emergencies happening never really crossed my mind when it came to animals until one rainy day, a man burst through the doors of the clinic cradling a large German Shepherd. The man was in hysterics and soaking wet, dripping water onto the ground while the dog dripped blood from a gaping hole in its chest.

"He ran out in front of my car! Please! You have to help him!" the man shouted desperately.

I had sprung up from my chair behind the desk, completely at a loss for words. My mind was yelling back at him: *What happened? Is this your dog? Hand him to me and I'll go save his life!* But nothing came out of my mouth. The words had been lost in fear. Lost at the sight of torn sinew and copious amounts of blood pouring out of this poor, innocent little life.

It was all happening too much, too fast. Since my attack on my sixteenth birthday, I hadn't been in a *too much, too fast* situation. I purposely remained a recluse, separating myself from the world and possible conflict to avoid these types of scenarios for this exact reason: I just couldn't handle it.

The man's eyes widened with disbelief. "Hey! Are you listening to me? Call a doctor out here!" His words echoed, his voice became distant, and I was still frozen in place.

Eventually, the man's loud yelling alerted the doctors and vet technicians in the back. They came rushing out, retrieved the dog, and after about thirty minutes of working on it, it was declared dead. As it turned out, the dog didn't stand a chance against the man's car, the tire having rolled over its body, applying so much pressure that its chest literally exploded open.

Needless to say, I felt like scum. Worthless. Like I could have done...*should* have done more. I went home to my tiny apartment that night, popped a couple of my anxiety tablets, and wallowed in my own self-pity until I passed out on my futon.

Before that happened, I had never seen the insides of any living being before. And the moral of the story wasn't to shed light on how meek and helpless I became at the sight of something so dramatic and gruesome, but to somehow demonstrate the extreme differences between seeing the insides of an animal versus a human being. Even an immortal one.

Because there was a difference. Not in the color of blood or viscosity of tissues. It was more of feeling. Seeing the dog like that had left me heavy-hearted. Seeing Pandora made me feel faint.

Landon stood erect in his gentleman's coat and top hat, arm out in front of him with his hand gripping Pandora's still heart as the thick vessels drooped over his knuckles. He stared down at her body at his feet, and then dropped her heart. It plopped onto the concrete next to her, sending out a sickening plonking sound that resembled a wet rag. It sent what little food I had in my stomach creeping up, up, up into my esophagus until I could taste the metallic bitterness of bile in the back of my throat. I pressed the back of my hand to my mouth, breathing in and out slowly until I felt I had full control over my gag reflexes again.

"Now, we need a fourth member for our nest," he said casually as he wiped his blood-soaked hand on a handkerchief.

Madame Clara didn't look at all disturbed by the fact that her son had just killed one of their own. More irritated than anything. "Landon, really. This isn't the time for showboating." She turned her back on me, stepping closer to Landon and Chef Winston, and they all hovered over Pandora's body.

"Please, Mother," Landon said. "As if you liked her in the least. You only tolerated the wench because she maintained the drudgery of the manor. Winston will just have to pick up the slack from here on out."

"Well, it will only be fair that Miss Harris pick up where Pandora left off." My ears perked up at the sound of Chef Winton's short-winded, raspy voice saying my name, finally pulling me out of what happened just a second ago and into the now.

Landon's smoldering red eyes met mine, his lips curling upward into a calculated grin. "No, I have other plans for *Miss* Harris."

Pinpricks of dread admixed with flattery crawled up my spine. There was no way of knowing what Landon's plans were for me, and I wasn't entirely sure how long I would be able to keep from opening the enormous can of what-ifs his words carried with them. And yet, I was perversely charmed by his alluring gaze. I only locked eyes with him for a few seconds longer before realizing that I better stop. What if he compelled me into doing something right here, right now? What if he—

Blinking rapidly, I moved my focus past him, to the door in the back of the room. There was something in the next room, and I had to find out what before I was either going to die or become whatever it was Landon wanted me to be. His next meal? His sex slave?

"Pandora was nothing short of a daft newbie who couldn't control her urge to feed, but so were you at one point, Landon," Madame Clara said. "Shall we carry out the same punishment on Winston? After all, he was the first to slip up with those dreadful children."

The children. She meant Max and Missy. But I couldn't stop to wonder what horrible things Chef Winston might have done to those kids. The three of them weren't paying any attention to me, so this was my chance to somehow slide past them into that other room.

I moved one foot in front of the other, slowly and soundlessly taking tiny steps forward. The weird ominous music was still playing in the background, but either Madame Clara turned it down, or my brain was choosing to block it out because it now sounded like instruments whispering from a distance.

"Madame, I misunderstood. They were misbehaving and broke a crystal glass. I assumed it would be best for those children to suffer the consequences for disrespecting our things," Chef Winston tried to explain.

Landon scoffed. "That is a complete load of shit, old man. We know how much you enjoy drinking from the young. Neither of us are fooled."

A few more steps to go and I was going to be standing parallel to Landon, Madame Clara, and Chef Winston. I imagined that as soon as they noticed, one of them was going to pull me by my hair and drag me back. After all, they did have that whole teleporting ability. In a single flash, someone's hands could be around my throat and snapping my head right off my body.

"I appreciate your concern and devotion to the manor, Winston," Madame Clara said. "And I also understand that it must have been hard for you to restrain yourself considering the low inventory we've had to work with over the past year. That damn pandemic really muddled our routine. Regardless, we are no longer in the business of terrorizing humans. That ship sailed decades ago. And now that we may have a new member of our nest, we must show her that we are not to be feared."

There was silence. I was about halfway across the room, just past where they were standing over Pandora, when I turned to find all of their red eyes on me. Madame Clara frowned and rolled her eyes, as if to be disappointed by my weak attempt at running away. Landon simply smirked at me, as if to be amused.

One more moment of *oh shit what do I do?* passed before I finally just bolted, reaching that door in the back of the room in the cellar and slamming it behind me, leaning back against it and letting out a big breath of *thank God* and praying no one on the other side tried to kick down the door while I was resting my shaking body against it. One strong shove from a vampire would probably send me flying across the room.

But the thought of Landon, Madame Clara, or Chef Winston getting to me was quickly replaced with something else once I was able to focus on what had been on the other side of this door. It was panic. Sheer panic. The memory of the exploded dog came flooding back. This was a *too much, too fast* situation, and I had no idea what the fuck to do.

The first objects in the dank room to command my attention were the two bodies hanging upside down and side by side from the ceiling and in the far-right corner, their ankles tied together by chains. My eyes traveled from their bare feet down their legs and to their backs, which were facing me. They were clothed, but even then, I could tell which was the man and which was the woman by their hair—one had long hair, the other short. The man's arms draped over a wooden bucket overflowing with inky liquid, which was positioned just below his head. The woman's hair floated on top of an equally full bucket of her own. It was then that the stench of death and decay finally wafted into my nostrils, testing my gag reflex once again. It was a wonder I've managed to keep anything down having been surrounded by so much gore.

I managed to pull my gaze away from the two obviously dead people and onto the...gurneys. Like the kind that rolled and what paramedics used to transport patients into the back of an ambulance. There were around five of them lined up against the far-left concrete wall. Two of the gurneys were empty, with just the black, torn cushion visible from where I stood. Someone occupied the one in the middle. It took me a second, but I soon realized that it was Aidan lying on the gurney, the top half of the cushion reclined up to reveal his face looking worse for wear.

"Aidan!" I scurried over to him, noticing then that the two other gurneys next to him were also occupied, only by white sheets in the shape of human bodies. I reached Aidan and attempted to touch him, but my hands could only hover over his shirtless chest. I recoiled my fingers for fear of hurting his wounds. There were puncture marks all over his torso, small round holes multiplied by twos, each individual one leaking blood. His abdomen was moving up and down and relief rushed through me. Aidan was still alive, but after one look at his face, I knew it wouldn't be for much longer. His normally olive-complected skin was ashen, his cheeks sunken in and gaunt.

He looked to be sleeping, but his eyebrows were permanently drawn together as if to be wincing. As if he was in constant pain.

It was when I reached down to take his limp hand to offer some kind of comfort that I noticed the needle embedded into the veins of his arm, connected to a tube that snaked down the side of the gurney then up to a large bag hanging off a metal stand. The bag was nearly full of Aidan's blood. My stunned gaze drifted from the hanging blood bag down to the bucket on the floor where multiple bags of blood lay. I gasped. How much blood was that? Judging by how close to death Aidan looked, it had to be mostly his. How much blood could be possibly left inside of him?

Instinctively, and surprisingly, I yanked the needle out of Aidan's arm and immediately applied pressure with my palm. If another drop of blood left his body, it was sure to be his demise.

"Aidan, we need to get you out of here," I whispered into his ear. He stirred, but I could tell his movements were sluggish. My mind raced. How was I supposed to get him out of here if he was too weak and near death? There was no way I could do it on my own. It was already amazing that I'd built enough courage to be helping him out, and I was afraid that this newfound conviction could just as easily vanish as quickly as it developed. My unstable anxiety disorder could have me cowering in a corner at any second, hands over my ears and shaking uncontrollably until one of those vampires just ate me already.

But I decided to take advantage of it while I could. After all, this was supposed to be the weekend of new beginnings. Not exactly what I had in mind for the way to find my bravery again, but I had to take whatever the universe was throwing at me.

"Aidan, listen to me," I urged. "You have to find the strength. You have to help me. If you don't, we'll be stuck here and we'll die. They're going to kill us."

His eyes fluttered and he attempted to moved again. "Mc... Call?"

"Yes, please. Open your eyes, Aidan. We have to go."

I hadn't a single clue how we would get out or where we would even go, but I knew that if there was a chance of us surviving, we had to get out of this vampire nest.

And just as Aidan's eyelids flitted up, the door to the room busted open. Literally exploding into a million pieces. I bent over Aidan's body as pieces of wood rained down on us.

"For God's sake, Landon! Was that honestly necessary?" Madame Clara chided as she carefully stepped over the mess her son had just made. Landon strode in behind her, all cool and calm.

"Oh, Mother. Live a little. I'm just having a little fun. Besides, you know the blood is better when it's mixed with fear."

"I thought you said we weren't going to kill Miss Harris," Chef Winston reminded Landon.

"Doesn't mean I don't want a taste," Landon said.

The vampires all finally noticed me. "You stupid girl," Madame Clara said, pounding her heels over to me. "That man is already dead. There's nothing you can do to save him."

I shook my head and peered down at Aidan again, laying a hand on his chest, praying that he didn't just die on me. He hadn't. His breaths were shallow, but he was still alive.

Madame Clara snatched my wrist and yanked me away from the gurney. "They are all dead. There is nothing you can do for any of them," she said, and it was just then that it all came down on me like an anvil.

For some reason, I didn't connect the dots earlier, probably because it was all too much to take in, too much to comprehend, but the other four people in the room were the other guests.

Tom and Ellen hanging upside down in the corner. Preston and Gwen under the white sheets. And she was right, there was nothing I could do to save them. But Aidan and I were still alive, and I wasn't about to go down without a fight.

I shoved Madame Clara away and pulled my arm out of her grip. It was incredibly hard to do and I had to use almost all the strength I could muster, but I still managed to break free. Without turning my back on them, I carefully walked backward toward Aidan again. "He isn't dead yet, and I'm not going to let you kill him."

"He's well on his way there," Madame Clara said. "And we don't have time for this. You need to decide between an immortal life or not."

Yes, that was a conundrum, wasn't it? I didn't want to die, so it seemed like I might not have that much of a choice. Did I really want to become a vampire and a part of this vampire nest? Hell no! Especially not one that was run by the Wicked Witch of Hazelhurst Manor. But what else could I do? There was no way I could get past three powerful vampires. And even if I could, it was raining blood with lightning bolts of fire outside, rendering it pretty impossible to navigate down a steep mountain.

I had to think, think, think. My options were death or... death. Death was death, but becoming a vampire meant that I was dead but not dead. Let's kick around that idea for a moment.

"Miss Harris! We don't have all day," Madame Clara barked.

"Give me a moment to decide," I shot back, startled by the snip in my own voice. This was no delicate matter. I had to choose wisely.

On the downside of becoming a vampire, I'd end up having to live at Hazelhurst Manor. But did I really have a life back in

Miami? I don't get along with any of my siblings, and my parents might feel a sense of relief if I wasn't around for them to worry about anymore. Well, I said *worry*, but it was more like *financially support*. My parents weren't exactly too compassionate about my mental struggles. They were around if I needed them, but they didn't quite understand what it was like to have anxiety or PTSD. They barely even believed it was a problem, and the most anxiety they ever experienced was whether or not the gardener trimmed the bougainvillea back too far.

I was assuming that if I lived here, I wouldn't need money. The vet clinic wouldn't miss me, and it would mean that I could concentrate on my writing. I would also have access to an amazing library. Pro: Madame Clara might somehow have connections in the publishing world. I didn't know how often or if the vampires ever really left the manor, but they'd been around for centuries. That meant they had to know at least *some* important people, right?

There was the possibility that Landon wanted to use me as some kind of personal toy, but maybe I could somehow make that impossible for him. According to Aidan's S.O.U.P. knowledge, vampires had to be taught most of their supernatural abilities over time. But maybe it was possible that I'd have some power to start out with. I had no idea if it would be enough to handle Landon, but you better believe I would at least try. The man was dreamy in a Gothic kind of way...with a hint of Dracula flare, but it didn't mean I would automatically surrender to becoming his vampire girlfriend.

Another con would be that I'd most probably have to drink blood. Although, that really didn't bother me so much. I was assuming that my taste for it would naturally adapt once I *changed*. My main concern was how I would acquire it. I didn't want to kill people.

I turned to Madame Clara. "Would I have to...feed...on people?" I asked. Landon rolled his eyes and sighed dramatically. Chef Winston released a cackle, and Madame Clara simply pressed her lips together into a hard line.

"Miss Harris, under usual circumstances, we operate professionally. We do not normally condone the *feeding* on mortals. If you shall choose to become part of this nest, you will be thoroughly educated on how Hazelhurst Manor is run."

That was a little reassuring. But there was one more important question I had to ask. "You said that the transformation can fix me. That it can take away all my problems—"

"Now, Miss Harris, let's not get ahead of ourselves. Becoming one of us does have its perks, but I cannot guarantee anything. Each individual is different, and how you take the transformation is completely subjective."

Dammit! That wasn't exactly what I wanted to hear. If she had guaranteed it, that would have made the decision much easier. The possibility of the transformation taking it all away might have been enough for me to just say yes, because it was a chance of finally living a life without fear. Without the constant twisting knots and nauseating churns in the pit of my stomach. And daily dread of someone jumping out and attacking me at every corner. The weight of apprehension bearing down on my shoulders, every second of my life. And never having to swallow another pill again.

I could be different. I could be me again, but maybe even better.

There was slight pressure coming from my hand, and I glanced down at Aidan. He was squeezing my fingers the best he could, his eyes like saucers now, brow furrowing and displaying obvious concern. He was clearly too weak to speak, but I knew exactly what he was trying to communicate to me. Aidan knew what was happening. He was coherent enough to understand that I was seriously considering becoming a vampire, and he didn't want me to do it.

But I was a grown woman who could make my own decisions. For most of my life I had allowed fear and anxiety to choose for me. Now it was finally time to take control.

I met Madame Clara's ruby red eyes. "I'll join your nest, but only if you allow Aidan to live." Sounded fair enough. Take a life, leave a life.

For the first time, Madame Clara seemed to be amused by something. She chuckled. "Miss Harris, Mr. Moreno isn't going to make it much longer."

"The man is a corpse," Landon chimed in.

But he wasn't. Aidan's feeble grip in my hand was proof that he was not dead yet.

"He's still alive," I said. "And I know you can do something to help him." It was a lie. I had no idea if these vampires had the ability to heal or cure. If there was any truth in any of the fictional books I had read in the past, a few swigs of vamp blood could have Aidan up and out of that gurney, ready to run down this mountain to safety in no time.

"Whether or not Mr. Moreno lives is not included in the proposal. He is only one bag away from serving his purpose. You either become one of us or begin filling up your own bags for our inventory. Decide now," Madame Clara demanded.

Who was I kidding? Did I really think I could persuade a bunch of old supernatural beings into saving a life that was practically already gone?

I couldn't bear to look down at Aidan. The tears were already stinging, threatening to fall on top of him as I stood next to his gurney, my hand in his. I couldn't help him. I tried, but there really wasn't anything else I could do. With no powers of my own, forcing the vampires to save Aidan was out of the question. All there was left to do was to decide my own destiny.

The last time I made a big commitment was when I received the vaccine for the virus that killed thousands around the world. There was a lot to consider, as far as how it would affect me long term, but I did it anyway. I remembered feeling accomplished, maybe even a little powerful that day. Like I had a say in my future. But the feeling only lasted about an hour before the anxiety kicked in and I had to knock back a few pills to stop the incessant what-ifs.

What if the vaccine didn't work and I got sick from the virus and died? What if I was allergic to the vaccine and died? What if the vaccine turned me into a mutant...then I died?

It took weeks for me to finally calm down and keep myself from worrying about the vaccine. Long enough for me to find something else to obsessively worry about.

Three vampires were leering at me, their red eyes attacking me, applying so much pressure on me. My breath hitched. They wanted me to make a decision, and they wanted it *now*.

With my mind reeling, trying to make the right decision for myself, I finally dropped my eyes down to Aidan one last time. He was still looking at me, but his eyelids were slowly opening and closing, and I knew he was trying to fight the darkness that was bound to overcome him.

And then it hit me.

I squeezed Aidan's fingers, hoping it would wake him up a bit and keep him with me long enough for me to make my final declaration. I turned to Madame Clara.

"Change me. I'll join your nest. Turn me into a vampire," I said with clear intent.

Yes. Turn me into a vampire so that I *can help Aidan.*

Chapter Twenty-Nine

The truth was this: there was no guarantee that I could save Aidan. In fact, I still wasn't completely sure that vampires had the ability to heal the wounded and the sick. Madame Clara didn't exactly clarify whether or not she could when I pleaded for her to help him just a few minutes ago. On top of that, I had no idea what the transformation entailed. How long was it going to take? What kind of strength or power would I automatically gain from the beginning? And to throw fuel on that dumpster fire of an idea, there was no telling how much longer Aidan would be able to hold on to his life. For all I knew, he could die any minute now, before I even had a chance to change.

But it was my only chance. It was a shitty chance, but it was something and better than no chance at all. It was either die or die trying. Becoming a vampire was going to give me some kind of power. I wasn't sure what that was, but I was going to find out.

"Are you choosing to become one of us?" Madame Clara asked. I was assuming for clarification.

"Yes," I said with no hesitation, standing up straight to match her poise. My insides were thrashing, stomach flipping, nerves vibrating all through my limbs. Silently, I was praying to God, asking him to please give me the strength and courage to stay calm. To hold it together. Refrain from passing out from fear or vomiting all the anxiety out of my body.

Landon stepped forward, his face donning a crooked grin. "It will be my pleasure."

Of course he would be the Creator of the group. He had "God complex" written all over him. Two long strides and Landon was nearly on top of me, but my reflexes got the better of me. As he descended upon me, I fumbled back, knocking into Aidan's bucket of blood bags before pressing myself flat up against the concrete wall.

"Oh, careful," Chef Winston warned before scrambling over to retrieve the bucket. He quickly hunched down, picked it up, then scurried away and out of Landon's way.

Landon obviously sensed my fear and eased his movements. Leaning into me, he opened his mouth slightly and pulled his top lip tight over his teeth, revealing two canines slowly morphing into pointy fangs. It was hard not to marvel at what I never thought could be possible.

"Now, now, little bird. I'll be gentle with you. Soon you'll have nothing more to fear." His hooded eyes took hold of mine as he reached out for me, placing a hand on the back of my neck and closing the space between us in one fluid motion.

My entire body froze, and all I could do was stare into Landon's beautiful crimson eyes in awe as the apprehension inside me began to dissipate. A small piece of my brain was still coherent and able to recognize what he was doing. Hypnotizing me, taking away all of my worries. Holding me in place so that I wouldn't run away. Allowing him to do what he needed to do.

A passing forethought of the next few seconds skittered across my mind in tiny fragments. His teeth sinking into my neck. My blood rushing from my open vein and filling his mouth. I wanted to be scared. I felt like I *should* have been scared. After all, it was the bite of another man who ruined my entire life, causing years and years of mental health issues.

But his last words stood out like a blinking sign. *Soon you'll have nothing more to fear.*

Suddenly, there was nothing else I wanted more in my entire life. Becoming a vampire sounded not only like my only option, but the best one. Finally, there would be relief. I would be free of the anxiety and the depression and the constant worry that had me shackled all these years, chained to the four walls I had built around myself to hide from the world. From people who could hurt me.

Without another thought, I gave into Landon's hypnotism, releasing the tension in my muscles, softening under the weight of his body, which was now pressing into mine. He draped over me like a well-worn coat, bringing his mouth down closer to my neck. I tilted my head, extending until my ear touched my shoulder and the tendons in my neck stretched tight. Time felt like it had slowed down, but my heart raced, the blood pumping loudly in my head in anticipation of when his fangs would finally make contact.

And then they did.

I gasped and winced, and then nearly cried out loud when I heard the *pop* of my skin tearing open. And when Landon began to suck, my fingers curled into the concrete wall, fingernails clawing so hard into the solid surface that I thought I might have broken a few.

Those fiction writers who claimed that being bitten by a vampire was a sexual experience had it all wrong. It hurt. It hurt like a son of a bitch. It hurt so badly, I wanted to yell and scream, push Landon away and beg Madame Clara to take me to a hospital. There was nothing arousing about it, but I could tell it was for Landon because his fingers wove into my hair and pulled. He thrust his pelvis into me, only it was more on my stomach than my pelvic area because he was much taller than me. It was definitely an awkward feeling, the way he seemed to be so into it and how inside, I was in agony. And it only got weirder when he started shaking, which I assumed meant that he was climaxing.

How the hell did this happen? How did I end up inside a cellar surrounded by corpses, my blood being sucked out by a vampire who was having an orgasm on my stomach?

The shaking intensified and relief washed over me when Landon pulled his fangs out of my neck. I was thankful he was done, but I wasn't completely sure what came next. When would the *change* begin? When would I start to crave the blood of living things?

The questioning in my head didn't last long, though. Landon stumbled away from me, the shaking clearly morphing into violent convulsions. Blood dripped from my neck down to my chest, and I immediately placed a hand over the puncture marks and applied pressure as I watched Landon's body thrash before he dropped to the ground. Lying on his back, he gurgled then coughed up black liquid mixed with foam. The smell of it instantaneously found its way into my nostrils and I nearly gagged. It was rotten. Like the odor of something that had been dead for centuries.

The same substance began leaking from his ears and his eyes and his nose. Something was definitely not right about this picture. My knowledge about vampires was not vast in the least, but it didn't take a genius to know that this wasn't supposed to happen to a vampire after he drank the fresh blood of a human.

"Landon!" Madame Clara shrieked, rushing over to his side. Chef Winston's red eyes were wide and staring at me, a look of distrust and terror taking over his face. He slowly stepped back, away from the scene on the floor and toward the door. His freaked-out stare remained on me as he lifted his hands into the air, as if surrendering to something, and he slowly shook his head. Then he turned around and bolted through the door and out of the room.

Madame Clara clung to Landon's side, hovering over him but not touching any part of his body. He was still seizing, but now the inky, acrid liquid was oozing out of his skin. Areas on his face began to blister and pop open, more of the black pus foam pouring out of him. His three-piece old-timey suit made it impossible to see if more of these revolting bubbles were erupting from the rest of his body, but judging by the rivulets of black liquid streaming down from the cuff of his jacket onto his hands, I could assume so.

I had no idea what was happening to Landon, but it seemed Madame Clara knew. "No, no," she whispered next to him. "This can't be. How could this be?" Then her grief-stricken gaze met mine. "You did this. You've killed my son!"

I shook my head in disbelief. "I didn't...I didn't do anything."

"What are you?" she asked me. "A witch? A vampire huntress? Is your blood spelled?"

A vampire huntress? I didn't even know those existed!

Smoke began to rise off Landon's body as more and more blisters formed and burst. The fabric of his clothes began to tear with each pop, finally revealing his bare skin. It was boiling, the nauseating sound of liquid rumbling subcutaneously before spurting out. Madame Clara stood up and stepped back, bunching her dress in her hands and lifting it up off the ground. Clearly, something terrible was about to happen. Why else would she be retreating, away from her dying son?

I tried to mimic her, but there was no place for me to go. I was stuck between two gurneys, with a concrete wall behind me. The seconds passing by felt like hours as I watched the horror unfold on the floor and waited for some more horror to happen.

Before I could decide to close my eyes, to shield myself from something that could possibly cause even more PTSD than I already had—*BOOM!*

Landon exploded.

I wiped my face, clearing away a chunk of something spongy and wet from my cheek. Glancing around the room, I spotted gobs of Landon. On the walls, on the floor, on Madame Clara, on the white sheets covering Preston and Gwen. On Aidan.

Aidan's chest was still rising and falling, but it was apparent that he was struggling. I was surprised that he was even still alive, but relieved, nonetheless. Now all I had to do was turn into a vampire. It wasn't clear how long it would take, but hopefully it was in enough time to save my friend.

And before Madame Clara tried to kill me for killing her son.

She stared at me from across the room, pieces of her son dotting her dress and her face. Landon's hypnotism was no longer suppressing the fear. The anxiety was back, full force, making my hands tremble and my knees weak. What was Madame Clara going to do to me?

She didn't move. "You did this," she hissed.

"I...I didn't do anything. I let him bite me," I said, my voice wavering between pleading and certitude.

"Your blood is cursed," she said, pointing a long finger at me.

I shook my head vehemently. "No, it's not. My blood is not cursed! I have normal blood." That I knew of. The only time I ever had to go to the hospital was when that asshole hobo/might-have-been-vampire bit me years ago. Other than that, I barely even went to annual checkups for fear that some doctor would give me a horrible diagnosis, or worse...take advantage of me in a way that would be considered assault or rape. The last time I had seen so much as a nurse was just a couple of months ago when she poked me with a needle full of the virus vaccine.

Silence. Madame Clara stood still, glowering at me, her once neon red pupils dulling. They weren't glowing anymore, and I wondered if it was because she had just lost her son or because she was getting hungry. I prayed it wasn't the latter. At any moment, she could just flash herself over and rip me to shreds. Drink my blood out of the base of my body like it was a pitcher of sangria.

Except she didn't move. The room remained quiet, only the sound of the *drip drip drip* of Landon's remains falling from the ceiling, along with Tom and Ellen's blood dripping into their buckets.

Finally, Madame Clara straightened herself, gathering back all of the dignified poise that managed to escape her when her son blew up. After smoothing out her dress and setting her hair in place, pretending like clumps of Landon hadn't even touched her, she said, "Leave."

It was such a simple thing to say at the moment, I had to make sure I'd heard her right. "What?"

"I said leave. You are not welcome at Hazelhurst Manor ever again."

I shook my head slowly, confused. Wasn't she going to kill me because I killed her son? "But Landon..." I felt stupid, reminding the woman of what I'd just done, as if to be arguing against myself.

"And take Mr. Moreno with you. He won't last much longer, anyway."

I turned my attention to Aidan and the shallow breaths he was taking. It was loud and raspy now, like his throat was closing and only small amounts of air was finding its way out. His forehead glistened from the sheen of sweat on his forehead. His eyes were closed, a deep crease etched on his brow. He was clearly in pain. It was a miracle he was still alive. He wasn't going to last much longer.

With a pleading glare, I asked Madame Clara the question one more time. "Can you please help him?" I moved toward her in an attempt to somehow show her how much I needed her to fix Aidan. How desperate I had become. If I had to, I would get down on my knees and beg. But when I'd taken two steps toward her, she took two steps back.

"Stay away from me! Do not come any closer."

I paused, dumbfounded by how a S.O.U.P., a centuries-old vampire who had the ability to manipulate the weather, could be acting like...she was afraid of me.

Then, as my foot sloshed in a puddle of Landon's bloody remains, it hit me. Madame Clara *was* afraid of me. Somehow, I'd killed her son, and she was scared that I would kill her.

With this newfound information, I had to think fast. I had to take advantage of this. Alas, this was my chance to take *control.* To reach deep down inside of myself and pull the McCall that has been buried all these years out of the ashes that she had become.

"I won't leave without him," I said firmly, standing erect and confident. "If you want me to leave, you'll have to heal him. If not, I'll...I'll kill you." I might have looked like I meant what I said, but inside, my heart was drumming outrageously in my chest and my entire nervous system vibrated. I prayed that Madame Clara couldn't sense how unsure I was of my own words. There was no guarantee that I killed Landon, and even if I did, how the hell would I get my deadly blood inside her mouth?

For good measure, I decided to add, "And if you don't heal him, I'll tell everyone I know about this place. I-I'll go to the police, tell them that you are performing heinous acts on people." A chuckle nearly escaped my throat after I'd spat out the threat. The police would most certainly laugh in my face and send me to the loony bin if I claimed to know *vampires*.

But surprisingly, my threat managed to work.

"Fine. But you will stand in the far corner, away from me while I revive Mr. Moreno." She pointed to the corner where Tom and Ellen hung from the ceiling, their blood still dripping from giant gashes across their throats.

Hesitantly, I shuffled over to the two of them, forcing my gaze anywhere else but on their lifeless bodies hanging unnaturally upside down. It was hard not to imagine how they died, if Landon had tortured them or if Chef Winston used one of his carving knives to hack through their skin. Believe it or not, the only one in the nest who seemed to have mercy was the only vampire I truly feared, which was Madame Clara. I didn't know for sure if she had a hand or not in the deaths of Gwen, Preston, Tom, Ellen, or the kids, but she was the only one to have shown self-control. The only vampire who hadn't exhibited any desire to drink blood straight from the source. Landon, Pandora, and Chef Winston all had longing in their ruby red eyes when they had looked at me. A very obvious thirst for what was pumping through my veins. However, Madame Clara was different. She didn't wear her desire on her sleeve, which was much more frightening. She had the strength to conceal her fondness for blood, which made me wonder just how powerful a vampire she could be.

It also confused me. How could such a strong and ancient vampire be afraid of little old me? To be fair, my blood might have killed her son, but Madame Clara could still be capable of killing me without biting me and draining me of my blood, couldn't she?

Craning my neck and standing on my tippy toes to get a better view, I surveyed the situation at Aidan's gurney, trying to assess whether or not Madame Clara was really going to heal him or just kill him. Honestly though, what could I possibly do to stop her from finishing him off?

I took a quick inventory of the room and started imagining all the ways I could attack her if I had to. The room was nearly empty except for the gurneys and dead bodies and buckets of blood lying around. The metal IV stands seemed like the only possible weapon. I could stab her through the skull with it, but I couldn't be sure if it would completely kill her. Vampires were immortal. They healed. Maybe I could slash my wrists and throw my raw blood at her. Maybe it would melt her skin like acid. Except, that would leave me in a terrible position, and I'd end up dying from my own wounds.

Hold on. Landon bit me. A vampire bite meant that I should be changing soon. Did that mean that my own blood would kill me?

Holy shit! This was not good. There was no way of knowing what Landon's bite would do to me now. I could ask Madame Clara, but she was busy saving my friend. Besides, she was allowing me to leave Hazelhurst Manor without killing me. Should I really start questioning anything at all?

There was movement. Aidan released a low moan and his legs twitched underneath the white sheet. Madame Clara's body hovered over him from the side of the gurney, blocking me from seeing what she was doing. If real-life vampires were anything like TV vampires, she could be feeding him her blood. Her magical, supernatural blood. The same blood that my blood could be morphing into as I stood there, waiting.

I could become a healer. If vampires existed and were able to cure the sick and dying, why were they too busy hiding? The world would accept them and their ability to save lives. Because that was what I would do. Save lives. Well...unless I murdered myself with my own blood. Of all the bad luck...

After just a couple more minutes, Aidan sat up in the gurney, bent at the waist and stretching his arms up over his head. Madame Clara backed away from him, her pointy fangs extended and resting on her lower lip, a thin smatter of red along the corner of her mouth. She pulled a lacy handkerchief from the inside of her cuff and wiped daintily at her face.

Aidan's eyes scanned the room, a mixture of confusion and concern creasing across his forehead. Until his gaze landed on me. His big, brown eyes widened, and he gasped. "McCall," he said, removing the white sheet from his legs and scooting off the gurney.

I took a quick glance at Madame Clara, who was already on the far side of the adjacent wall, as far away as she could be from me. Then I rushed to Aidan, nearly collapsing into his open arms.

"Are you okay?" he breathed, taking me in and wrapping himself around me. He felt so warm. So strong. Nothing like the dying man on the gurney literally just minutes ago. When he pulled away to look me in the face, I noticed he also had remnants of red near his mouth.

"I'm fine," I lied. I wasn't fine, but Aidan's hands were now on my cheeks, and he was staring at me with so much concern I could cry.

"Get out," Madame Clara demanded. "Leave and never return."

She didn't have to tell either of us again. Aidan reached down and gripped my hand, wrapping his long fingers around mine, and then guiding me past Madame Clara and the vampire coffins in the next room, out of the cellar and into the foyer of the house. We climbed the stairs to the second story together, down the Hallway of Death to his room. When he let go of my hand to pack his luggage, I hugged myself and waited, trying to hide the sudden vulnerability I'd felt without his touch. Once he was done, he reached out for me, and I happily took his hand again.

We hurried down the Hallway of Death again and to my room. Aidan helped me gather my things while I purposely avoided the portrait of the woman on the wall. I didn't want to risk discovering that she was watching us, although I already knew she was.

Landon's manuscript lay on the wooden desk, and I picked it up, bringing it downstairs with us. Before Aidan made it to the front door, I stopped and set the book down on the accent table, hundreds of pages that were bound together by worn leather. There were probably so many things I could do with it, something so old and unique. Sell it for a lot of money. Submit it to a museum. Or even use it to write that bestselling novel. But it wasn't my story to tell, and Madame Clara deserved what belonged to her son. The son I killed.

After leaving the book behind, Aidan and I rushed out of the front door, the welcoming bell chiming overhead in a sequence of dings that I could have sworn sounded more like a ghostly *goodbye* instead of the cheery *hello* I heard when I first arrived.

As we trotted down the steps of the veranda, luggage hanging off our shoulders and hands, I was surprised to see that the sky had opened up. There was no longer an enormous, angry-looking gray cloud looming overhead. No evidence on the mossy ground of a blood rain having showered the area. No blackened remains of a tree that had caught fire. It made me wonder if I'd imagined it all, but then I quickly remembered where I had been the whole weekend: a fucking vampire den. If *that* was possible, anything was.

We reached the graveled circle where the bus had pulled in to drop us off and I slowed to a stop, my breath heavy from running and hauling bags. "Wait," I wheezed.

Aidan skidded to a stop, his shoes kicking up a cloud of dust. "We should go. We don't know if Madame Clara or anyone will try to catch up."

"Landon and Pandora are dead," I panted, gulping in breaths of air. "I killed Landon. Madame Clara let us go."

"What do you mean *you killed him*? How?"

My lungs were finally feeling properly inflated again. "My blood. He bit me and it killed him. I don't know how it happened."

The strap of Aidan's camouflage backpack slid off his shoulder and his weight shifted as he just stared at me, mouth agape. "He bit you?"

"Yes. And when he drank my blood, he just...imploded. Madame Clara said my blood was cursed. She didn't even want to be near me. It's why she healed you. I told her I wouldn't leave unless she made you better."

"But Landon bit you. That means—"

"That means I will become a vampire," I confirmed.

Then we stood there, silently staring at each other. There was clear hesitation on Aidan's face and my anxiety was getting ready to surge through my body like a volcano shooting lava. All of the pent-up nerves I had managed to keep held tight and in place were getting ready to unravel. And when he'd taken a cautious step away from me, I knew it. I knew right then that he wanted nothing else to do with me.

Suddenly, I had gone from the victim to the predator. A weekend that was meant to make me brave and strong again actually turned me into a monster. I hadn't transformed into one yet, but I might as well have by the terrified look on Aidan's face. The way he was slowly but surely backing away from me.

And what about when the time came when I couldn't control my need to kill, when the thirst for blood was just too overwhelming, like it had been with Landon and Pandora and Chef Winston? I was going to become what ruined my life all those years ago. My own version of the alleyway hobo.

It was painfully clear what I had to do now.

I took one last look at Aidan, the guy that maybe in another life could have eventually been my boyfriend, then turned around and began walking back to Hazelhurst Manor. Back to the vampire nest. My new home.

Chapter Thirty

There was a long, narrow road ahead of us. The seat warmer was on full blast, keeping my butt warm. The back of my chair had been slightly reclined, just enough to relax in a comfortable position and still be able to see over the dashboard at the road ahead. Beige mountain ranges surrounded us in the distance, the outline of them climbing high and low under the cloudless blue sky and blazing sun. Not a single tree could be seen for miles. Nothing that contained any color of the rainbow in sight. There was only beige sand on both sides of the two-way highway, with the occasional beige tumbleweed rolling alongside us as our vehicle carried the wind. Every twenty miles or so, a dilapidated house came into view that seemed like it had been abandoned for decades, only kept standing by the occasional meth addict or gangbangers seeking a place to hide from the law.

The clock on the dash read 3 p.m. When I was reading up about Arizona, I learned that three o'clock was the hottest time of the day in the summer. But it was nearly Christmas time in the desert, and the weather was a perfect 71 degrees.

It had been hours since we'd eaten, and now my stomach was roaring with hunger. I reached behind the driver seat to retrieve the Yeti Daytrip bag, grateful to feel that it was still cooling our sandwiches. Definitely worth the money. I unwrapped his and handed it to him, then peeled the foil off mine. He lifted his roast beef sandwich in the air, waiting for me to lift my turkey wrap. When I did, we toasted, touching the crusts of our breads together before we each took a bite. I smiled as I chewed.

"It's pretty good," Aidan said before taking another bite, one hand steering the SUV.

"Just pretty good?" I asked, only half pretending to be hurt. The other half had hoped that he'd think the sandwich was scrumptious. The last hotel we'd stayed at had a kitchenette, so I was able to do a little grocery shopping to prepare for the final leg of our trip. Over the many years of self-isolation and living as a recluse because of my debilitating anxiety and long stints of agoraphobia, I'd learned a thing or two about cooking my own food. Assembling a sandwich didn't take a five-star Michelin chef, but I thought my mayo-to-meat ratio was excellent.

Also, I really wanted to impress my new boyfriend.

Aidan tore an enormous piece off with his teeth and chomped while moaning, "Mmmmmmm."

I rolled my eyes and grinned. "Whatever."

After he swallowed, he leaned over the center console and kissed me on the cheek. "I'm just kidding, babe. It's delicious. Thank you for making it."

I giggled, and the spot where his lips touched my skin flushed, like I was some kind of smitten little high schooler. I was no high schooler, but I was definitely smitten. A smitten kitten for sure.

Gazing out of the passenger window at the desert landscape, I silently munched on my sandwich and took a moment to appreciate where I was: in a car with someone I truly cared about. Alive and breathing and happy.

Aidan had almost walked out of my life two months ago. According to him, he came very close to hiking down that mountain in Maine without me. He said he didn't know how to handle my situation or the fact that I had been bitten by a vampire, which would inevitably turn me into one too. It was more than he had signed up for when he had become a Chaser. But during the course of our short time together over that weekend at Hazelhurst manor, he started to like me. He claimed he wouldn't have been able to live with himself if he'd left me behind, alone to fend for myself with vampires.

He grabbed me before I could even make it back inside the Victorian mansion, and together we trekked down twenty-five percent of the mountain until we hitchhiked the rest of the way. The entire journey lasted nearly three days, mainly because of the lack of other human life. It was a miracle we even came across Lars, a nature photographer from Australia in search of a rare bird. We told him that we got lost while camping, which I was pretty positive he didn't buy considering we had no camping gear. There was no way we could tell him the truth, and if we had, there wasn't enough energy between the two of us to answer the ass-load of questions Lars was bound to have.

By the time we made it to the nearest town, Lars dropped us off at the nearest hospital to get checked out. Thankfully, we had both washed the residual blood and guts from Landon's explosion off in a small waterfall before we had even met Lars the Bird Man. Otherwise, more questions would have been asked.

I panicked the entire time I sat in the hospital examination room, worried that the doctor wouldn't be able to find a heartbeat, or that I'd transform right then and there and attack a nurse's carotid artery. But nothing happened. In fact, day after day passed, and there were still no signs of me changing into a vampire.

It was extremely difficult to control my anxiety during this time. Every second of every day, my stomach was twisted in knots. Panic attacks would come and go, my body trembling in fear and my skin breaking out into hives from so much worry. I couldn't eat from the nausea, couldn't sleep from the constant loop in my mind. Over and over, I replayed what happened at Hazelhurst manor, what could have happened, what would happen in the future. The only thing that kept me from walking into the Atlantic Ocean with cement blocks strapped to my ankles was...Aidan.

He agreed to fly home to Miami with me to make sure that if I was going to turn into a vampire, I wouldn't be alone. He called all of his Chaser friends, getting as much information as he could about vampire bites and what it would be like to turn. But as the days and weeks passed, we began to realize that it just wasn't going to happen. If I hadn't turned into a vampire when I was sixteen and the alleyway hobo bit me, then I wasn't going to turn into one now.

Aidan did confirm with his fellow S.O.U.P Chasers that it took more than just a bite to turn someone into a full-bred vampire. But there was also another revelation that proved our assumptions to be true—it was the vaccine that killed Landon. The ingredients used to create the recent virus vaccination seemed to have caused my DNA to produce vampire-killing cells. It was all really scientifically complicated, but several Chasers in the community had reported similar effects on vampires. Whether or not the vaccine affected other S.O.U.P.s was still unknown but seeing as how I was the only one of the guests that weekend at Hazelhurst Manor to have been vaccinated, and it was *my* blood that killed Landon and not any of the other guests he had bitten, it only made sense.

Aidan's mind and body recovered well over the weeks we spent in my apartment together. However, it was that Madame Clara healed him from blood loss made it seem like nothing had even happened to him. I worried that mentally, he would develop PTSD just like me, but it turned out that having someone around to talk with day and night, who experienced the same things you did, really helped in preventing depression and further damage to your psyche.

I didn't know whether or not it was a good thing, but Aidan had become my Dr. Finn, which was for the best considering there was no way I could open up to her about my weekend stay with a few bloodsuckers who killed people. And before too long, I found myself using less and less of my anxiety meds and cherishing more and more of Aidan's encouraging and uplifting presence. He was such an optimist, which clearly explained his interest in chasing magical beings.

As far as the other guests, Aidan and I felt it best to keep our mouths shut about the murders. We just didn't know what the outcome of that would be. Would the police think we were crazy? Would they choose to investigate and ascend upon the manor, only to find nothing of what Aidan and I claimed happened was real? No evidence. No bodies. After all, Madame Clara and Landon and Chef Winston did sound like they knew how to clear up a crime scene.

Slowly but surely, the two of us healed each other. I talked Aidan into getting the vaccine, convincing him that not only would it protect him from a killer virus, but from killer vampires too. If we weren't supernatural with supernatural abilities, we could at least have vampire repellent coursing through our blood.

After about a month of mental recovery, our friendship blossomed. Aidan asked me out on a proper date, which I thought was romantic considering he'd been living with me. And from that day on, we officially became a couple. It wasn't surprising in the least. We'd spent every hour of every day together, and neither of us grew tired of each other. If anything, we only wanted to be together more.

Then one day I asked, "What's it like being a Chaser?" Aidan's eyes sparkled at my question, my apparent interest exciting him. He cooked me dinner that night and we sipped on red wine in my living room, surrounded by candles, as he explained everything he knew about being a Chaser. Hours passed of intense conversation before we finally made it to bed, and after making love, I gazed into his big brown eyes and said, "I want to be a Chaser."

Now, here I was, sitting in Aidan's SUV, eating a sandwich and marveling at terrain that I had never seen before in a part of the country I had never been. Just a couple of Chasers going to investigate skin walkers in the Arizona wilderness.

I glanced over at Aidan, and he glanced back, grinning before reaching for my hand. I watched as he wrapped his fingers around mine and squeezed, sending a surge of gratitude and appreciation through my arm and up to my heart. It took me a very long time to find this kind of happiness. Years and years of self-doubt and melancholy. There was a time when I was convinced that I would never get better. That my mind would never be healed.

What if all that despair finally led to something good?

I understood that I might not have been completely cured

of my anxieties and the what-ifs, but for now, I was better. And that was something.

Acknowledgements

I can't even believe I'm here again, writing many thanks to the people who are responsible for helping me publish yet another book. I'm going to make this one short and sweet. Much thanks to the best editor a girl could have, Precy Larkins. You make my stories come to life.

To Murphy Rae, who yet again, somehow traveled deep inside my brain and managed to create the exact book cover I had envisioned. We literally worked on it in no time!

Elaine York, thank you for working your formatting magic. Otherwise, the pages of this book would be so lame.

And to Ashley Quick, thank you so much for the Hazelhurst Manor floorplan. It really adds a special touch to the readers' experience.

Finally, to all my friends and family who have supported me through my writing journey, my life would be crap without you.

About the Author

J.Q. DAVIS is from New Orleans, Louisiana. She has a bachelor's degree in healthcare but chooses to pursue her dreams of being a writer. Her husband is a retired Marine (23 years!) who works with surgical robots. They don't have kids but spoil their pups as if they were real little girls.

Her other interests include reading, watching true crime shows, and reading some more. She is also a video gamer and candy lover.

She is excited to continue this journey through writing and hopes that her readers enjoy her books.

Follow J.Q. Davis on:
Instagram: @authorj.q.davis
Website: www.jqdavis.com

www.ingramcontent.com/pod-product-compliance
Lightning Source LLC
LaVergne TN
LVHW091107080826
845145LV00008B/1836